A NOVEL BY
JOSEPH OLSHAN

NIGHTSWIMMER

SIMON & SCHUSTER
NEW YORK LONDON TORONTO SYDNEY TOKYO SINGAPORE

SIMON & SCHUSTER
Rockefeller Center
1230 Avenue of the Americas
New York, New York 10020

SIMON & SCHUSTER and colophon are registered trademarks of Simon & Schuster Inc.

Designed by Carla Weise / Levavi & Levavi

Manufactured in the United States of America

1 3 5 7 9 10 8 6 4 2

Library of Congress Cataloging-in-Publication Data

Olshan, Joseph.
Nightswimmer : a novel / by Joseph Olshan
p.   cm.
1. Gay men—United States—Fiction. I. Title.
II. Title: Nightswimmer.
PS3565.L8237N5   1994
813'.54—dc20   94-12617
CIP

ISBN: 978-1-4516-6719-6

For Margaret Edwards
and
for Charlet Davenport

ACKNOWLEDGMENTS

I would like to acknowledge the following people who, in various ways, made the completion of this novel possible.

Charles Sprawson, whose *Haunts of the Black Masseur: The Swimmer as Hero,* was an excellent guide to swimming in literature as well as to the many writers and poets who were obsessed with the sport;

The late Allen Barnett, in whose short story collection *The Body and Its Dangers* I have found much inspiration;

Andrew Sullivan, whose article "Ecstasy and Intimacy" in *The New Republic* was a great inspiration when I was beginning this novel;

Peter Davenport, who, along with Charlet, time and again provided me a place to come away to and write;

Margaret Edwards, who gave me a careful and insightful reading of the manuscript;

Eric Steel at Simon & Schuster, New York, and Liz Calder

and Maggie Traugott at Bloomsbury, Ltd., in London, who gave many helpful comments and encouragement;

Steven Gaines, who provided me with emotional support and encouragement;

Gordon Robinson, who gave me insight into growing up as a military brat in Okinawa;

John Lynch, who sang while I wrote.

And there's another reason for my sorrow:
it's no great sea that sunders him from me,
no endless road, no mountain peak, no town's
high walls with gates shut tight: no, we are kept
apart by nothing but the thinnest stretch
of water.

—OVID, *METAMORPHOSES*, BOOK III

PROLOGUE

EVEN NOW, TEN YEARS LATER, I'M WAITING FOR HIM TO COME BACK. Still out there at the buoys, treading water, I'm waiting for the sun to rise over the Los Padres, for the far horizon of the Channel Islands to reappear. I know that he'll surprise me, the way he used to, and I'll give him a hard time for scaring me, for staying out in the Pacific so many years.

As I picture it, he suddenly surfaces, swims over and slips his arms around my shoulders. We take the last two hundred yards leisurely into the beach, throw on our jams, stroll along the boulevard back to my apartment, make love like the familiar strangers we have become, then sleep through the day.

The first to awaken, I lie there listening to the cackling Santa Ana winds, to the frenzied blades of fan palms outside my window. Finally I look over at him. He sleeps on his stomach, and his back, stretching wide like a cobra's hood, rises and falls in the proof that he's actually alive.

The first time I ever saw him was at the campus pool the day

I quit working out with the swim team. The water polo players were milling on the Astroturf deck, strands of chlorined platinum glinting in their hair as they clowned and shoved one another into the water. I'd gone into a dark office, told an unconcerned coach that swimming 15,000 meters a day was interfering with my studies, and was just leaving when I locked eyes with a man. Something inside me was stilled as he pivoted away from me, raced along the deck and leaped up in the air. One of his friends lobbed a yellow polo ball in an arc over the water. He caught it with one arm back, and then, cradling it to his chest, plunged into the aquamarine.

Now ten years have passed and I have been loved by others. And yet, after all this time, there's a part of me that believes he's out there swimming the thirty miles across the channel to Santa Rosa. There's a part of me that believes one day he'll break the cryptic embrace of that ocean. And so, no matter where I am, I remain exactly where I lost him.

PART ONE

WEAVER

1

SOMETIMES I GET CONFUSED AND THINK YOU'RE *HIM*. *YOU, HIM*. JUST
as I get confused when I swim beyond the breakwater and forget
what ocean I'm in: the Atlantic, the Pacific. Or when I wake up in
the arms of a stranger and it's too dark in the room to see a face
that I suddenly cannot remember.

You asked me to tell you what happened, and so I will. It starts,
of course, the day you began. Sunday a year ago, August, I was a
houseguest out on eastern Long Island, on what the newscasters
were calling the perfect weekend of the summer. I'd volunteered
to pick up someone arriving by train and was waiting at the station among a crowd of impatient Manhattanites, who were anxious to collect their visitors and head to the beach. Leaning against
my car, reading a *New Yorker* article about surfing, every so often
I looked down the fretwork of tracks shimmering in the heat as
they slowly bent toward Southampton.

I was thinking about the "Morning Party" going on right then
in Fire Island. Thinking about the parade of men who'd worked

out for this day, and even shaved their chests for the occasion. Thinking how the Morning Party must also be the *Mourning Party* inasmuch as while there were thousands of men dancing, there were also, hovering above them, the thousands of souls of the newly dead who had danced on that beach just a year or two before. Thinking, as I had been vaguely all summer, about falling in love again.

Those first few days and weeks with someone new makes the whole world feel like a Tanqueray ad: everyone is dressed in loose linen and holding their martinis at the edge of the cobalt-colored bay. If I met someone, I knew I'd spend the first possible weekend in Vermont in the converted red 1800s schoolhouse I was renting at the time, making love in the loft beneath a skylight, going for late night walks in a cemetery across the road among the old Revolutionary War tombstones.

But the train did not arrive. A woman wearing a black sleeveless blouse and cut-off jeans began complaining to me, and she decided that I should call the Long Island Rail Road from the pay phone. I was put on hold and just as my change was about to run out, a clerk came on and said that the train was being held one stop before Sayville. I asked what was causing the delay and he told me quite matter-of-factly, "Some guy threw himself in front of the train."

These words were spoken just as my money ran out. Because I really don't know what happened to him, I reel from stories of untimely deaths, of disappearances. I make grim assumptions. I felt shaken as I came out of the booth. "So what happened?" asked the woman in black.

"Somebody apparently threw himself in front of the train."

"Oh, for crying out loud!" exclaimed a middle-aged lady dressed in a caftan who was standing nearby.

"Boy, that really fucks everything up!" said a guy holding a motorcycle helmet under his arm.

As news of the delay spread, many people began leaving the train station. Deciding to wait for a while longer, I took off my shirt and put on some sunscreen. When I tried to finish reading the surfing article, I found myself unable to concentrate. I imagined a whole life for the dead man, his awakening on this the last morning of his life with the realization that without warning, his lover had arisen earlier than was ever customary on a Sunday and had gone to the Morning Party. And such a furtive departure could only mean that among the five thousand men converging on the beach, the errant lover was planning to meet and steal away with someone else, perhaps to a guest room of one of the gray pine houses rented out in half shares.

Such fantasies led me to remember the last night before *he* disappeared. We lay in bed after making love. Outside, the Santa Anas whined like a turbine, but I was feeling calm because he was with me. No arguments, no emotional tug-of-war, just our limbs casually entwined. He lay there, his arms cocked behind his head, eyes flitting around the room. He was restless.

"Hey, Will," he said in his sweet, hoarse voice as he leveraged himself up onto his elbows and scissored his legs away from mine, "how about a half mile out." He leaned his head toward the Pacific.

"Not tonight," I told him. "I'm exhausted. And it's too windy besides."

He shook his head and grinned. "Come on, let's just get in for a while." He took a playful swipe at me and sprang off the bed, naked. Cupping his hands around his eyes, he peered out the window. His back was casually bronzed from being outdoors, thickly corded with muscle, elongated from swimming so many millions of meters, his buttocks a white band of flesh preserved from tanning by a Speedo. *He* was the more beautiful.

"Why does it always have to be at night?" I asked him.

"It's more of a kick at night." He flattened his forehead against the window, staring out into the darkening red-roofed city of Santa Barbara. "You said so yourself. You even bragged once that we were probably the only ones in California who swim at night beyond the breakwater."

"But I also said we were crazy. A stunt like that quickly loses its appeal."

"Not for me."

"Then go by yourself."

He turned around and looked doubtful. "Come on, Will," he said softly. "You know it's cardinal never to swim alone."

"Swimming after dark isn't exactly forgiven."

"Just an easy half mile, out and back. It'll be over in twenty minutes. Over before you know it."

I told him he would make a good proselytizer, and that made him keep on.

"Yeah! Swimming at night. Think of it! Being out there in the swell, in the black belly. Not seeing ahead of you or behind you and just counting strokes until you know you've done your half."

"Can't we just go to the pool?"

He remained resolute, crossing his arms. "You know it's not the same thing, Will." His eyes told me we'd make love again if I gave in to what he wanted.

That mid-November night, the last night we ever swam, he held my hand as we descended the tile steps from my apartment onto Mason Street. Below me lived a rowdy Mexican family who would good-naturedly broom-handle their ceiling whenever we got too loud, and they snickered as they saw us leaving. We wandered shirtless along the waterfront of West Beach, among the palms and jacarandas, where construction had stopped for the day on the old harbor pier. Santa Barbara was pouring money into the refurbishment of its wharf, and it was only a matter of time before there'd be restaurants out there teeming with tourists and local pleasure seekers, in their faded Hawaiian shirts and sunburnt hair, getting blitzed on tequila and rum. But that night the wharf still held its condemned abandoned look, and the only people venturing out there were true derelicts, the drug addicts and the fair-weather bums who commuted from one mild southern California town to another.

The moon rising over the Los Padres frosted the water, and we could see the dark landmass of the Channel Islands twenty miles across.

He turned to me with a jittery smile. "Ready?"

A moment later I was watching him dive through the middle of a wave. Then I was right behind him, yelling from the shock of the temperature. Whenever we went in at night, I felt as if I were testing something, or teasing the temperamental universe. I started counting how many strokes it would take to reach the white plastic buoy line. It was two hundred yards offshore, a line used by the long-distance fanatics who always swam the stretch between the beaches of Ledbetter and Coral Casino. Those buoys were nearly halfway to our imaginary destination.

We ran into several kelp beds on the way. The instant I felt those slimy necklaces of seaweed I thought for sure I'd run into a shark. Why do you keep doing this, Will, I kept asking myself as I swam farther from shore. Months before, when we'd first met, I had felt the need to swim with *him* at night because I thought it would guarantee his love. But now I believed he would refrain from being more daring if he were forced to reckon with the company of another swimmer.

Just as we were closing on the half mile, I heard a kind of churning explosion. I stopped swimming and eggbeatered my legs and peered around until I saw, coming straight toward us, a whale-shape of boat outlined with what looked like Christmas lights. I gaped at it until I realized it was a barge dredging sand from one part of the harbor and dumping it in another. The boat would suck up whatever it came across: kelp, fish—and us if we happened to be within range. He somehow didn't hear it because he kept swimming, and I had to race to catch him, until I could grab his arm and scream, "Look at that fucking boat! Let's get out of here!" He mumbled something and I thought he'd said, "Okay."

I began sprinting back to shore. I swam my guts out until I finally hit the white buoy line. Stopping for a moment to recover my breath, I peered around, looking for him. Listening for him.

Admittedly, my circle of perception was limited by darkness and by the sound of surf pounding the shore, but in an instant I realized he wasn't with me, that I was completely alone out there.

Now, ten years away, and three thousand miles, I suddenly heard a railroad bell tolling the train's arrival. When the cars finally pulled into the station, I watched all the disgruntled passengers getting off until I finally spotted the guy who was getting a ride from me. He was one of these eternally pale East Village types who dress from head to toe in black. We barely knew each other.

"Hey, Will, sorry about the delay." He tossed an overnight bag in the back seat of my car and climbed in front. He had a long pointy face, small glittering pebble-gray eyes. "Hope you didn't have to wait too long. The Summer Express turned into the Suicide Special."

"That's what I heard," I said as we drove off.

"One stop before Sayville. You should've seen the guys trying to make the Morning Party. Fit to be tied. 'How long does it take to remove a mangled body from some railroad tracks?' " he mimicked.

"Fucking New Yorkers," I said. "So, did you see anything?"

"You mean like a severed head?"

He hadn't.

The conversation lapsed until we were driving through the town of East Hampton with its rows of expensive clothing stores and food shops. "By the way," my companion said, "I ran into your ex on the train. On his way to the Morning Party."

"Was he with a dog?" I asked.

"Are you for real?"

Then I remembered it was Metro North that allowed dogs, not the Long Island Rail Road. "Forget it."

"That's right. I remember hearing from somebody that you guys have joint custody over your dog."

"His name is Casey."

"Whatever. But it's so nineties, joint custody of a dog."

"What else should we do if we both love him?"

I couldn't wait to drop this drippy guy off at the house where we were both staying and head to the beach. It was a red-flag day, the combers crashing far out and unevenly, and the Atlantic's mood was in sync with my own. The beach swarmed with people and I trekked down the strand until the oiled bodies began thinning out. I spread out my towel, dropped the hardcover that I was reading and wandered down toward the lip of the water.

There'd been plenty of men in my life since *him*, and Greg Wallace was the latest in the succession. Recent memories tended to blend together, whereas *he* of ten years past had managed to remain relentlessly distinct: the dark unruly hair matted with salt, the colorless down on the back of his neck, his scent of chlorine and sweat and eucalyptus, the ardent black eyes that perhaps he had inherited from his one Latino grandparent. In the last few weeks he'd been on my mind a lot more than usual. Ten years is a wicked anniversary.

On that crowded beach, no one dared to enter the treacherous surf past their knees. Without a second thought, I waded out to the critical point between shore and breakwater, dove through a wave and surfaced beyond, swimming. Another roller snapped on me, twirled me up like a ribbon and charged me down to the bottom. I clawed my way up through sandy darkness to the surface, just as another one was beginning to cave in. I dove right through its belly and cut out another twenty-five yards to where there was less chance of being churned up. The water was all murk and I could feel the tongue of the tide trying to swallow me as I settled into long strokes, conscious of rotating my shoulders, inviting danger.

I finally stopped swimming to tread water. I'd ended up pretty far out, maybe two hundred yards offshore, much farther than ordinary swimmers go even when the water is serene. A cluster of concerned people were already gathering at the tide line, waving me in. But there was part of me that wanted to keep swimming, for miles and miles until I was forced finally to give up. Realizing this, I started feeling panicked and swam back until I caught a wave at its curl and body-surfed in.

As I walked back to my towel, I reminded myself that things were okay, that it really wasn't so bad to be single. For once, I didn't have to worry about a relationship, being a part of what seemed like endless compromising. I was a free agent, right? But of course I'd think that on the day of meeting you—you who, at that very moment, were riding the ferry back from Fire Island. I remember looking at my watch, which read five minutes before five. You would tell me much later that something had compelled you to leave the Morning Party earlier than you'd planned, that you'd barely caught the five o'clock boat back to Sayville, where a medical examiner was pondering the mutilated body of a thirty-two-year-old man. Little did either of us know that you were on your way into my life. Little did we know that his death had something to do with you.

2

But of course you wouldn't know the particulars of this death until the next morning. You would first hear general news of a suicide—I would be the one to tell you, that same night—but you still wouldn't know who. As for the media coverage of it, I think the incident never went beyond what was probably informal newsroom gossip, an inconvenience to thousands of New Yorkers. Never was it mentioned in the *Times* or the *Journal*, papers I sometimes write for. I probably should've checked the Long Island coverage in *Newsday*.

When I arrived back in Manhattan that Sunday evening, I parked in a lot on Lafayette, across from World Gym. I grabbed my overnight bag and was heading across the street when I spotted Peter Rocca, a red-haired psychiatrist whom I'd been dating on and off over the summer. Wearing the sheerest of orange tank tops, he was standing in front of the gym's huge plate glass windows, as if waiting for someone. I thought, he's back from the Morning Party conspicuously early. Stopping to watch who might be joining him, thinking how throughout the past few months with Peter I'd been waiting for the single act of tempestuous lovemaking, the act of casual cruelty that would seed a romantic obsession, I stood there on the curb.

Then you. You walked out of World Gym.

Peter nudged you playfully with his shoulder and you both began strolling along Lafayette. I thought jealously, How sweet: they went to pump up together before getting it on. This must be some hunk Peter snagged at the Morning Party; no wonder he got back so early.

Sure, I would have liked to subvert this pickup, but I knew there were no grounds for doing so. Peter Rocca and I had never had any real commitment. Throughout our fling, he'd remained attached to another man with whom he'd been involved intermittently for a couple of years. What first drew me to Peter, in fact, was the Saturday afternoon I was walking down this very street when I saw his superhero's build tumble out of World Gym, closely trailed by a compact swarthier version, a man who wore his hair in an exaggerated pompadour. The other man, whose name, I learned, was Sebastian, began screaming obscenities at Peter. Initially Peter tried to walk away, but when the litany kept up, he finally whirled around, rushed back and tackled Sebastian right there on the sidewalk. I watched them struggle until Peter seized the advantage, pinned Sebastian and began strangling him. "I love you, Peter, I'll always love you," Sebastian garbled as he was being choked. Yet before I could figure out what to do, a couple of other guys from the gym came out and broke up the fight.

What compelled me was how the pompadoured man, in the midst of being throttled, could keep declaring his love. Some might call this a sick desperation, but I have to say there's something in me that respects people who put themselves on the line, who risk appearing like complete fools.

From my distance I could see that you were broadly built with

ashen coloring and tight black curly hair. I was as yet too far away
to see your small piercing eyes. Peter spotted me immediately,
however, and waved. I tried to keep walking.

"Come on, Will, stop acting like an asshole and get over here!"
he trumpeted. "This is Sean." He introduced us immediately.
"Sean Paris."

You barely said hello; it was hard to tell if you were shy or ar-
rogant, and I dismissed you the way I figured you dismissed me.
Good solid body, I'd give you that. Great legs of the hockey player
variety—okay, so legs are my particular weakness. I figured that
Peter was in the midst of leading you back to his apartment, fourteen stories above Sixth Avenue, with panoramas of downtown
and of the Empire State Building, whose upper-story lights would
die out romantically on the stroke of midnight. Those were the
lights that he and I had often watched expire after sex.

When Peter invited me to walk with the two of you along Wa-
verly Place, it was an invitation that both confused me and created for us all an awkward silence. I remember noticing the way
you floated along the street, wide shoulders slumped slightly forward, the sort of body whose gangly magnificence at rest would
come gracefully alive with speed. You inhabited every inch of your
body, unlike Peter, who, though bigger and sexier by gym stan-
dards, would always strike me as a skinny boy silhouetted at the
core of a muscle man.

Once we reached Peter's building, he invited us both upstairs.
I accepted, you declined and then we all said goodbye. Peter and
I proceeded into the lobby. "I'm glad you're coming up, because
I think that guy was after me."

"I think it was mutual attraction, Peter."

"I'm not bullshitting, I'm telling you the truth."

"Truth notwithstanding, he's beautiful."

"Shaddup, you." Peter punched me in the arm and then bit
my shoulder. He was fidgety and I could tell that he was horny.

Fine with me, I thought in a sudden rush of arousal as Peter rang for the elevator.

Then came the knock on the outside lobby door. You'd changed your mind.

You'd left the Morning Party on a hunch that something was supposed to happen back in New York City. At first it seemed what was going to happen was Peter Rocca, whom you'd met on the ferry crossing back to Sayville. But then the moment you began walking away from his building that night you realized that what was going to happen was me.

And so we all sat in Peter Rocca's pristinely decorated living room—you and I on a chintz-covered sofa. There was a lamp made from a carved crystal globe and a reproduction Louis XIV writing desk. The gleaming parquet floor was covered by a Turkish area rug that had burned my knees the first time Peter and I went at it with the abandon of complete anonymity. He was hardly a stranger to me by now, and yet, Peter's double invitation made absolutely no sense at all.

When it came to sex, Peter certainly had his share of quirks. He was a morning-sex person. Whenever I would spend the night he'd wake up early and, before we did anything, would jump out of bed, and, still naked, vacuum the rugs in his apartment and polish the glass coffee table and furniture with a vengeance. Then after he was done cleaning and before he rushed off to patients suffering from phobic disorders, he'd be ready for a berserk ten-minute quickie. He loved getting it on all over the apartment. Standing by the picture windows in full view of the apartment house across the street, either he'd lift me up or I'd lift him up and we'd hike to the next location. We did it on the kitchen counter, on the kitchen floor, and then finally, predictably, ended up in the shower. I called this routine our Sexual Stations of the Cross. Thinking about all this, I chuckled.

"What's with you?" he said.

"Nothing, leave me alone."

"Then tell me, what do you want to drink?"

"Beer."

"How about you, Sean?"

"Do you have Red Label and soda?"

"Sure do."

God, are you as pretentious as your taste in alcohol, I nearly asked. "So, where are you from, Sean Paris?" I said instead.

Detecting my sarcasm, you frowned at me. "From here."

All transplanted New Yorkers get defensive when you ask them this question. "I mean, from originally."

"A lot of places. My father was military. The last place I ever lived with my parents was Okinawa."

"How long in the city?"

"Four years."

"You're still in the honeymoon period," I concluded rather abruptly and then asked what you did for a living.

"Landscape architecture."

"Must be slim pickings in all this concrete."

You rolled your eyes. "Everybody always says that." Then you explained that most of the firm's work was out-of-town business.

I pegged you for one of those really cute but ultimately boring out-of-town boys, ones who have come to the city to reinvent themselves, who can't stop reveling in all the heathen pleasures: late-night discos, jack-off clubs, designer drugs. Had you learned to commit all the sins of the eye? Perhaps you were just shy—I tried to give you the benefit of the doubt—not the sort of man to effuse conversation.

Suddenly the phone rang and Peter grinned maniacally over his shoulder as he went to answer it. Overhearing his frantic chatter, I knew he was speaking to Sebastian, the pompadour. You were now sitting sightly hunched over, staring rhapsodically into the cut crystal glass of good Scotch. Slowly, however, you shifted your vulpine gaze and caught mine. And I think that must've been the first time I ever saw you straight on. I was singed by a split-second glance before you looked away.

"Were you at the Morning Party?" you said.

Suddenly nervous about meeting that eerie gaze again, I was barely able to explain that I'd decided not to go, that I have difficulty with crowds. What was wrong with me? I now ventured to look at you, and this time your stare forcibly struck. Then I knew who you were. I knew why you'd changed your mind. I knew why you had to come back.

"Is he heading over now?" I asked when Peter returned from his telephone call.

"I explained that the two of you were here and told him I'd call back later."

"You sure he's not going to just show up like he did last time?"

"Why should he? He doesn't like you."

"And who could blame him?" I laughed.

"He thinks Will is keeping us apart," Peter explained to you.

"Certainly it's easier for him than facing the fact that *Peter* is keeping the two of them apart," I quipped. Turning to Peter, I said something like "I don't know why you put yourself through all of this nonsense. Either marry him or move on," when behind me you said, "Leave him alone, Will!"

I spun back around, but was paralyzed by your dimpled, mischievous grin. And by something else, too; something that you gave off—a loaded calm. A midwinter feeling, like standing in a pine forest, watching the snowflakes fall, hearing their soundless bedlam.

"Part of the reason why Sebastian wants to come over is that we were supposed to meet out on the Island," Peter went on, "but he could never get there. Apparently, all the trains got screwed up."

"That's because somebody jumped in front of one of them."

Then I explained how I'd come by the news.

I distinctly remember that you looked perturbed for a moment and then the placid look resurfaced. Suddenly you were standing. "Well, guys, got to go."

"Me too," I chimed in, standing also. Peter cast me a baffled glance and I claimed that I was tired.

Finally alone as we stood together in front of Peter's building, you and I were making up our minds. It's amazing to think how the outcome of a single conversation can break open a whole new territory.

"So which way are you headed?" you said.

"I can head your way."

"Come on, then."

And somehow I knew that fourteen stories above us, Peter was watching to see if I'd accompany you. At one point, halfway down the block, I even swerved to look back; and Peter saw that, too, the guilty gesture, the futile wish to cover my tracks. Later on, Peter would tell me that that image of me walking away with you, then swiveling around in a moment of hesitation, would be the one summer memory that would stay with him. Not the rooftop barbecues on Twenty-third Street, not the pickups at Splash and Fire Island, not even the Morning Party. No, the remembrance of two dark figures walking away, and then one turning around like Lot's wife looking back at the cities of the plain.

3

WE WERE STROLLING WEST TOWARD YOUR NEIGHBORHOOD OF CROOKED brownstones with chipping paint and quiet, in some cases neglected, gardens. We were walking through what seemed like a fissure of the night. The full moon brushed the streets with a tingling opalescence and a hot wind spiraled through the rest of Greenwich Village. Gates of town houses squeaked and cawed as people passed through, their muted conversations just beyond us. The whole city seemed to become our encounter, or, better than that, our encounter seemed to be at its heart.

"So who is he?" you asked after several minutes of silence.

"What do you mean, *who is he?*"

You could have meant Peter. Or even the railroad suicide. But, most mysteriously, you had guessed the secret of ten years. "The guy that burned you," you said.

"I don't know what you're talking about. Nobody burned me."

Your eyes held me steadily. "I don't believe it."

So strange, your insistence, and so frightening. Such a twist on the fact that I am usually the one who makes overly pointed conversation with complete strangers. You walked along a few paces ahead of me, leading the way to wherever we were headed, and your question continued to fluster me even though you said nothing more. You were the first person who had ever sensed immediately that his life still stalked mine.

"I loved him like a fucking idiot," I said finally. "Okay? Like nobody before or after."

"So what happened?"

"What difference does it make? I'm here, aren't I? He's obviously not in my life anymore."

"Is he still alive?"

I told you right away that I didn't know and declared that I would speak no more about him.

As we walked along Seventh Avenue you told me that you'd developed a skill at "sussing out" new people. As a child of a military father, you'd grown up in different parts of America, as well as in Okinawa, and that meant sitting around lots of dinner tables where you were expected to be quiet. And so you became astute at observing peccadillos, picking up the telltales of people's character. Sometimes you'd even been able to sense which of your parents' friends were cheating on their spouses.

As you spoke to me, however, all I could think about was the first electric touch of you, a caress of my fingers along your pale, beautifully formed arm after a soft collision of our shoulders. We finally reached your place on Grove Street, and just outside the building entrance you turned to me.

"Will, I'd like to invite you in. For a few minutes. But for an innocent few minutes."

I frowned. "And what's that supposed to mean?"

"Just what it says."

Finding you even more compelling now that I was beginning to strike the flint of a personality, I told myself I would not take no for an answer, and that I would have you. I would have you that very night.

You lived in a fourth-floor walkup, whose stairwell was paved with a runner of red carpeting and hung with antique Buddhist tankas. As we climbed to the top floor, I confessed to owning several tankas myself.

"I used to follow Buddhism," I said, explaining that for me it had been an erotically driven interest. One of my ex-lovers was Buddhist, and by following his religion, I had once made myself indispensable to him.

"The same guy that burned you?"

"No. Somebody else."

"Been busy in your life, haven't you?" You grinned.

A tall door opened into an apartment with high ceilings and grand windows facing Grove Street. We were hit with a gust of pent-up heat and the smell of laundry starch that would soon become one of the scents of you. You crossed the room to raise all the windows and lean out for a moment. The night was sonorous with the drone of air conditioners, Manhattan's own species of cicada. Full moonlight was reaching through the massive arms of an ailanthus tree that loomed up from the small courtyard below. In the dim glow I noticed the dark shape of a piano, its sullen gleam.

Once you switched on the lights, I could see that the piano keys were covered with all sorts of bills and papers, the piano bench was strewn with underwear and socks and workout shorts—the apartment was a holy mess. The floor was littered with T-shirts, canvas carry bags, army fatigues—both full-length and cut-off—a Patagonia shell that hinted a sporting life, and all sorts of dog-eared seed and bulb catalogues. One wall held framed mounts of exotic butterflies; and on the fireplace mantel, on either side of a curious-looking basket that looked to be woven out of 16-mil-

limeter film, were two stuffed wood ducks with emerald heads and
rings around their throats.

"I see you like dead things."

"Well-preserved dead things. My uncle was a taxidermist."

Beneath one of the windows sat a square mahogany dining
table that was covered with jelly glasses sullied with fruit pulp,
white plates bearing remnants of several-days-old salad. Quite a
contrast to the fastidious preservation of taxidermy. Next to the
dishes was a small pile of slim blue aerograms, those nearly
weightless letters that, I imagined, had been written by old lovers.

Every single guy I'd ever loved had been meticulously neat
and had always derided me for being a hardcore slattern. When
I remarked, "You're even messier than I am," you surveyed the
room with a bemused expression and said, "Lately it's gotten out
of hand." Most people would have apologized; you hardly seemed
to care that I might judge you.

There was no sofa, and so you sat down in one dining chair
and offered the other one to me. The place had been very run-
down when you first took over the lease. That you renovated,
scrubbed the fireplace, scraped the walls and repainted them (and
probably ingested lead)—all this was explained to me. And as
you talked I noticed a blush in your cheeks that usually vanishes
by the age of twenty-five, but whose lovely tint had obviously remained with you at least as far as thirty-one. Soft tight dark curls,
those pale wolverine eyes.

Jesus Christ, he's really stunning, I said to myself. Not the
sort of beauty that turns heads in the street, but rather the wan
beauty that gains dimension the more you look at it.

I found myself unable to make any more superficial conversation. All I cared about was making my move in full challenge
of the fact that I'd been invited to this apartment "for an innocent
few minutes." I managed to cantilever myself forward and squeeze

my two knees around one of your massive legs. I was rewarded with a wary look. "You think I'm going back on what I said?"

"People do."

"Not this people."

"So you're stubborn."

A shrug. "I'd like to have dinner with you sometime."

"So what's precluding that?"

"Nothing at all. Except, uh, you're squeezing my leg."

I must have looked pretty crestfallen because you went on to say, "Look, Will, I think you're attractive. What's the big rush?"

"We could have fun now and eat later," I suggested.

The wary expression ripened into annoyance. "Are you always so insistent? Do you always expect to have everyone you want?"

"Do you always expect people to tell you their secrets?"

"I left off, didn't I?"

"For the time being."

You wrenched your leg out from between the press of my knees, leaned back in your chair. "This is going to be a tough tournament."

"Why does it have to be a tournament?"

"I'm just calling it the way I see it."

One look at me, you now explained, and you knew we were suffering the same affliction: that a part of ourselves had been torn out, stitched to some stranger's heart and gone molten in the heat of other loves. There were others like us roaming the cities of the world, the broken homeless ones sifting through the litter of one-night stands, of short-term loves, for that missing piece. You said that our hunt would probably take us to the ends of our lives and that in all likelihood we'd never become whole again.

"What's this, your Vampire Theory?" I asked.

"But you know it's true," you said just as the telephone rang. We both glanced at the bedside clock, which read 12:35. "It's kind of late. I'm not going to answer it. If they want me they'll have to leave a message."

So we listened to it ring two, three, four times, waiting for a voice to print on the answering machine.

Hello, this is Sean, can't come to the phone right now, please leave a message. Beep. "Sean, this is Gary, Bobby's roommate." Pause, and then the message continued tremulously. "Look, you've got to call me as soon as you get this, I *don't* want to speak to your tape . . ."

An ember of alarm in your eyes, but the rest of your expression was frozen, cadaverous.

Then you jumped off your chair, dashed to the answering machine, switched it off and grabbed the phone.

"What's going on, Gary? No, I was actually awake. What is it?" Then, in answer to whatever he said to you, your voice warbled, "Come on. You can't be serious. Don't tell me this!"

I was fascinated, of course, and I noticed your gestures, how as though in some kind of trance you methodically began to order the chaos of letters and bills that were scattered all over the piano keys, categorizing them into several neat piles. But then you stopped abruptly, and with a sharp movement dispersed all that you had collected.

"Why, Jesus Christ!" you said numbly, pivoting away from the piano. "No, what did *that* say?" And a silence. Then: "Okay, I'm coming now. Hold on to it until I get there."

You put down the phone and in a moment of indecision stared at me with your frozen look.

"Where do you live, Will?" you said vacantly. "Maybe we can share a cab."

"What happened?"

"I can't really talk about it. There's just something I've got to go deal with immediately."

"But will you tell me eventually?"

"Sure, at some point."

"Why do I not believe you?"

No response. You collected your wallet and keys from the cluttered dining table and then opened the apartment door and waited for me to walk out ahead of you.

"I just want to know if that phone call has to do with some guy," I said, stepping over the threshold.

You followed close behind me, slammed the door shut and hurried toward the staircase. "What do you think?"

"Aren't you going to lock the door?"

You stopped, glanced back and shrugged. "I don't give a shit. Let them steal whatever they want. Everything I have of value is purely sentimental."

Seventh Avenue was desolate as far as taxis were concerned, and so we headed along Bleecker Street toward Sixth. Several of the Italian bakeries were taking on deliveries of bread, the whole street aromatic with yeast. You acknowledged your hunger with a grunt and then a wistful look as we passed cartons full of loaves that stood upright.

"Can I do anything?" I asked after we'd walked half the block in desultory silence.

"Just leave it alone for now, Will. That's what you can do."

As we skirted a Korean fruit market that was surprisingly thronged for such a late hour, you suddenly said to me in a tone of wounded innocence, "I wonder what it is, anyway, about all of us, Will."

Unsure of what exactly you meant, I said nothing. We reached Sixth Avenue and stood for a moment at the corner, watching hordes of empty taxis wheeling by. As you raised your hand to flag one, you turned to me. "I'll call you tomorrow, how's that?"

"You don't have my number," I said. "You don't even know my last name."

And then that silly look I've come to expect, to hope for, capered across your face and right in front of the cabdriver I was given a swift, dazzling kiss. "I read your first book," you told me in a near whisper. "I cried at the end of it. And I know you're listed because I once looked up your telephone number."

When I arrived home, my answering machine was blinking three messages: the first from Greg Wallace, my ex, reminding me that we were supposed to meet the next day. The second two messages were from Peter Rocca: one at 11:45 saying, "You're not home yet, give me a call when you get in. I wanted you to spend the night with me, fuckhead!" The next one at 12:30: "So it's obviously a night of debauchery." No trace of irony.

I only wished it *had* been a night of debauchery. Pent-up and horny, not wanting intimacy with anyone else but you, only wanting to get off now, I decided to try my luck with a phone line. I picked up the receiver, dialed and got a busy signal. Here it was 1:15 A.M. on a weeknight and this particular phone line, which could handle hundreds of calls simultaneously, was overloaded with people hoping to find just the right voice to get off to over the phone.

For years now, my phone line alias has been a guy named Jim. I'm Italian, not Jewish, an inch taller than my actual height. I tell the truth about my build, which I describe as water polo player; however, I hedge somewhat on the hairline—I say it's thinning just a tiny bit—and lop five years off my age. When I'm asked what I like, I say muscular men, straight-acting, preferably married types who wear wedding bands. I put more bass and languor into my voice and speak with a southern California lilt that I acquired easily when I was living out there. And if they ask me what I do, I say I'm a journalist, never a novelist. It's amazing how you can get people ready, willing and able to get off on the phone at all hours of the day or night—even early in the morning. Sometimes when I reach the line in the afternoon, guys' voices sound constrained, clandestine, and often I hear other phones upsetting the silence around them. "Are you in your office?" I ask. "Yeah," they murmur. "I'm looking to hook up with somebody after work."

"But you'd rather get off in your office, wouldn't you?" I say. "I bet you'd like me to come up there right now and do you under the desk while you take phone calls"—a twist on Philip Roth, I joke to myself.

There are certain voices that make me a little insane, certain timbres of male vocals that can make me come several times in succession. I like deep Southern overtones, Texans, guys from D.C.; California will always do it for me because of *him*. The voices have to be pure, resonant, American. When it comes to phone sex I'm incurably redneck, a white-bread-eating patriot.

I'm always casting for a way to say things simply but potently. In a slow, confident voice I'll tell them how they're going to be lying on their sofas when I walk in the door, what they're going to be wearing, how they've prepared themselves for my arrival. But it's not hardcore smut talk, it's always romantic: a promise to spend the night, to cradle someone, to kiss them with everything I possess. I never get very far with people who claim they want to be abused and debased in the act of lovemaking. Just recently I was talking to a guy about an encounter (a favored subject of phone fantasy is one's last real-life sexual experience), and he admitted to fucking someone without a rubber. When I asked him if he was telling me the truth, he swore up and down that he was, that this other person didn't care whether or not he was taking a risk. Abandoning all pretense now, I said evenly and sadly, "You shouldn't do things like that. You should take some responsibility, too." The guy slammed his phone down on me.

That night when I finally got through to the line, I spoke to each person one-on-one. If I didn't like whoever it was, I simply pressed the pound key (pound!) and was connected to someone else. Sort of like a computerized Rolodex of live male fantasy. In this way, I scrolled through the variety of offerings until I found a guy with a hoarse, heavy Italian-American accent calling from Queens. He claimed to be six feet two inches, a thirty-inch waist, a forty-seven-inch chest, the perfection of Tom of Finland. Big, gruff-sounding guys often start off talking all macho and dominance, but many of them finally admit that they just want to get fucked. "I want you to wrestle me to the ground," the guy was saying. "Come on, show me you're stronger. I want you to pin me, make me give, then I want you to shove it in hard!"

Suddenly, not more than three strokes from orgasm, I got Call Waiting. I might have ignored it, but for some reason I thought you were calling me. With a murmur of apology to my phone sex partner, I clicked over to the other line.

"I can't believe you finally made it home!" said Peter.

"What do you want?" I said, looking down at my swollen cock, throbbing just shy of what had promised to be a spectacular orgasm.

"You on the other line?"

"Yeah."

"Who're you talking to?"

"My mother."

"This late?"

"She lives in California. What's this, twenty questions?"

"Is *he* there?"

I sighed. "No, Peter, I'm all alone."

"Well, I hope you've had your fun. With your night of debauchery."

This made me yell out, "A little less teeth! That's better! More lip action. Use the roof of your mouth!"

Peter waited for me to quit teasing and then said somberly, "You meet a friend of mine and then nab him for yourself. Right before my eyes."

"He's hardly a friend of yours, Peter. You were trying to pick him up yourself."

"Who could get anywhere with a barracuda like you around? I asked you to come along with us because, believe it or not, I was actually hoping that you and I could spend the night together. I figured Sean would buzz off eventually. But instead—"

"Peter. Come on, let's not do this." I tried to be compassionate, having lost my hard-on and all but abandoning any hope of getting off with the guy from Queens. "Nothing happened, okay? All we did was talk."

There was a pause on Peter's end and then he said, "When I saw you guys walking away and you, obviously feeling guilty, looking back like that, I went nuts. I couldn't sleep after that."

"I'm sorry. You should've jacked off."

"I did twice. I just don't understand why you didn't spend the night with me, Will."

"Because I got distracted. *You* get distracted sometimes . . . by Sebastian."

"We've got a long history, Seb and I. Besides, this guy Sean, he's a pretty loose cannon, you know."

"Come on, now, don't malign him."

"I'm just repeating what I've heard at the gym. Sean Paris gets around."

"Suddenly you're taking what those queens in spandex are dishing for gospel?"

"It's convenient."

"And like you don't sleep around?"

"All right, so I'm jealous!"

"Fair enough. I accept that. Now, why don't you try to get some sleep? I'm alone. I didn't do anything."

"Sure you don't want to come over and keep me company?"

"It's late and I want to sleep in my own bed. Good night, beautiful."

I clicked off from Peter, completely wired, and figured I'd call back the phone line for a quick release. As I started punching in the numbers, I heard somebody trying to talk to me: "Hey, hey!"

"Hello?"

"It's me," said the voice. "I'm still here." The man from Queens had latched on to Call Waiting.

I'd already forgotten his name. Not that it mattered, because he'd probably given me a phony name anyway.

"Wow," I said, "you waited!" I felt an amazing tenderness for this disembodied voice who probably lied about the way he looked, but who was obviously patient, maybe even steadfast. Suddenly I thought I could feel his loneliness there in the outlying borough that bordered La Guardia Airport and Flushing Bay, a residential area dismissed by the Manhattan elite as being déclassé. And it occurred to me, as I began urging myself and this guy toward a late-night climax, that perhaps I could persuade him to become my monogamous phone lover.

4

THE NEXT MORNING AT TEN O'CLOCK I WAS AWAKENED BY MY EDITOR at the *Wall Street Journal*. I had neglected to file a review the previous Friday. Promising it by noon while simultaneously flipping on my computer, I sat for twenty minutes trying to compose my lead paragraph. But my thoughts kept roaming back to you and your apartment and the strange phone call that had interrupted us. You said you'd call, but maybe that was just a line. On impulse I punched Information and asked for a Sean Paris on Grove Street. Nervous that the number might be unlisted, I was relieved to hear the operator say, "Hold for the number," and quickly jotted it down.

I fought off the urge to call until after I'd downed a mug of coffee and cranked out the first draft of my critique of a long-winded Danish novel. When I first dialed I figured I'd probably reach your recording, it being Monday morning and you would be, like the vast majority of Manhattanites—everyone except me, it seemed— at your office. But your phone rang and rang until I remembered that you'd switched off the answering machine.

I tried to tackle the review again, but got nowhere. I remembered your saying that you'd cried over my book. It almost made me want to start writing another one. Almost. People think that I started writing journalism because I "lost it" as a novelist. I find this irritating.

My first book had been relatively successful, both in America and abroad. I'd almost dedicated that first book to *him*, but was advised by a friend that it would put too much pressure on him to contact me. Better to let him think that I'd gone on with my life, had even found a certain degree of success, better to let him think I had flourished without him.

Once the novel appeared, I was contacted by all sorts of people I used to know, some of whom I hadn't heard from as far back as kindergarten. The moment I received each letter from my publisher and glanced at my name scrawled in handwriting, I half hoped that *he* had seen the book in a shop somewhere, read it and now was compelled to contact me. But I never heard from him.

In the midst of writing my second novel, I suddenly realized that one of the driving forces behind the first one was that without knowing, I'd been writing it to *him*. In a way it was as though I were sending out a message in a bottle, a message that would never be found.

I dedicated the second novel to Greg Wallace. The reviews were lukewarm, and I was so disenchanted with myself and the public's response that I decided for a time to focus on journalism.

My phone began ringing and I pounced on it.

"What's going on? You didn't call me back. Are we on or not?" Who else but Greg.

"We are, I'm sorry. I've been on deadline."

"I'm about to go to the park."

"I'll meet you," I said.

I grabbed my keys and walked one flight downstairs and out

the door of my apartment building. I was all too aware that a phone call from Greg, who once meant everything to me, had become just another perfunctory communication.

Nevertheless, for the last eight months, our Casey, a Labrador mix, had been shuttling between Greg and me. There had been times when, because of logistics involving the dog (separate sets of keys to each other's apartments), Greg and I had been forced to witness telltales of sexual activities: a packet of open condoms, a crusty towel lying next to the bed. Once I even discovered a blurry black-and-white Polaroid of a muscle man with his white shirtsleeves trashily rolled up. As far as I was concerned, sharing the dog equally had been forcing too much contact between us, and now it was time to map out the future.

The moment Casey saw me, he began taking great leaps, trying to scale the fence of the dog run. I stuck my hand through and let him lick me.

"You coming in?" Greg asked.

"Yeah, in a second. Let him calm down first."

At first glance one never would have thought Greg was twenty-seven. Already lines were etched around his eyes; his pale skin was starting to freckle, and there were even thinning patches visible in his blunt-cut fair hair. He wore a plaid button-down shirt cut off at the shoulders, a fad that made the arms look bulkier, more chiseled. The shirt was open to the navel. He looked like a wild hot Marine.

"I heard you were at the Morning Party," I said after we'd embraced over the top of the fence, after I'd smelled Greg's familiar sweet scent that gave me a stab of confusing desire.

He frowned. "Who told you that?"

"What difference does it make? Half of New York City was there."

"I decided to go at the last minute," he admitted bashfully. "I was bored."

"So how was it? Did you . . . enjoy yourself?" I asked, wanting but not wanting to know if Greg had met anybody. Eight months into a breakup, on a migration toward emotional autonomy, we'd traveled enough distance from each other by now not to cave in emotionally at the thought of the other making love with someone else. And yet we hadn't gone quite far along enough for our romantic adventures to be an easy topic of conversation.

"How could you meet anybody at one of those events? Or I should say, how could you *believe* you'd meet anybody, since nearly everyone except me was on Ecstasy?"

"I'm your best friend," I mocked.

"Your best girlfriend," Greg said.

"Who are you, again? Where did we meet?" we both said in unison and laughed.

"Fucking grim, isn't it?" Greg said.

"Fucking grim to be single again."

For some reason I remembered the first time we'd ever made love, how Greg had presented me with a gift-wrapped condom and how corny I thought it was at the time. I'd gone through that period where I thought it was charming, but now it seemed corny again.

I walked the length of the dog run and passed through the gate. Casey rushed me, jumped up and gleefully placed his paws on my shoulders. He had a taller, lankier frame than most Labradors, splashes of white on each of his paws as well as on his chest; his head was slim like a hound's. The blue squash ball in his mouth was dropped at my feet, and I picked it up and heaved it. By the time I reached Greg, he was looking wistful.

"What's wrong now?" I said almost accusingly.

"Something just made me sad, okay?" he said defensively.

"What is it?" I wondered if I should put my arm around him.

He fought to steady his voice. "Just that we seem to get along better now that we've broken up."

"Is that so uncommon?"

"But you keep your distance. In order to skip over everything that makes you feel uncomfortable."

"What am I supposed to do? Continue to beat my breast?"

"I'm not saying that."

It occurred to me that exactly one year had passed since Greg had announced to me that he was having a summer affair. Ironically, he'd broken the news not ten feet away from where we now stood, while Casey was chasing a ball. Although it was not quite clear at the time, it turned out that Greg was retaliating for the fact that I'd left him in the city for the summer and brought Casey up to Vermont, where I had tried to write another novel in a rented house, a novel that I ended up abandoning.

"So are you always going to keep me at arm's length?" Greg asked me now.

"I didn't know that I was," I said, although the words echoed with what some other ex-lovers had told me.

"Come on, of course you are. And doesn't that have something to do with the fact that you don't want to share Casey anymore?"

I began digging a hole into the layer of wood chips that cushioned the ground of the dog run. "We've been through this so many times, Greg," I said. "I mean, as far as I'm concerned, outside of the fact that we don't sleep together nothing is all *that* different. I may not trust you as much as I used to. But that's not really required, is it?"

Casey had plopped the ball at Greg's feet and was still waiting for it to be tossed. As the dog's patience began to wane, he cocked his head from side to side, as if trying to understand what we were saying. Finally a frustrated whine escaped him, and Greg picked up the ball and threw it. Casey took off.

I said, "I've always held that there shouldn't be something between us like Casey that forces contact. We should choose when we want to see each other."

"The thing that bugs me, though, is sometimes you give me the impression that you think this has all been so much easier on me, that I haven't gone through it, too."

"Easier only in that you've had your diversions."

"Look, you're no angel either, big guy."

Greg was referring to the fact that once he'd ended his affair—to my way of looking at it, conveniently at the end of the summer when I was ready to come back to Manhattan—I had had an affair myself. The Domino Theory of Retaliation. But what disturbed me was that all too quickly it seemed possible to veer beyond the crisis with Greg into self-sufficiency. Quite the opposite of what happened with *him*, when for too long I was marooned in depression and grief. Nevertheless, Greg and I had dutifully tried to revive the relationship with marathon conversations that seemed to go nowhere, with separate weekend vacations during which we each tried to figure out what exactly we wanted from the relationship. But what emerged was the fact that we were each polarized by distrust, by the sense of betrayal that flourished in the wake of our affairs. Our relationship finally died during the winter.

Even so, Greg still wanted some form of contact to continue between us, whereas I leaned toward collapsing the shell of a bombed-out structure. Then there was Casey, whose unconditional devotion to each of us had become more and more insistent. It was hard to know what to do about him.

Two and a half years ago we had adopted Casey from an animal shelter on a cold, blustery morning. Greg and I caught the Long Island Rail Road out to the North Shore of Long Island, where, among hundreds of puppies, we were both drawn to a seven-week-old Labrador with blue eyes and a whip of a tail that had a white tip like a little penlight. The train home didn't allow dogs, and we had to take him back to the city in a cardboard box that, we pretended, held a television. Whenever Casey began whimpering I'd elbow Greg in the side, and Greg in turn would make diversionary noises.

The first night Casey lived with us, we tried to make him a bed in the kitchen, but whenever we left him alone, he'd let loose this heartrending bleat. I never wanted the dog to bunk with Greg and me—it took a lot of convincing on Greg's part—but once he finally convinced me to bring Casey up into bed, the dog instantly fell asleep. He'd slept between us ever since until the day Greg finally moved out.

"So are we agreed to stop trading him back and forth?"

Greg responded almost immediately to my question, as though he'd rehearsed the entire conversation. "Your parents got divorced. You're more used to the idea of having to give things up."

"You could also say it makes everything more traumatic for me."

"I suppose."

So easily does a dog become the child of two lovers who will never have children.

"Listen to me for a second, Greg. You spend less time at home than I do." He looked at me, alarmed. "But we both know you're more bonded to Casey," I added.

"Now you sound like you don't even want him."

"Come on, this is hard enough."

"You're right. I'm sorry."

I knew that Greg was grateful to have me spell everything out. "You'll come and see him a lot, though, right?" he now said.

"Sure, and every time I go to Vermont he can tag along."

For many months I tried to blame our breakup on extracurricular liaisons. And yet, in my heart, I knew that I had failed Greg in a much more fundamental way. For in the wake of losing *him* I'd barricaded the deepest corridor of myself from anyone else. And in a way, that was a much more profound infidelity.

"I'm thirty-five years old, Greg," I suddenly found myself saying. "I'm just beginning to understand things. I can't imagine what it must be like for people who realize that when they don't have a lot more time left."

"Well, of course, then their priorities change."

"I guess they would have to."

There was a sullen silence before Greg said, "Will, I don't think our decision should be irrevocable. I think you'll agree we should try Casey living with me and see how it works out."

My meeting with Greg might have exhausted me if I hadn't been fueled by the anxiety of waiting to hear from you. However, there were no calls on my answering machine when I returned from the dog run. I kept warning myself that nothing yet had happened between us and that it was foolish to expect anything. Nevertheless, all throughout the rest of the afternoon, I felt a kind of tentative emptiness that I could identify all too well, and by the end of the day this mood had assumed its familiar ache.

For me, expectation quickly turns into discomfort: waiting to hear from someone, knowing that as the afternoon diminishes, there are fewer chances of a call. Why do all the potent experiences reduce to this terrible yearning, the *him* at the center of me? It's no wonder that in the last ten years I've deliberately chosen men whose emotional reach falls just shy of that region of desperate desire.

By the time five o'clock came around, my mood had turned vile, and this, I knew, was the beginning of trouble. Then, suddenly, a remedy struck; and having a plan, a purpose, momentarily stilled my uneasiness. I recalled your mentioning that your office was in Turtle Bay; surely one of my architect friends would know a bunch of firms in that neighborhood. I managed to get hold of my friend Sheldon, who rattled off a half dozen companies until I heard the one that jogged my memory.

"Sirjane, Wallis and Moody," said the receptionist.

"I'm trying to reach Sean Paris."

"Hold on," she said, giving me classical music to fret by. She came back on, saying, "I'm sorry, but Sean Paris is at a doctor's appointment."

"A doctor's appointment?" I heard myself saying. (Were you okay? Was it HIV? Was that why you'd eased away from making love to me?)

When the woman asked for my name, I managed to think quickly. "I'm a friend of Sean's from graduate school who's in town for the day."

She offered to relay a message but then stopped short. "Oh," she said. "It's marked down here that he's leaving town afterward. I guess he won't be back until tomorrow."

Leaving town? You had never said anything about leaving town.

Now I was really on edge. I decided the only way I could gain any relief was by hurrying to the six o'clock masters' swim practice that I attended three times a week at New York University. But I was too preoccupied to work out properly, and in the midst of leading a set, five people behind me, I ceased swimming in the middle of a lap. A very competitive woman who was trailing me slammed into my feet and roared, "What the fuck are you doing, Will?" I apologized to her, because I always hunker down when it comes time for swimming sets, then surprised everyone by vaulting from the pool.

There were no messages when I got home.

I tried calling your house. Still no response.

That night I attended a book publication party held at a SoHo art gallery for an outspoken Latin American novelist whom I'd profiled for a glossy magazine. I had several drinks, tried to make conversation with the people I bumped into, but all I really wanted to do was rush home and see if the message light on my answering machine was flashing seductively. No such luck.

My frustration got channeled into the annoyance of two take-out menus slipped under my door in my short absence—a pet peeve of mine—in defiance of the sign I had posted downstairs in ten languages, including Chinese and Korean, asking that all printed matter, including menus, be left in the vestibule. I promptly picked up the telephone and called both restaurants and warned that if another menu was shoved under my door I would call back with a hundred-dollar delivery order and leave a phony address. When I put the phone down I felt powerful and right-eous, but only for a few minutes. Until I tried you again and your phone just rang and rang and rang. Perhaps it was better if you never contacted me again, for surely, after a week of separation, you'd clear out of my system like an airborne malady and my emo-tional temperature would drop to normal.

Nevertheless, I barely slept that night. At some point midway between midnight and dawn, I woke up and saw the red 0 on my answering machine. A red zero on an answering machine is like an infinite ellipse of loneliness. A 1 digital readout looks like a strike or a hit, a glimmer of possibility that there might be inter-est from someone else. A 2 spells an even greater hope of proba-bly one business or unimportant call and the call that you're really waiting for. A 3 message is more promising and subversive in its suggestion of at best two romantic possibilities. A 4 is definite popularity, business and love all mixed together. And a 5 with its S squiggle promises a full life to someone who is as swift as Mer-cury. Beyond 5 is pure chaos.

I'm obsessed with the telephone. But it has to do with the in-ordinate amounts of time I spend working alone. Alone. I know that during certain months when I'm depressed or anxious, my phone bills rise. For two weeks after Greg broke the news of his affair, I hardly slept and ran up quite a phone bill calling far-flung friends who lived in time zones so distant from my own that calling them at four o'clock in the morning didn't seem, in their time, like such an act of desperation. To have neurotic conversations relayed by satellite beguiles me. The latest advances of science can touch the backward human heart.

I try to imagine the nineteenth century when lovers were sometimes separated by great continental and oceanic distances, when, in some cases, letters required weeks to voyage back and forth between the tolerant and the cherished. How did people wait so patiently for word? What sustained them during those long, attenuated silences? What made them keep believing that at the end of a long separation they would still be loved?

5

ONLY THREE DAYS WITHOUT WORD, AND I ACTUALLY STARTED WON-
dering if I'd invoked you like some kind of demon lover, if you
even existed at all. For there had been a time in my life ten years
ago, the dark August after he vanished, when I was having trouble untangling real events from my fantasy life, a time when all
the edges seemed to blur.

For the first few months his memory became like the phantom feelings of an amputated limb that injured war veterans talk
about. I felt his presence tingling just beyond my fingertips, the
eucalyptus/sweat smell of him coming to me at odd times. As I
took long, solitary walks along the Rincon's curving beach, I
thought I saw him out with the surfers, the glints of the sun's fil-
igree in his salt-glossed hair. At night I could swear he climbed
in bed and brushed up against me with the silken muscles of his
cobra's-hood back.

I began pondering the idea that he might have unwittingly
slipped into some parallel world. Sometimes, after driving for

hours at a time, I suddenly have no recollection of navigating my car. I wonder if I've been in an accident, catapulted into a dimension of those who have also died in auto wrecks and who keep driving on some celestial high-speed road, as yet unaware of their sudden transmigration.

In my mourning, I became a solitary nightswimmer. Swam alone out to the two-hundred-yard buoys and beyond, breaking the cardinal rule that he and I laid down. Swam that dark half mile, swam until I panicked that the ocean had become my own private black hole. Swam recklessly close to the shoals because only when I feared for my own life was I able to dull the pain.

Three days without word from you, and then I was riding in a taxi up Sixth Avenue, late for a dinner engagement with a German publisher. Waiting at a red light, I suddenly thought I spotted you sailing along the street in a pair of cut-off army fatigues. At such a pace your body had now assumed the perfect balance of its proportions. Like a ray of light you effortlessly rent the slower-moving clouds of city dwellers. And through the window of the cab I just watched, stupefied, afraid that I was imagining you, afraid that my voice would fail me if I called out. Even if I did call out—"Sean Paris!"—I'd only watch you pivot and look around. And that would be even worse, to see you search for me. However, once the taxi started moving again, I realized that at least I should've tried to get your attention. Because now in addition to not knowing why you hadn't called, I would never know for sure if I'd actually seen you. The moment I reached the restaurant, I used the phone. No response on your line—and still no answering machine.

I stood there, composing myself before sitting down with the publisher. It was a Vietnamese place, the telephone located in a small enclosure whose walls were covered in rattan and drawings of sampans gliding along swampy rice paddies. Whether or not I'd seen you, either way the situation was grim. If I *had* seen you, then you weren't out of town (as the receptionist had claimed) and purposely you were choosing not to call me. If I'd imagined you, that meant . . . ten years ago was happening all over again.

Six months after he left me, I thought I began to see *him* all over Santa Barbara—the first time, weaving in and out of the crowd at the Summer Solstice Parade, wearing a loosely fitting Hawaiian shirt. I rushed after him, knocking into people, who cursed and grappled with me until I just plain lost him. And even after I called his family, who'd gone ahead with the funeral and had accepted the fact that he would never wash ashore, who kept assuring me that it was unlike him just to disappear, I couldn't sleep for days, suddenly believing that he'd been deliberately avoiding me.

Then one night I was driving past the Paradise Café. I was driving in his Volkswagen, given to me because his parents could not bear to keep it. I thought I spotted him with a woman; I recognized his swaggering movements, his unique gesture of patting the scruff of his neck. When I slammed on the brakes and screamed his name, he darted into an alleyway. I quit the car in the middle of crowded Anacapa Street and sprinted after him. But he was nowhere. Cars were honking at the Volkswagen abandoned in the middle of traffic as I ran back to the Paradise Café and described him: a guy wearing a black T-shirt and turquoise drawstring pants. But no one seemed to remember him. And that was when I finally began staying home.

For six months I barely left my apartment. Listless, totally without energy, I suffered from strange night fevers that hovered around a hundred degrees. In those days, the early eighties, it was one's privilege to come down with a fever and not be frightened of what that fever might forecast. Mornings I'd wake up completely doused in my own sweat. A doctor at Student Health Services told me that I had some kind of low-grade blood infection, for which I was given a course of colorful-looking antibiotics. But the medicine did very little. For other reasons, mainly that I

didn't like any of the professors in my graduate program, I ended
up leaving the University of California without completing my
master's.

I slowly got better but my funds dwindled. The days accu-
mulated as slowly as prisoners' scratches on the walls of a holding cell. I did absolutely nothing day in day out, pent up in my
own little hell while, just outside my Roman-arched windows, the
southern California weather remained unblemished and dry. The
same whetted-looking leaves of the fan palm trees kept scraping
against the window glass. Down in the front garden, the birds of
paradise menaced me with their orange beaks; and a century plant
began perishing right before my eyes, a last spurt of life shooting
up from its dying heart, a spear that looked silly, too much like an
asparagus.

The publisher sensed immediately that something was amiss but
said nothing at first. His accent was quite heavy at times, and I
had difficulty understanding him. And since I tend to speak rather
quickly, particularly when I'm perturbed, the man kept asking
me to repeat myself. "You don't look very well, Mr. Kaplan," I was
told as we were waiting for the check.

"I think I'm a little under the weather. I'm actually feeling
somewhat feverish," I explained.

"I hope I don't get sick from you. Because there are many people I have to see on this trip," the man said rather irritably. I knew
that his sudden impatience in part had to do with his discovery
that I had not yet begun writing another book.

I was shivering by the time I arrived home. I took a comforter
down from the upper reaches of the closet; and it was the oddest
sensation, climbing into bed and trying to stay warm in the middle of August amid the smell of mothballs. And as I lay there trying to warm myself, I wondered if some piece of *him* had managed

to live on inside me, dormant for all these years until you came along. Because I was suddenly remembering details and situations I hadn't thought of in so long.

I'd first heard of him as this crazy grad student in philosophy who loved to swim alone at night in the fifty-meter pool, a guy who'd already been All-American in college water polo at Stanford and had been invited to work out with U.C. Santa Barbara's water polo team. I'd heard about how his activities, well known to the maintenance guys, were too much admired to be reported to Campus Security. The first afternoon I ever locked eyes with him, I'd gone home and nearly wrecked my closet looking for my favorite LONG COURSE NATIONALS T-shirt that an acquaintance of mine had brought me back from Tennessee. When I arrived at the pool that night I'd noticed the chain-link gates were slightly ajar and heard the unmistakable splashing rhythms of someone doing butterfly.

I ventured just inside the enclosure, saw one silver depth lamp illuminating a swimmer performing that power stroke that can be executed only by the most conditioned of athletes. I watched him rip out of a turn and start weaving through the water on his way back, and I listened to the thunderous sound of his dolphin kick. It is difficult to keep up butterfly for more than a hundred meters, harder still to surpass two hundred. But there he was, turning over fifty-meter lap after fifty-meter lap, his stroke long and steady. I kept waiting for his rhythm to flag, for his energy to wane, but his speed remained constant for three hundred, four hundred, five hundred meters. When he finally stopped, I left the shadows and ventured on deck.

"Hey, Will." He saluted me and then his arm slapped on the surface of the water. "What are *you* doing here?"

How the hell did he know my name already?

A moment later, he had vaulted from the pool, had crossed

his arms over his chest and was darting through the chill air toward the shower room, his dense upper body giving short fatless
jerks as he moved. Noticing my bewildered expression, he said,
"Don't look so shocked. I've been sitting in on *The Divine Com-
edy*," referring to an overcrowded graduate lecture being taught
by a visiting scholar from Yale. "I've been sitting a few rows behind you. Now get a hit of that night jasmine, will you." He passed
me with a playful slap on the forearm, leaving it tingling with
droplets of water. "Pretty strong?"

Maybe he's just being friendly, I said to myself.

But then he continued, "Why don't you give me a few minutes . . . hang by the pool. I'll be right back." And so, terribly nervous, I waited for him out in the cooling night air, smelling the
jasmine and even the pittosporum trees, until he came back in a
pair of loose green sweatpants and a V-neck T-shirt, closed the
chain-linked gates and secured them with a padlock.

"Some night when the weather gets itself right again, I'm going to sleep out in the pool," he said as we began strolling toward
the parking lot. "Haul in one of those plastic rafts, lie out and
count everything up there I see. What do you think of that?"

"I've heard about you," I said, stopping. "You're the guy who
swims at night."

He gave no reaction other than automatically increasing his
pace. "So what are you up to, tonight?"

I shrugged.

"Take a ride with me," he cajoled. "Yonder go the wheels."
He pointed. The Volkswagen Beetle was illegally parked a few
yards away in a faculty spot. A *Harvard* decal was affixed to the
back window, and there was a bumper sticker for *Save the Whales*
as well as a three-pronged peace sign—obviously plastered on
the chrome bumper during Vietnam.

"Did you go to Harvard?"

"Belongs to my old man—he went. They drove it out here from Boston in '65."

"That where you were born?"

"Mass General Hospital."

The cramped interior of the car reeked exotically of dank vinyl and carpeting. A frayed umbrella lay in the back seat. He fired up the car and we began driving without an agreed-upon destination. I suppose I didn't really care where we were going. For a while we followed the circuit of campus roads, passing saltwater lagoons and towering Australian eucalyptus that punctuated the sandstone quadrangles of the University of California.

Something was rolling around the floor. I finally looked down to find an old pulpy orange. I batted it back and forth with my feet.

"How about we head up San Marcos Pass," he finally suggested.

"Isn't that kind of far?"

"You got someplace to be?"

"Not really."

"What's that burning smell?" I asked when we were halfway up to the Santa Ynez Mountains.

"Needs a new clutch." His eyes remained riveted to the road.

"Will we make it?

"I do this drive a couple times a week. It's been hurting like this for a month or so. We'll more than likely run out of gas." He was squinting at the fuel gauge. Suddenly letting go of the steering wheel with his right hand, he deftly reached around into the back seat for the umbrella, which he then brought forward, choking the lower portion down near the tip.

"What the hell are you doing?" I asked as he banged the metal point on one of the glass circles covering the dashboard. He shrugged as he tossed the umbrella behind him. "If you don't bang on it, it won't register." He leaned forward again and studied the dial. "Eighth of a tank. Jeez, I didn't realize it was that low."

"Are you doing this on purpose?"

He leered at me and I noticed how long his lashes were. "Look, it's faulty. Sometimes I forget to check it. I get distracted. You're actually the first person I've ever brought up here with me." He suddenly seemed bashful. "I usually come up here to get away from everybody."

The burning smell of the faltering clutch miraculously vanished as soon as we reached the summit of San Marcos Pass. He pulled off the road onto the dirt shoulder. If we'd kept going, the road would have begun a steep descent into the desolate Santa Ynez Valley, a region that people say resembles the East African plains.

Two thousand feet above sea level, we leaned against the hood of the car and peered up at the stars. Overhead, clouds were shredding themselves into rags. You could see the firmament better, the air was so much warmer up there in the mountains than it was down by the coast; and breezes riffling through the chaparral were spiked with sage. We stared out toward the black outlying mass of the Pacific, where a lighted strand of oil derricks, hugging the bend in the coastline, draped down toward Los Angeles like a bejeweled, celestial runway.

Something strange happened to me as I stood there on that mountaintop. Only years later did it seem portentous. But that night, looking at the panorama with *him,* I actually abandoned myself. I became the distance, I became everything I saw except for who I was. No longer myself, I got frightened that I would never be able to reenter my own body. Was this some kind of premonition of his vanishing and of what would eventually happen to me? Was it some little gremlin out there, tempting my soul to disembody, like one of those Chumash Indian spirits that supposedly gather up the coast at Point Conception and fly across the Pacific Ocean with the speed of darkness?

But I was yanked back to myself when I felt his arms winding around me from behind. And I jumped.

"What's wrong?" he said.

At a momentary loss to explain, I said, "Nothing, just a little dazed."

He twirled me around, kissed me once and, parting his lips, took mine just inside of his. How could he so boldly assume that I would allow him to do that? He just didn't care.

I was elated as we drove back toward the city of Santa Barbara. After the engine sputtered and failed, gravity pulled us down the mountain road, and it was like being in a glider, hovering in wind drafts above a mountain range, hoping for a flat valley in which to put down. He was adept at maneuvering the car around all the hairpin curves that remained on the descent. He took the last two much faster than safe, the Volkswagen's wheels bellowing and nearly slithering off the road.

"You can come down off the roof now, Will." He grinned, as the car coasted into the flats and finally stopped a quarter mile from a BP station. He got out and pushed the rest of the way while I steered. We finally edged into the gas station, wheels squeaking over the well-oiled smoothness of the concrete islands.

As he pumped the gas I watched him talking to a young, skinny attendant. They were standing rather close to each other while he held the nozzle in the tank, and he kept grinning and gesturing with his free hand. And I actually felt jealous that he might be flirting.

That scared me. I sat there half wishing he'd drive me back to my car so I could go home and try to unravel my emotions. But then he jumped in, and as we drove off I found myself unable to look at him. Finally I couldn't help myself and glanced over. He was peering at me, despite the fact that he was supposed to be driving, and the fervor in his black eyes was startling. He roared with laughter and I let my head fall on his shoulder.

"You're soaked," I commented.

"I worked up a sweat, pushing you," he boasted. "I think I need a swim."

"Where?"

"Where do you think?"

"The pool?"

"Noooo." Then he tilted his head toward the ocean, as though it were a given.

"I'm not going in there at night. It's dangerous at night."

"Says who?"

"No way am I going in!"

"Even if I tell you I'm a certified beach guard? Even if I promise to bail you out if you get in trouble?"

"A lot of good that's going to do if you're in trouble, too."

We suddenly swerved into a mini-mall, notable for a 7-Eleven that sold soft drinks out of a fountain—rare in 1981—as well as a chartreuse-colored thing called a Slurpee. He told me he'd be back in a minute, threw the brake, trotted around the front of the car, jogging down the row of shops past the 7-Eleven to a small lighted storefront. He reappeared a moment later with a small brown bag, asked me to open the glove compartment, where I'd find a Swiss Army knife. He yanked a lime out of the bag and then a bottle of Cuervo tequila.

He switched off the engine, commandeered the knife and cut neat, practiced lime wedges, which he then balanced on top of his squeezed-together knees. He scored off the plastic bottle cap, raising the tequila to his lips, and threw back a hard slug. He sucked a piece of lime, smiled at me with the green rind between his teeth and said, "Kiss me."

"Give me that." I wrenched the bottle and the lime from between his legs and took a gulp of tequila.

I was feeling numb and daring by the time we reached West Beach. The moonlight stretched like a bridge over the water and went as far as the Channel Islands. A collection of Speedos clustered on the floorboards of his car, and combing through them, he gave me the skimpiest, most revealing one he could find. "I want to see how you look in *that*," he said.

"But I'm pretty wrecked," I complained.

"Good, because you might not have done this otherwise."

No, but I would've done you, I thought to myself. Even without the tequila shots.

He peeled off his clothes, and I looked at him unclad for the first time: the olive complexion with a cool bronze patina from months of casual sunbathing beneath an unobstructed sun, large sensual nipples the color of caramel, each with a sparse sprouting of dark hair. I wondered if I'd ever be able to absorb what his body had to offer, the twin mounds of pectorals, where his back flared wide, the dark obscenity of his armpits, of his groin.

Before I had even taken my shirt off, he was in his Speedo, carefully watching me undress. And when I stood there, naked finally among the shadows on the beach, he shut his eyes halfway, reached forward, combed his fingers through my chest hair. In response, I made my hand into a tight rake, ran it up the scruff of his neck until it caught on his salt tangles. I slowly wound his head back until a groan inadvertently escaped him and I kissed his taut, corded throat. Then we fell to the sand and started going at it.

I ran my tongue along his tan line, buried my face in the tangle of pubic hair, gulped the sac that was as tight as a pear. "Baby, we've got to stop," he moaned finally, giving a long tender kiss. "For crying out loud, we can't do this here." A moment later, I was watching him dive in and disappearing through a crashing comber.

I hesitated, of course, but I had to follow.

Once I'd broken through the chill black wall of the first wave set, I sobered up. As I swam out beyond the breakwater, the ocean still seemed so amorphously deep and wide, an even greater mass than it appeared by daylight. Waves rolled over me like tall dark shadows. And there were times during that first reckless swim that I lost track of where I was in relation to the beach or the outer islands thirty miles across the channel.

But he was vigilant, never swam too far ahead of me. That first night, with each stroke away from shore, I felt as though I was trespassing beyond my own instinct for survival. Even though in the coming weeks we'd venture out even farther, sometimes with surfboards, sometimes sharing a single raft, I knew we could commit a fatal error of judgment that would allow us to be swept under, hauled back to our moment of entry into the world. The whole uncertain future could be decided by a single, wayward glance.

That first feast of another man's body is both joyful and confusing. I want to fill myself with everything, every nipple and biceps and every inch of cock, but I want to savor it and that demands more than one occasion. When I know a man for a while, when the parts of his body become familiar to me, as his own scent that I carry on my clothes, on my forearms, when he ceases to become just a name and becomes a familiar man, that's when the real sex begins. By then he's told me private things, and I know something of his story; and when I reach over to touch him in a bed that we've both slept in night after night, nothing casual, no matter how galvanic, can rival the power of that touch. For that touch is now encoded with the knowledge that I could lose everything, and movement by movement, as I make love, I'm more completely aware of what I stand to lose.

6

THE TELEPHONE RANG. DRENCHED IN MY OWN SWEAT, I KICKED OFF the quilt and grabbed the receiver. "Hello," I said, "hello," as I heard the noisy background of what I assumed was a bar. "Is *he* there?" somebody finally asked.

"Is who here?"

"You know who." The person sounded more sad than menacing.

"What number are you trying to get?" I asked and then whoever it was slammed down the phone.

I was unable to sleep after that. I do get my share of crank phone calls and wrong numbers. This must happen more in cities, where within a single exchange there is a higher density of numerical sequences that are slight variations of one another, and it's easier to reach a working number if anyone dials incorrectly, or randomly. However, I had the feeling that the person who'd called somehow knew me.

I tried to get up and begin working on a travel article that I

was writing for the *Los Angeles Times*, but felt too weary and distracted to concentrate. I ended up heading over to the New York
University pool. I swam a straight 2,500 meters, pushing the last
500 as hard as I could, in pursuit of an endorphin fix. I was toweling off in the locker room when I overheard two guys discussing
Splash, a recent addition to the bar scene that, on certain nights
of the week, featured go-go boys in G-strings who took showers in
front of the patrons. Splash was also known to play video footage
from previous weekends at Fire Island. "Last night I saw myself
at the Morning Party," one of them remarked.

Listening to them, I realized that Western life was truly becoming saturated with all new kinds of media. And that people
were becoming less selective about what images they chose to
preserve—now every stupid bacchanal weekend at the Fire Island Pines was certain to be recorded by somebody. I tried to
imagine the sheer space taken up by memorabilia all over the
world, and it occurred to me that the ratio of what was recorded
to what had actually happened was constantly growing at an
alarming rate.

Not much of a barfly myself, I'd never actually been to Splash.
But now I was curious to see what it had to offer in the way of Morning Party footage. I left word on Peter Rocca's Voicemail, sug-
gesting that we go out for a drink later that night.

"Gee, I wonder if that T-shirt could be any tighter on you," I said
to him the moment he strolled in and gave the crowd his once-
over. He grinned tensely at me, then glanced down at his chest
straining against a skin of gray cotton, and at the tips of his shiny
cowboy boots. "Shaddup," he said. "You don't come to these places
to be inconspicuous."

"So you're going to start man-hunting right in front of me?"

"No better, no worse than somebody else I know."

"Now, wait a second, Peter, let's get this straight. You're the one who said 'no commitments.' "

"Only because I'm not yet commitment-free . . . Jesus, what's with you tonight, anyway?"

"I've been having trouble sleeping, for one thing."

"Well, if it stays like this and you need a prescription, let me know."

It dawned on me that having a doctor for a friend could be handy. "Do any drugs exist that can wipe out selected memory?" I asked.

"Believe it or not, the best way is still electroshock."

Electroshock, I admitted, might be pushing it just a little bit.

"Particularly if memory is how you make your living." Peter put his elbow on my shoulder. "So why haven't you been sleeping?"

"Let me ask *you* something. What would *you* do if one of your patients came in here right now and saw you dressed like this?"

"Highly unlikely, but I could deal with it." Self-consciously crossing his arms over his chest, Peter squinted at me and said, "There are one or two I might even take home with me."

I guffawed.

Splash was brimming on a Wednesday night, late summer, only a few days beyond the full moon. White T-shirts, tans, the latest pump at the gym being advertised. The more revealing the outfit, the loftier the attitude, and, quite often, the deeper ran the rut of insecurity.

In the late seventies and early eighties, it used to be that you could surface in such a bar and know instantly who wanted you and whom you could have. But these days, with sex-at-the-first-encounter not necessarily first on everybody's agenda, there was more caginess, posturing, an element of wiliness. These days people basked in being sought after, being desired, not necessarily needing to make sexual contact.

"See that pumped-up guy, the one with his shirt off?" Peter

asked. "Well, he's made himself a couple of million on Wall Street."

"Then I think there should be a cap on income."

"Why? Let the guy have his fun . . . as if *you're* not into money and power."

"Peter, if I were into money, believe me, I wouldn't be doing what I'm doing. I'd be trading bonds or brokering stock."

"Making a lot of money is just another form of vanity."

"Is that why you shrinks make so much of it?" I laughed.

"I don't know about the rest of them, but I make as much as I can so I can take my boyfriends on expensive vacations."

"So, if I'd hung in there a little longer, I would have hit the jackpot?"

Peter shrugged. "Who's to say?"

"And just when would you have sprung the trip to Istanbul on me?"

"Probably in another week or so."

"And what about Sebastian?"

"Oh, he would've come along—as the towel boy . . . Look, why are we here together, anyway?" Peter's tone became irritable. "We didn't have to come *here* in order to squabble."

"We came here to see that," I said, pointing to the television screen directly opposite us that was playing shots of the Morning Party.

"I've seen it. I was there, remember?"

"All right, so you're keeping me company," I said.

I bought the first round of beer, and then Peter and I wedged ourselves into a corner and began watching the video screen. All over the bar stood clusters of men, riveted to the footage of the summer's most popular bash, where the worship of hairless muscle was celebrated en masse. In living color, men gamboled on a huge dance floor that was erected right on the beach at Fire Island. Necklaces made with what looked like ball bearings strung together were all the rage this year. Clutching cups of frothy beer, glassy-eyed, tribes of torqued-up bodies danced together under the influence of the great friendship drug Ecstasy.

"What a pain it must be keeping the whole body shaved," Peter said in response to all the smooth torsos.

I imagined thousands of guys rising at the crack of dawn, steaming up their bathrooms, shaving their balls, their assholes, their chests. Battalions of odalisques. No expense spared to create an illusion of youth. But, quite obviously, only an illusion. Fascinated by the procession of hairless guys, I said, "Jesus, they make me feel like a fucking ape."

"You better not start shaving anything," Peter warned me.

"What difference does it make? You and I will probably never do it again," I found myself saying.

Peter looked at me, injured. "Why did you say that?" he demanded, clenching his jaw and raising his eyes once again to the video screen. "You know, you're lousy to me sometimes."

"You're right. I'm sorry, I shouldn't have said that. I guess I'm in a bad mood tonight."

"Why are you in such a rotten mood?"

Obviously I wasn't going to explain. "Probably some kind of chemical imbalance," I said. Looking around the bar, I couldn't help wondering what someone from another culture would say upon entering this place: why are there only men here, and wearing white T-shirts; why are they all watching television monitors? "Seen yourself yet, Peter?"

"I was in the water most of the time. Believe it or not, there was hardly anybody in the water. Five thousand guys strutting their stuff up and down a beach and maybe twenty of us were in the ocean."

"Obviously, they didn't want to screw up their hairstyle," I said, nervously patting my own thinning scalp. "Must be nice to have to worry about that."

Peter grinned and then took a playful swipe at me. "Don't

worry, you don't need a full head of hair. You're a bona fide tamale," he said and kissed me.

Some of the guys were fondling themselves self-consciously as they danced, looking guardedly down at their pumped torsos as if to make sure that everything was there, if it still worked, as if their bodies had been borrowed from someone else and had never belonged to them to begin with.

Will, what are you looking for, I remember asking myself, even though I knew I was searching for your face. Your face as it would have looked only hours before you entered my life. Searching for the dark curls, for the wolverine eyes. Until I became aware of a couple of Latino hunks clustering near Peter and me. There were fast-track glances in our direction, too swift to necessarily mean interest. "What do you mean?" I heard one of them say nastily. "He did have someone. He was dating Sean Paris."

"Well then, it's no wonder," someone else murmured.

They were peering our way, at Peter's bulging fairness, his overpumped cliffhanger tits.

The reference to you made me gawk at the group of men, something one never should do at a *posing bar* such as Splash; gawking is immediately interpreted as some sort of self-abasement.

"Why are you cruising *them,*" Peter wanted to know, and I told him why, that they'd mentioned you.

"Sean Paris?" Peter looked irked. "You seem inordinately interested in Sean. You seen him since that night?"

I shook my head.

"Seriously?"

"I told you, no."

"How come?"

"Just haven't seen him, that's all."

"So, is *he* your next quarry?" Peter was someone who had already inspired deranged behavior in another man, yet he knew

that I'd gone cool on him in the heat of you. He wasn't used to being in this predicament.

"*Quarry,*" I repeated, "that's an odd way to put it."

"Not really. Because you can't completely immerse yourself
in an experience, you're always one step back, studying it. You'd
have made a great doctor," he exclaimed, looking at me solemnly.
"A much better shrink than I'll ever be."

"You make me sound awful, you know that?"

"It's true, though, isn't it?"

I hesitated and then I said, "I think it might be why all my recent relationships have ended."

"So then where exactly does Sean fit into all this?"

"Don't be jealous of him." I tried to soothe Peter. "You're a
good friend."

"Oh, Jesus, now I'm just a *good friend* to you. That's not what
you were saying last week when I had your dick in my mouth."

"I just want to get to know Sean Paris, that's all. There's something about him—"

"I'll tell you what it is about him."

But Peter never got a chance to say. Time and space collapsed
as I looked up to the video screen and saw a flash-frame of you
grind-dancing with a black man, both of you glistening, two so
distinct from those surrounding you. Your eyes were closed, lust
scrawled all over your face, and the other man was more divine
than any line that I could ever write.

"Shit, there he is, that fucking little heartbreaker, that bitch!"
one of the Latino boys cackled. "She deserves a cannonball up
her humpy little ass."

Bewildered, I glanced over at the group of them again. Why
were they so angry? But then an almost psychic current swerved
my attention toward the door, where, completely unaware that
your video doppelgänger was making an appearance on twelve

different television monitors all over the bar, there you stood. You were dressed in a loose white T-shirt and the cut-off army fatigues I'd noticed the other night when I was riding in the taxi, when I was unsure whether or not I'd spotted you. So you *had* been in the city all along, you just hadn't called *me!*

As you scoured the far corners of Splash with the most dismal of expressions on your face, the moment you noticed me, the silly grin appeared. Without even considering whether or not it would be a romantically politic move, I began walking toward you, and as soon I arrived you gave my shoulder a playful squeeze.

"Hey, I just left you a message."

And I actually tried to sound calm and detached when I answered, "Hey, I'm not home."

"What are you doing *here?*"

Looking for you is what I should have said. "I'm hanging out with Peter. You remember Peter Rocca," I joked as we strolled over to where he was standing.

"Hey, Sean," Peter said, clearly uncomfortable.

Your eyes bored into me. "So what's the story, Will? Your phone isn't listed anymore. I've tried to get ahold of you."

"Didn't you know, he's too important now to appear in the white pages," Peter said.

"Now, wait a minute," I objected. "I'm supposed to be in the latest phone book."

But I explained how there had been an error; when the last telephone book had been printed the number was mistakenly listed only under Greg's name. "I called to have it changed."

"Well, it never got changed," you said. "I finally had to go to the library to look it up in an old phone book."

"To think that you of all people aren't listed," Peter murmured. "It's kind of amazing. Considering that you'd shrivel up and die without a telephone."

"Do you have to broadcast every one of my weaknesses?"

Peter looked annoyed. "It doesn't take a rocket scientist to figure you out. Anyway, I think I'm going to move on. This is getting a little cozy. And"—he pointed across the crowded bar—"I see someone over there that I'd like to get to know. Catch you guys later." He strolled away toward the muscle sea that eventually parted and took him into its steroid depths.

"What's with *him,* suddenly?" you said.

"He spied us leaving his place together the other night. He got bent out of shape."

"Doesn't he see somebody?"

"You mean, is the shrink in therapy?"

"No, I'm saying doesn't he have a boyfriend?"

"As if that means anything." I sounded a little more cynical than I'd intended.

"Well, there are all kinds of relationships," you said and then winked at me. "So how are you doing?"—resting your hand on my shoulder.

I wanted to tell you how difficult the last few days had been, but felt foolish—yet again—for collaborating on my own misery. "God, I wish I'd known my phone wasn't listed," I said. "I actually tried calling you a couple times myself."

"Look, don't sweat it. I don't give a shit about the telephone, as you probably can tell."

This sobered me. Did you know how many times I'd tried to call, had you been hiding out in your apartment, listening to it ring and not answering it, mocking my persistence?

Wanting to move on to another subject, I pointed to the cavorting bodies on the video screen. "Hey, I just saw you."

"Saw me on the hit parade, huh?"

"You were dancing with a beautiful black man."

"Oh yeah?" you said shyly.

"I mistook him for God."

You laughed and the hand on my shoulder slipped around un-

til your forearm was resting on my neck. "Let's get out of here,
Will."

A perfect night for strolling, dry, with river wind slapping us
as we headed down Seventh Avenue. We moved together grace-
fully, as though accustomed to walking in each other's company.
The peacefulness I felt suddenly made up for the last few days of
fretting. Why had I tortured myself so?

"Been away, haven't you?" I said finally.

A nod.

"You never bothered putting the machine back on."

"I know."

"Don't you like getting messages?"

"People have my work number; they can always leave word
for me there."

"So where did you go?"

"Down to Pennsylvania . . . a friend of mine passed away. The
funeral was held in his hometown."

"Young?" I said, which tactfully meant "AIDS?"

You nodded.

"What a shame," I said.

At your lead we'd turned off onto Twelfth Street and traveled
west toward the Hudson. And then I had the oddest sense of the
air around my ears warping as something whizzed by. A thudding
sound echoed from the hubcap of a parked car. Somebody had
thrown a rock.

We both jerked to a halt and saw the shadowy forms of people standing under a street lamp next to a warehouse. One of them
grabbed something that looked like a pipe, banged on a car wind-
shield until a horizontal rain of green shards showered the street
like crushed ice. "Hey, Sean—ice princess!" somebody said. A
warble of laughter echoed through the street as they vanished into
the alleyway.

You shook your head dumbfounded and then looked at me, alarmed.

"What's all that about?" I asked.

"How do I know what it's all about? They're obviously drunk."

"Cut the bullshit. Why did they call you that?"

You frowned at me and said grimly, "Your guess is as good as mine." Hesitating another moment, you eventually said, "But I think I recognize one or two of them from the funeral. They all seem to know one another."

"So what's that got to do with you?"

"You certainly ask a lot of questions."

"Come on, what's going on here? What's the story?"

You sighed. "I dated the guy, the guy who died, for a while."

"How long ago?"

"We met around a year ago. It took a few months to get involved. The last time I saw him was way back in February."

I couldn't help asking, "Are you at all worried about yourself, your health, I mean?"

You shook your head slowly as you fitted the toe of your tennis shoe on a single fragment of glass that had managed through the impact to scatter like a seed as far as where we stood. You tried to break it down even further, but it refused to pulp. "I recently got tested again . . . I was negative."

I waited for you to ask me my status, and when you finally did I stammered, "I've never taken the test."

"How come?"

Like a recording on an answering machine, I announced how there was no tried and true early intervention, how for years I'd been practicing sexual behavior that assumed either I or my partner might be HIV-positive. That there were just too many opinions of what safe sex was, too many variable possibilities of becoming infected. Which meant, if one stayed single, running on the treadmill of having to get tested every six months. HIV-negative or -positive were labels that reminded me of Jews being constrained to wear yellow stars during World War II. No matter what anybody said, HIV-positive still spelled discrimination—outside as well as within the gay community. For the sad fact remained that many HIV-negative people were finding it difficult to make love to an otherwise healthy HIV-positive man. This made the otherwise healthy HIV-positives feel like outcasts.

And finally I explained that, for myself, keeping my HIV status a mystery made me live harder, kept me aware that I could not necessarily count on being in the world for more than the next few years and let me identify with both camps.

You were looking straight ahead, toward the West Side Highway, and I almost thought that you'd lost the thread of our conversation. But then you said, "Sounds like a lot of justification to me, Will. Sounds like you're just afraid of getting it—getting the test."

It was difficult to disagree, because I knew there was some truth in what you said.

We started walking again and the silence held sway over us until I remembered the point we'd been arguing before we hit the subject of HIV. When I remarked that I still didn't understand why anybody would blame you for a man's death, you shrugged and said you couldn't think of any other reason than you were the last person he'd been involved with. And that it didn't work out and that he was really upset for a long time afterward.

"Was he sick when you dated?"

"Not at all."

I thought how horrible it would be if your lover, whom you hadn't really loved, had sickened. Then you'd be faced, morally, with caring for him, but not caring—the most horrible paradox.

You were now gazing at me with the dismal expression I'd seen at Splash. "Things ended badly between us. I mean, I was only involved with him for around four months. But I was honest with him the whole way, honest from the very beginning."

The guy just never believed that you wouldn't eventually fall in love with him.

Yet I sensed something was being withheld about this man. I felt I was trying to grope my way along the dark borders of your story. But then you told me the real reason why you'd left your machine off, why you weren't answering the phone. This man's ex-lover, someone he'd been involved with before he met you, had been calling and harassing you.

We'd reached the West Side Highway, the body of the Hudson a dark void pearled with searchlights from Circle Line boats. I thought I heard music being piped in from somewhere.

Remembering the phone message the first night I met you, I said, "This guy who died, his name was Bobby, right?"

"His name was Bobby Garzino."

"So how exactly is Bobby Garzino's ex-lover harassing you?"

"Well, he's basically trying to get stuff back. Stuff that Bobby gave me. This guy thinks he deserves it all back because he really loved Bobby and I didn't. And I've refused because Bobby made them as gifts for me. Naturally I consider what Bobby gave me is mine."

Earlier in the day, Bobby's ex had managed to get through, and when you'd balked at his demands, he told you there were people he knew who wanted to ruin your face forever.

The horror of this idea stunned me for a moment and then I growled, "Not while I'm around."

"Come on, Will, he couldn't have been serious. He was just trying to scare me. And I certainly don't need you to be my protector. I can deal with this on my own."

"Now, wait a second, Sean. Just one second!" I stopped walking to emphasize what I had to say. "If somebody came up to us right now, am I supposed to just stand back? Let them hurt you?"

You laughed scornfully and faced the Hudson.

We continued to stand there in suppressed indignation, bracing ourselves against the wind. The moment passed, and when we started walking again, you turned to me, your eyes glistening.

"What would you do if I came up to you one day and my face was completely wrecked? Would you dump me then?"

"I didn't even know I had you to get rid of."

"Come on, you know what I'm saying. Let's say you did have me . . . to get rid of."

"How about this, Sean: I'd blind myself so I wouldn't have to see what had been done to you."

You threw your head back and howled with laughter. "Oh, God, so grandiose. So nineteenth-century."

"Don't knock the nineteenth century. Some great novels came out of the nineteenth century."

"Yeah, and so did some bad operas," you said.

7

YOUR APARTMENT WAS EVEN MESSIER THAN IT HAD BEEN SEVERAL DAYS
ago. The pile of clothing and magazines in the middle of the floor
had continued to gather and there was a daunting collection of
dirty dishes on the dining table. Yet there you sat wearing a crisp
white T-shirt and those military shorts with a razor-sharp crease
down the front. I noticed clusters of cut flowers everywhere: on
the mantel white roses floated like lilies in a glass bowl; the vio-
let faces of pansies draped over a short stubby vase, their thin
stems bobbing on the surface of the water. All the flowers looked
as if they'd come from a backyard, not from a store, a fact confirmed when I learned that you spent weekends tending a brownstone garden that you'd designed on Charles Street.

You retreated into the small dressing area, where there was
a drafting table and a bulletin board filled with photographs of
yourself with friends, a single hanging strand of pearls that once
a drag queen had thrown around your neck; a chain dangling a
rainbow assortment of freedom rings; a pair of blue undershorts

that had belonged to an especially memorable sexual encounter. You removed a thumbtack from a snapshot and brought it over to me. "That's Bobby Garzino." I flinched, half-expecting to see an emaciated face, an ethereal portrait of someone fast leaving the world behind. But this turned out to be a photo of a healthy man, no doubt taken before your first acquaintance with him. I contemplated a goofily handsome man whose chin had an appealing spoil of cross-hatched acne scars, whose ears were a bit large, whose dark eyes were soulful and turbulent. In them it was easy to see the glint of a wounded past.

"He was a gifted man," you explained. "He was a weaver." I frowned. "You know, like weaving baskets and silk fabrics. All these woven things he made." You led me to a closet near your front door where there was a small, square wall hanging composed of threads of varying thicknesses that were woven in a Hopi-like design. "That Egyptian-looking basket on the hearth, the one made of sixteen-millimeter film? That's his work. I've got scarves made out of nubby silk. A couple of lamb's-wool sweaters. Anyway, Bobby had his own custom-weaving business. He called it 'The Loom's Desire.' "

It was now hard for me to look at the photograph, which I still held. Almost like looking at a photograph of myself after you'd told me that I could never be your lover.

"He has—*had*—two looms in his apartment. They took up most of the main room. He could spend hours weaving the most amazing things." You frowned and then shrugged. "Probably why his old lover wants it all back. Anyway, I used to hang out with him while he worked and do some of my own drawings. He would go into a kind of trance. Almost like he was playing a silent harp."

The last time you'd seen Bobby Garzino was when he showed up at your apartment unannounced late one night in February in the middle of a severe snowstorm. You'd been out of touch with him for over two months, although somebody had been calling you at home and at work, hanging up as soon as your voice could be heard on the line.

You faltered for a moment. "He did the wildest thing, Will. He sat down in the middle of this floor, in that pile, although it was a different pile then, and he told me . . . he told me that this apartment was the most beautiful place he'd ever been to in his entire life. He said it was like being at a shrine."

I know exactly what he means, I thought, as I looked at the wings of the butterflies, veins of exotic deep pastels that would be impossible to re-create on any palette, the likes of which I'd seen only in tropical fish. And from across the room, the iridescence of the wood ducks' heads.

You continued, "He told me that since we'd ended it he'd been unable to take up his loom. That he'd just sit there and stare at it. And that the only place he thought he could do his weaving was here."

"You mean, he wanted to bring his loom over?"

"When I told him he really couldn't do that, he broke down and just lay there in the middle of my clothes. He kept telling me that I'd done something to him that made him feel stuck like . . . 'like a needle of a throttle' was the way he put it."

"But then you made love to him?"

"Yes."

"But why, if you knew it would only make his misery worse? It would only give him false hope."

You looked tormented and then made a fist and banged it on your chest. "Maybe I didn't realize that yet, okay? Maybe I thought he was finally going to get through to me." You paused and scowled at me, breathing swiftly. "When he came over here that night and put himself on the line, I really admired him for that and I thought maybe I'd . . . I don't know!" you cried out. "I don't fucking know."

And then I was all over you. Couldn't wait any longer, I just had to kiss that soft bud of a mouth. And as you resisted me I remembered California, afternoons of argument that he and I spent in my apartment, foolish arguments, in retrospect, urged on by the fact that one of us was in the mood for sex and the other was not. When chemistry is great between two guys as it was with *him*, it can bond in a way nothing else can. And yet I've come to believe that great chemistry is, more often than not, paid for by some equally great antagonism that has yet to be discovered, and once discovered, then mastered, and that, in all its mystery, galvanizes attraction.

I remember how he and I would argue until we'd finally reach a stalemate and, falling into silence, he would peer sullenly out my window at the pastel waterfront buildings and the rows of king palm trees that lined Cabrillo Boulevard. But then smelling *his* sweat-with-chlorine-and-eucalyptus, I thought I'd crack if one of us didn't break the barrier and initiate sex.

But with you it was different because you made clear from the beginning what ailed each of us. And there wasn't a mystery that needed to be unraveled as much as there was a history that needed to be revealed.

You gently extricated yourself from my embrace. "I don't know if I can do this right now, Will. I'm upset. Do you understand?"

"All too well."

"I mean, when I first met this guy, he was completely self-sufficient. He was joyful, he loved his work. And his stuff was beautiful, too. He had tons of commissions lined up: wall hangings, designing fabric for custom-made clothing. But then after a few months with me he was completely miserable."

"Sometimes I think that some of my loneliest times were when I've been involved," I said.

"You mean with the guy whom you haven't talked about?"

I hesitated. "I guess . . . with him, yeah."

"The guy whose name you won't even tell me."

"That's because I don't allow him to have one . . . Anymore," I added after a moment.

"Come on, Will, you make it sound so melodramatic. Like you're still so devastated ten years later that you can't even speak his name."

I glared at you, then realized how deftly you had changed the subject. I said matter-of-factly, "I can easily speak his name. It's a rather uncommon name." I found myself looking at the arcing neck of your trout fishing rod, at a pale blue oxford shirt hastily draped over a hanger that dangled from a closet doorknob. "But if you really want to know, I'll tell you what it is. His name"—I hesitated—"is Chad."

A short silence followed and then we heard a warbling sound, a soft clamoring of wings, as though, just by mentioning him, I'd roused a nest of pigeons from the building eaves.

"So what bugs you so much to say his name?"

"What bugs me is that I'm still angry." You frowned and then I added, "I don't say his name because I don't know if he died or if he left me. I don't say his name because if he left me, it's my only way of . . . I don't know, Sean, it's been a lot worse living with the idea that he might have wanted to disappear."

"But what exactly happened to him?"

I gulped and couldn't answer at first, couldn't get the words to come. Had to wait for them, still afraid to admit why it had been so hard for all this time. "You see, we became . . . we were nightswimmers," I finally began. "But it was *his* thing. He coerced me into swimming after dark in the ocean because *he* loved doing it. He was magnificent in the water, completely fearless. He was the only guy I ever knew who could do a thousand yards straight of butterfly."

I described that last swim and the sudden appearance of the barge coming toward us. How I thought we were turning around and swimming in together, but it ended up being only me.

You waited a few moments and then you said, "So what are you telling me? That he never came out?"

I explained how I'd waited for him by the two-hundred-yard buoys for what seemed like hours, how I'd ended up with a bad case of hypothermia.

"So then he must've drowned—like Leander drowned crossing the Hellespont."

I sighed. "We were close enough to shore that . . . let's put it this way, usually things as large as human bodies wash up fairly soon."

"Usually. Unless a shark got to him first."

A fate that I'd imagined hundreds of times. "Still, there'd be— almost always there's some trace or other that washes up: bones, parts. I talked to the Coast Guard many times. But they found nothing whatsoever."

"But there was that boat?"

I faltered and then continued with difficulty. "Even if he'd gotten sucked into the propeller, there would have been some evidence. It was actually the Coast Guard who suggested to me he might have swum somewhere else and just walked away. In fact, I think that's what they came to believe—though it wasn't official."

"But why? Why on earth would he do that?"

"I don't have a clue. I only knew him for eight months."

"What about his parents, what did they say?"

"That he just wasn't the kind of guy to vanish. But then again, what *would* parents say?"

"And you really loved him, didn't you?"

I lowered my eyes and nodded.

"And you really don't think he's dead?"

I now looked at you until I felt my glance piercing through. "I feel certain that he's *not* dead. And knowing that, knowing that he's probably alive right now, almost makes it worse."

"I don't agree. I think it's easier for you to believe that he's alive."

That made me angry. "I knew you wouldn't get it if I told you!" Again, I explained there would've been some trace, and how I'd done research into similar situations and learned that there were many people who did exactly that, "lost" themselves and were finally tracked down years later. "If you could've seen the way he swam, you would've understood there was no way he could've drowned. He used to go surfing in all kinds of weather and come out without a scratch. He used to go swimming in rough water when nobody else would."

"He sounds like one of those people who love to tempt the edge. But sometimes those sorts of people lose their gamble."

"He was a survivor from the word go. There was plenty of warning that the barge was coming. He obviously wanted to escape. And I'll just never know why."

You slipped your arms around me and held my head against your shoulder and stroked the back of my neck. And after a stint of silence you said, "You're too wonderful a man for anybody to want to leave you without at least an explanation."

Taking this as a signal, I drew a tongue line down your neck, and kissed arcs along your shoulders and gave you a small strategic bite that elicited a shudder, and only then did you begin to respond. Fixing mournful eyes on me, you sat up and took your shirt off with a deft, languorous motion. Pale, unblemished skin and muscles defined but not unnaturally chiseled. Gravity was just beginning to take its toll on you, but you didn't seem to care. You were one of the few men I knew with an attractive body who did not feel the need to wear clothing to show off what you had. That was probably because you'd had it your whole life, and in the healthiest way took it for granted.

We both stood up and now I stripped off my shirt. Hands on

my waist, you bent down and took one of my nipples in your mouth, gave it slight pressure with your teeth, then flicked your tongue at it. Lifted me and squeezed my back until it cracked, then carried me over to your bed, threw me down and jumped on top of me.

I often think of that first night when I told you about Chad; of all your weight on top of me, and myself pressed to your bed, hands pinned to either side of my ears, of how I pushed until I raised you above me and we formed this cage of arms before I lowered you into a kiss. I think about how your back widened dramatically, just as his did, but how your legs were much larger and as hard as a wall. And I think about how long it took you to warm up to kissing me, how you seemed afraid that my tongue would begin an invasion that might end up with my capturing yet another piece of you.

But when you finally gave in to those longer sensual kisses, the potency of each one was somehow a token history of your loneliness. It was then that I began to believe that we could be at par with one another. It was then that I felt a small warmth ignite in the core of myself, the place I had been afraid no one would ever reach again.

Then you stopped abruptly and turned your head away, and I could see a tear pressing out of the corner of your eyes. Your body convulsed in a single sob before you huddled into yourself. I was about to ask what was wrong when the phone jump-started our nerves. We listened to the machine pick up a boisterous message: that of a restaurant, dishes clacking, detonations of laughter, blares of jazz. No one spoke.

I suddenly remembered that I, too, had received a similar anonymous phone call. I asked if you'd received other calls like this.

You hurriedly wiped your eyes and said that you had.

"Because I got one myself. This morning."

"Probably just a coincidence. This ex-lover doesn't know we know each other."

Moments passed and we lay there without speaking.

"I think you do bring *him* out in me, somehow," I found myself saying.

You turned to me with a wet cheek. "What exactly do you mean?"

"Right off the bat? Something about your eyes." I hesitated and then I asked, "Do I at all remind you of . . . Bobby Garzino?"

You faced the ceiling again and smiled your silly smile. "Nah. You're very different from Bobby Garzino."

"In what way?"

"You're much more self-confident. Outgoing. He was rather quiet. Tentative. Incredibly intense. I think he was actually too fragile to live long in this world."

I let this idea creep through me for a moment. "Do you feel guilty about his dying?"

"It was *his* choice, wasn't it? Why, would you feel guilty?"

It struck me then that there are certain people who feel their vitality is enhanced when they help a person who is dying. Others feel their lives will be sucked away even if they so much as identify with somebody who is ill. "I think I would in some way," I remarked. "I mean, especially if I'd been the last person he'd been involved with before he got sick." I waited a moment and then I said, "Do I know everything, Sean?"

"What do you mean by 'everything'?"

"Is there something, anything, you're leaving out?" I still could not shake the idea there was a secret you held on to.

You suddenly grew impatient with me. When you spoke again, it was in a fierce whisper. And for some reason I didn't quite realize you never answered my question. "Look, Will, I told him that I'd been hurt badly before. That I'd never gotten over it."

Now it's clear to me that your answer was only a defense, the type of ploy a hardened seducer uses when he refers to a wife and kids whom he can never abandon.

"Was it really so bad?" I asked. "You've never really told me about what happened *before* Bobby."

"I don't create novels of my past. And I didn't tell Bobby much, either, because I never needed to. I wasn't in love with Bobby Garzino. And he knew it."

I reflected on this for a moment. "But you're going to tell *me* what happened to you, yes?" I'd wanted to add, "And you're not in love with me, are you?"

You fixed me with a spooky gaze and then, interlacing our hands, said, "Don't you see why? Because I think we're going to be able to help each other."

"But you once said it was going to be a 'tough tournament.' "

"I've gotten to know you a little bit more. I've changed my mind."

A chaotic chorus of late night voices passed below your window, and out of them we were able to distinguish a man singing "Wild Horses" by the Rolling Stones.

"So you'll spend the night with me?" you asked.

"Do you want me to?"

"Very much."

"Okay."

And once we settled into bed, your head resting on the crook of my arm, you quickly fell into a doze while I lay there, sifting through all the impressions of what you'd told me about yourself, about the weaver. More and more I thought I was beginning to see an outline of the affliction that your soul carried. The phone rang twice more.

I awoke to you kissing me. Long searching kisses. And I now knew that we couldn't plan, it had to happen of its own accord, we had to trick that locked-up part of ourselves into releasing. It must've been dawn, because the sky was a pearly blue, stars all dwindled except for one or two still winking at the tops of the building across the street.

Your mouth moved down my body slowly, taking it in. I watched your curls fall and brush my chest. Aiming my thighs around your head, you asked me to squeeze hard. Teased my shaft with your tongue, making me wonder if you'd give mouth or not, but then it happened and only a few strokes and I was brought to a terrifying plateau and had to ask you to stop. I made you switch places with me. Hugging your legs like trunks, I squeezed your inner thighs around my cheeks.

Sometimes when I'm making love the feeling changes almost inappropriately to a kind of spiritual elation. I start to remember things that are pristine rather than erotic, like being a child again, bundled up and warm in the midst of a cruel, cold afternoon, the sky an unblemished cobalt, and everything crystalline and pure liquid chill. And so I had this sudden vision of us in deep winter, months away, skating a frozen pond. You were teaching me the hockey moves, how to cross-over skate, how to do the T-stop, your face flushed, eyes ablaze with purpose. As I took your cock in my mouth, I could almost hear the sounds of the blades carving their purchase on the ice and sending up fine frozen powder as we flew across the glazed pond. And the trees on the opposite side were veined with snow and there was that quiet exultation that winter, my favorite season, brings.

"I hit the wall, I think," you said.

I turned and found a pale blot dripping down. "You did," I confirmed. "I wonder what makes it fly like that?"

"Pent-up emotion, probably."

And after lying there for a while in the narcotic stupor that follows sex, you suddenly turned to me. "So his name was Chad, huh?"

I nodded and I said, "Yeah, his name was Chad."

Moments passed and the dark sky was now burnishing. You made a move and I explained that I was fine the way I was. That I didn't need to come. That I just wanted to lie there and watch the light.

8

WEARING HIS <u>JOHNSON AND DIX PETROLEUM MARKETEERS</u> CAP, GREG stood in the midst of a tangle of frolicking dogs in the dog run, throwing Casey his ball. I stood and watched our dog maneuvering among the others, the way he kept snarling at any animal who looked eager to wrench his ball away from him. The moment he spotted me, Casey dropped the ball, ran over and jumped up onto the fence, barking exultantly.

"You're coming from the west," Greg remarked as he walked over to me.

"This is true."

"You're just dying for me to know that you spent the night out with somebody."

I frowned. "Oh, come on."

"Then why would you pass this way, when you knew I'd be here with Casey?"

At the mention of his name, Casey sat down, perked up his ears and tilted his head sideways. "I love that dog," I said. "And

I've always liked walking through the park."

"You're so full of it, Will. Completely full of shit."

"Let's not argue about this."

Casey dropped the ball at Greg's feet. Grabbing it, Greg threw it fiercely. When it bounced twice and cleared the fence, he turned to me. "Would you mind getting that? Since you're already outside."

"Only if you'll let up on me."

"I'll get it myself, then," he said, stalking toward the gate.

"What's *with* you today?" I called out, but Greg didn't answer. Casey followed and whined when Greg prevented him from exiting at the gate, then let loose a cry that reminded me of that first night he bleated like a lamb in our kitchen.

"I'm coming back, okay? Just give me a minute." Greg was all kindness and reassurance.

I tried to tell myself, Don't care too much for either of them, because that will tether you to the past. I wanted to burn off these old feelings, to suffer extravagantly from the new poison that was in my blood. This was my moment to leave, yet I felt compelled to conclude the argument Greg had started.

I finally held the advantage over Greg that I'd been seeking for so long. My sudden, almost corrupt numbness toward him was part of the intoxication of having just shared a bed with someone else. Someone who had completely overridden my attention, like a computer program replacing one file with another. And in light of last summer, when I had been forced to wait for Greg to come to his senses about his affair, I couldn't help but feel a great temptation to inflict my current infatuation on him.

Greg had sensed this change immediately, of course.

"So who is it, anyway?" he asked as he returned to the dog run and recommenced throwing Casey's ball.

"I thought we weren't going to discuss these activities."

He looked at me shrewdly. "We're not supposed to, but as far

as I'm concerned, coming from the west at this hour is the very
same thing as bringing up the topic. I can tell you're just dying to
tell me, and I don't want to ruin your fun. Go ahead."

"He would just be a name, anyway."

"Perhaps I know him. Believe me, Will, I can take it."

That last disclaimer enraged me. "Okay," I said, "his name
is Sean Paris."

Greg shook his head and let loose a repellent chuckle. "I'm
not going to know him, huh? I'm not going to know Sean Paris."

A nauseating fear settled over me. "Don't tell me
you've . . . done it with him."

"Doesn't that rain on your parade?"

"Did you?"

"That's for me to know."

"Come on, Greg, don't fuck with me!" I cried.

He now glared at me. "Why are you getting involved with
somebody like that, anyway?"

"Just tell me if you slept with him!"

"Is that all you care about? Mr. Depth-of-Soul who casts as-
persions on the rest of us for being shallow fuck-wads."

Greg's face was contorted, blotches of color blooming on his
pale cheeks. Casey was sitting at his feet, the muddy ball next to
him. Greg then asked in his most didactic tone, "Did you happen
to know that some guy who was dating Sean Paris did himself in?
Did you hear about that?"

The news bounced off me. "No. And I'm sure it's gossip. How
did you hear about it?"

"How did *I* hear? Plenty of people are talking about it is how
I heard."

"It's either ancient history or nasty rumors."

"Guess again, Will."

"What are you talking about?" I felt belligerent. "When?"

"Just recently!" Greg was looking at me with sudden recog-

nition. "In fact, last Sunday. Remember you told me some guy
threw himself in front of a train?"

But it couldn't be the same guy. I felt dazed and oddly pur-
poseful, remembering how much time I'd spent imagining who
the suicide was. And to think that he actually knew you.

"Sean didn't say anything," I murmured.

"Sean had already dumped him. A while ago. In fact, Sean
Paris has dumped a lot of people."

"You certainly seem to know a lot about Sean for somebody
who has never met him. Methinks you just might be a little
jealous."

"So what? So what if I'm jealous? I'll probably always be jealous of anybody you end up with. But that doesn't change the fact
that this guy is bad news. And he has been keeping this from you."

I forced myself to say, "Perhaps the news hasn't reached him.
He would've said something if he knew."

"I'm glad you think you know him so well that you can pre-
dict this."

"Okay, I'm *assuming* he would tell me."

Hesitating a moment, Greg said softly, "Will, you've always
been attracted to trouble, you know that."

"So then you admit that *you* were trouble."

Greg vehemently shook his head. "Only when I became unhappy. Only when I realized what you'd sacrifice: me—us—for
your work." His eyes clouded over. "I loved you as much as I was
able to love anybody. And I still love you, okay? But now I've got
to get away from this conversation."

Quickly he left me, heading for Casey on the far side of the
dog run. As I stood there watching him go, I noticed that Casey
had his head down and was heaving. Casey was rather tall and
slim, and whenever he threw up, his rib cage would expand and
stretch his shiny black coat. I figured the vomiting fit would pass.

When it continued, I hurried along the perimeter of the dog run and passed through the gate. Just as I reached the dog, he collapsed on the ground, his long, spindly legs convulsing as he lay there panting. I reached him first. Bending over him, I heard Greg running over.

"What the hell is wrong with him?" I cried.

"Jesus Christ, let's just get him to the vet!"

Lying on his side, Casey retched again and yellow foam bubbled out of his mouth. "I'm going to lift him," Greg announced.

The moment those words were spoken, Casey managed to get up. He stood there, legs bowed and trembling. "Let's see if he can walk," Greg suggested, attaching the leash.

As we slowly led him out of the dog run, Casey seemed to recover but then began dry-retching once we reached the boundary of Washington Square Park. Greg picked him up and carried him the rest of the way to Sixth Avenue.

At that relatively early hour of the morning there were plenty of vacant taxis swarming up Sixth Avenue. However, as soon as the drivers spotted Casey, we could actually see them shaking their heads, hear them gunning their engines to pass us quickly. Finally one stopped. I leaned down to see a portly Arabic man with mutton-chop sideburns shrewdly evaluating Greg and me and our obviously sick dog as though something might be wrong with the three of us. We dutifully waited for him to make up his mind whether or not he wanted our fare, and finally, speaking to me, he agreed to take us if we kept the dog on the floor and off the seat. Still cradling Casey to his chest, Greg began approaching the taxi, but I'd been made to feel so marginalized by the naked appraisal that I had to confront the driver. "Look," I said, angrily, "either you take us or you don't. He's obviously going to ride on our laps."

While Greg rolled his eyes at my inability to contain myself, the driver made up his mind and swiveled his attention back to the traffic, and just as the taxi was rolling away, I said venomously, "Don't you have any fucking compassion?" The guy slammed on the brakes and invited us to get in.

"I would've been so pissed off at you," Greg told me once we'd driven off.

"I would've been pissed off at me, too," I said.

Although I explained that we needed to rush to the animal hospital, the man drove as if he were bringing us to a picnic in Central Park. Greg took over from me, wielding charm to hurry him along. However, as soon as we hit a set of red lights, the driver turned around and snorted, "I will not drive fast."

I looked down at Casey, who lay still and panting on Greg's lap, his head spilling over into mine. "Somebody tried to poison our dog, okay?" I said. "And we're afraid he's going to die before we get to the hospital."

That seemed to work. The driver obviously didn't want a dead dog in his car and suddenly picked up the pace, weaving erratically around other cars. I ran my hand slowly along Casey's flank, then bent down and stroked his head, and when I straightened up again I could see that Greg had turned toward his window, toward the East Side where the sunlight, still low to the horizon, was sending out spokes of light through the streets. He was trying to keep his composure. And I sat there battling two fronts of anxiety: whether or not you'd purposely withheld the fact that you once dated the guy who threw himself in front of the train, and, of course, the more immediate concern, Casey's well-being.

A day or two after Greg and I had adopted him, Casey stopped eating altogether, the result of a virus that he'd contracted before his short stay at the North Shore Animal League. After we'd brought him to the vet and he'd been given a shot, we were told that turkey breast would jump-start his appetite. And so on the way home, we stopped off at a delicatessen and ordered some thinly sliced meat, and when we got back to the apartment and put it before Casey, he inhaled it. But no sooner did he finish eating than he promptly threw up everything he'd just devoured. Then, without missing a beat, he immediately consumed what he'd just thrown up, sending both Greg and me into great gales of laughter. The dog weighed a mere five pounds back then. Now he tipped the scales at seventy.

"I just hope it isn't some kind of poison," I whispered to Greg.

"I don't see how. I walked him from home right to the dog run."

"Well, I wouldn't put it past one of those nuts around there to put poison out," I said. People who lived adjacent to the dog run had always complained about the barking.

We both looked down at Casey.

"By the way, I'm sorry I got on your case earlier," Greg said. "About Sean Paris."

I told the vet's receptionist that I thought Casey might have been poisoned. She picked up the telephone, spoke to someone and after a few moments led us into a cubicle-like room that reeked of antiseptic and was crowded with tall glass-fronted cabinets whose shelves stocked vials of medicines and glimmering metal instruments. When Greg lifted Casey and put him on the metal examining table, his spindly legs began trembling.

"That's what he did when he first collapsed," Greg told a woman with bluntly cut salt-and-pepper hair who strode into the room wearing a starched white lab coat. The veterinarian introduced herself, then took Casey's temperature rectally and began palpating him. "His temperature is normal," she said. "How much has he been throwing up?"

"Just one bout, really," Greg said. "But he collapsed."

The vet listened to Casey with a stethoscope and then grace-fully extricated the apparatus from her ears. "Well, I don't think it's poison," she announced. "His stomach doesn't sound like it's in trauma, but I'll pump it anyway. I don't see any immediate dan-ger, however. Nevertheless, I'm going to sedate him," she ex-plained, turning to the display case. "Could you hold him while I do it?" She began to fill a needle with pinkish fluid.

Casey received his shot with a short, resigned whimper. Once the vet had disposed of the syringe, she glanced at each of us and said, "He lives with both of you, I presume."

"Well, not exactly," I said.

She looked puzzled.

"I mean, he used to," Greg explained. "Live with both of us. But lately we've been sharing him."

"Well, really, *he* has custody," I said, glancing sharply at Greg.

The vet smiled and shook her head. "Would you please just tell me where the dog lives."

"He lives with me," Greg said.

"I'm not prying," she told us. "I just need to know who is go-ing to be giving the medication."

Greg said that it all depended upon how many times a day the medication was supposed to be administered, explaining that he worked from 5 P.M. straight until midnight managing data systems at a corporate law firm.

The vet said, "Four times a day if it's what I think it is."

"Then you'll probably have to come over, Will."

"What do you think it is?" I asked.

"Well, let me begin by saying that the throwing up is not nec-essarily related to the muscular trauma. Except that it probably set off the other symptoms, which is actually a good thing. Be-cause now we know there's a problem. I just have one question: Has he been up to the country or out to Long Island?"

Casey and I had been to a friend's house in East Hampton.

"Well, that would support my hunch. He has some of the symptoms of Lyme disease."

"Lyme disease!" Greg and I both exclaimed.

The vet reassured us that Casey was going to be okay. "Why don't the two of you go back out to the waiting room while I take some blood."

We left the examining room and walked down a highly polished corridor. The animal hospital was cacophonous with yipping and mewing and even the exotic screeching of birds. Finally Greg turned to me. "Nobody seems to understand the idea of joint dog custody." He was smirking. "Anybody I've told thinks it's totally crazy."

I admitted having witnessed the same reaction.

Once Casey was checked out, we took a cab back to Greg's apartment. I always felt strange going to his new place. His clothing, his books, his artwork and kitschy mementos that once had commingled with my things had been uprooted and transplanted into a smaller studio space that in one room contained a sink, stove, refrigerator and bed. The apartment was on Carmine Street, a location for which Greg paid an exorbitant rent, as well as for its one winning feature, a working brick fireplace.

Despite the fact that it was still relatively early in the morning, the place was already hot when we walked in. Greg immediately went and switched on the air conditioner. I hovered by the door, hoping to make a graceful exit so I could go home, call you at work to find out what you knew and didn't know. Detecting my state of agitation, Greg probably assumed it had more to do with Casey's ordeal. "Let's just sit down together for a few minutes, have a cup of coffee and chill out," he suggested.

Casey, though still listless, seemed a little bit perkier. He made a few rounds of the apartment, his toenails clicking on the hardwood floor. Then he climbed up on Greg's futon bed, lay down and let loose one of his settling-down groans.

On one wall hung an all-too-familiar photograph of the moon, huge and pendant over the breakers of Monterey Bay, a photograph that I disliked but had once been forced to live with. On the fireplace mantel stood a gallery of framed snapshots, some of which were of Greg and me (cross-country skiing in Vermont, standing at Lands End on the blustery tip of Cornwall).

On the opposite wall I noticed something new, a poster hastily affixed with Scotch tape. Squinting at it, I realized that it was the view through a microscope enlarged perhaps a million times. In the middle of the poster was a line that divided what I recognized to be enlargements of two T cells: one perfectly spherical, the tendrils of its microscopic matter all flowing efficiently in one direction; and one no longer spherical, but rather in the process of disintegration, tendrils waving every which way like dreadlocks. *VISUALIZE THIS,* read block lettering beneath the healthy T cell.

"Why did you put that up?" I nervously asked. The last time we'd spoken, Greg was HIV-negative. He was facing away from me. Just then the tea kettle began to shrill, and he poured the scalding water through the coffee filter.

He finally turned to me. "Well, why not?"

"Is there something you're not telling me?"

"No!"

I turned back to the poster. The dichotomy between the two cells was distressing. I couldn't imagine, particularly after a bad night of sleep, getting up in the morning and looking at a poster of those paradigms of health and illness.

"I look at it to keep reminding myself what's going on," Greg explained. "I look at it and I visualize healing and finding a cure. I think it's important to do that."

I admired Greg's mature perspective, and remembering my own recklessness at his age, I also felt chagrined. Greg was young enough never to have known sex without its direct correlation to dying. Ten years ago, someone like Greg—someone like me—

might have tacked up on their wall a love aphorism, a message of inner forbearance, lines written by e. e. cummings or Kahlil Gibran. Now, looking from the decrepit, afflicted T cell to its smooth, well-heeled counterpart was like looking at the fates of two different generations.

9

WHEN I ARRIVED BACK AT MY APARTMENT THERE WERE THREE MES-
sages from you on my answering machine, spaced an even half
hour apart. It was the first time I'd ever heard you sound relatively
off kilter. In light of the psychological hoops I'd already jumped
through in regard to you, the worry in your voice gave me a burst
of satisfaction.

"Are you going to be there for five minutes?" you asked when
I finally got through to you at work.

I said that I would. In the interim, I sifted through my mail,
switched on my computer but refrained from working. Five minutes would hardly allow me enough time to begin concentrating.
When ten minutes had elapsed without your calling back, I retrieved a half-completed book review on my computer screen and
finally set down to writing. After another uninterrupted ten minutes, however, I'd grown so anxious that I was unable to consoli-
date my thoughts. Why had you told me five minutes? Was the
estimated time—of arrivals, departures, meetings—always go-

ing to be a stretch with you? Thirty-five minutes later the phone rang, and though I'd been anticipating it, I nonetheless jumped at the sound.

"I'm sorry I couldn't get back to you right away. Some shit has hit the fan in the interim. They've suddenly decided to send me out to Montana. To tag some trees for a job we're doing."

"When do you leave?"

"Tonight."

You were to be gone for five days, just when we were getting to know each other.

You added in a rush, "But look, I need to talk you to about something. I need to ask you a favor."

"What's that?"

And then you explained that shortly after I left at around eight thirty that morning, you'd received a call from Bobby Garzino's ex-lover, José. After he insisted once again that you return all the objects from The Loom's Desire, José said that if you didn't co-operate he'd conveniently wait until you were at work and then break into the apartment.

"So call the police," I said, "if he's threatening to break in."

"You think the police are going to pay attention to this—some dispute between two gay guys? Believe me, they won't end up do-ing anything about it. And anyway, I don't want José to be hassled by the police."

I grew immediately suspicious. "Why not?"

"Because he obviously really loved Bobby. And I respect that. And it's probably a lot easier for José to blame me for making Bobby unhappy than to accept the fact that Bobby died."

"So you're just going to let him keep harassing you?"

"I think he'll eventually stop."

But you wanted me to stay at your place while you were away. If José was actually keeping track of you, he'd soon find out that no one was staying there, and that would give him his chance.

Why didn't I suggest that you keep all the loomed possessions in my apartment—why didn't you suggest it, for that matter? Perhaps I was afraid that had I suggested this and you weren't keen it would mean you had some doubts about me, didn't trust me enough to take care of your valuables. Didn't want us that closely connected. But all this was getting ahead of what Greg had told me.

"Look, Sean," I said, "before we make any arrangement, I've got to ask you to clarify something."

No response. Just silence.

"Are you there?"

"Uh-huh. What is it?"

"I ran into my ex this morning on the way home. And then our dog got sick—" I began to explain the trip to the vet and was glad you interrupted to ask if Casey was okay. That interruption returned me to the point. "Before Casey got sick, Greg and I got to talking as we do sometimes . . . about guys we've been seeing, blah, blah, blah, even though it can get awkward sometimes. As it did today."

"Yeah?"

I couldn't believe how nervous the conversation was making me. My heart was fibrillating as it did when I finished a hard set in the pool. "When I mentioned your name he immediately knew who you were."

"What's his full name?."

"Greg Wallace."

"Can't say that I've heard of him."

"He told me something that I'm hoping is untrue." I took a breath and exhaled. "That you'd been involved with the guy who threw himself in front of that train a week ago."

"That's right, I was involved with him . . . at one time."

"Well, I mean, who was he, this guy who killed himself?"

"It was Bobby Garzino," you said without any noticeable hesitation.

Of course, I'd already linked the two deaths, immediately, the moment Greg told me. How eerie it all seemed, the instant feelings that arose in me the moment I heard about the train death, how I imagined that it was a man suffering from love, a man who couldn't be cared for.

"Now, wait a second, Sean," I said hoarsely. "You told me Bobby Garzino died of AIDS."

"No, I didn't tell you, you *assumed* he died of AIDS. And so I let you assume that because you weren't that far off. He *was* sick, and he would've died. And I was planning to tell you how he actually did die."

"But until that time, you would've withheld something pretty important."

"Well, okay, so I would have. But that was partly because it unnerved me that the first I'd heard of him dying was through *you*, of all people. I could've mentioned his suicide last night, and of course it'd crossed my mind any number of times. But last night was really our first night together. And I didn't end up saying anything because I was afraid it would . . . ruin the evening."

No, only the morning, *my* morning, I thought. I said, "Yeah, but look how open I was about myself and my own past."

"Precisely, because it *was* the past. This is the present. This is something that's going on, something I'm still trying to understand. I mean, in your friend's apartment, the moment you told me about a person who threw himself in front of the train, I went completely cold. I suddenly felt really queasy, and I couldn't figure out why. That was the reason I wanted to leave. Imagine later on that night when I found out I knew the person, and that it was Bobby. It was all too strange and creepy that I knew it before I knew it."

"But I felt creepy, too. That's why I brought it up to begin with. That's why you should've said something."

"I was afraid you'd make assumptions like the people starting these rumors."

"But who do you think started the rumors?"

You groaned and then concluded, "People always love this kind of drama. They'd love to assume that I had something to do with him dying, that he got AIDS from me."

A question flared, but I waited a moment before asking, "Are you really negative?"

"Yes, I'm negative."

"But you're supposed to wait six months."

"I did, but people don't know that. And even if they could know, they might assume that the stress of our relationship made him get sick a lot faster than he would have."

You repeated that you had not actually seen Bobby Garzino since that night last February when he lay in the middle of your pile of clothing. Since then he *had* written several letters to you that claimed he couldn't get you out of his mind, letters asking you to get back together with him. Rather than encourage him with any response, you chose not to contact him at all. Finally, one night toward the end of July, when the city was suffering from a heat wave, he called you out of the blue. Told you his health seemed to be going downhill and that he had scheduled an AIDS test. You made him promise to call you with the results. Throughout the conversation, he kept asking you to meet with him, and finally you agreed and set an actual date for dinner. But that was the last time you'd ever heard from him. On the day of the dinner he never even returned your phone call.

"So this is all assumption on your part. You never heard from him and so you're presuming he got bad news?"

"What would *you* think? Especially when he'd been insisting on getting together and I'd finally agreed to it."

"But why can't you ask around?"

"Who am I going to ask—José, who's been harassing me? You think he's going to be honest?"

There was the roommate who'd lived with Bobby, but the roommate had moved to the Midwest almost immediately after the incident. And yet, the more you thought about it, the more it made sense that Bobby wouldn't necessarily want you to know that he had HIV—anyone, for that matter, but you in particular. Because he knew you were HIV-negative and probably believed that if you knew that he was HIV-positive, the idea of a relationship would be an even more remote possibility.

Viral apartheid, I thought to myself.

"He chose not to go through all that suffering," you said with admiration. "He choose to die perfect."

I could tell that you were impressed by the fact that someone had taken control of his own death, had subverted the inevitable decline into emaciation, into ugliness, and had circumvented the renowned suffering of this disease.

But if Bobby had wanted to die perfect, why did he choose to throw himself in front of a train? I wondered. But it was too mean a question ever to voice.

From that pause, you conveniently eased us along to another subject, the fact that after the five-day business trip you were owed a week's vacation. How would I like to go away with you somewhere? Someplace quiet. "I have to catch up on a backlog of land drawings, but I can also work on them while I'm away and FedEx 'em back to the office as I finish."

"As a matter of fact, yes."

And so I explained how every summer for the past three years I'd been renting this little cabin in Vermont that used to be a one-room schoolhouse. You agreed it sounded perfect.

After putting down the phone, I reran our conversation. On the one hand I was inclined to suspect the staggered manner in which you'd told me the story of Bobby Garzino. On the other hand, I had to remind myself that, unlike you, I'm the sort of person whose imagination gets overstimulated from very little. And sometimes I get confused between what I've nakedly perceived and what I've varnished upon that perception.

1 0

SO THEN YOU WERE GONE AND I BECAME YOU. AND, STRANGELY, THAT was when I was happiest, alone in your apartment, those days before I met you in Vermont. Alone in your apartment when our idyll was still ahead of me like a harbor marking.

You had to leave town quickly without any time to tidy. Which suited me, because I wanted to turn the key in the door as though I were you at the end of any normal day. I wanted to shadow everything that I knew you were. To look around and sigh at the state of slowly accreting disarray. There are certain people whose natural style lends art even to their clutter. You were one of them. I found cut crystal glasses residued with Scotch; white ceramic plates encrusted with dried radicchio; a bruise of dessert wine on a ragged cotton place mat; an old tackle box filled with lead weights and flies that you'd tied by hand. And all the cut flowers that had almost immediately wilted, as though their very lives depended on your presence.

Instinctively I straightened up. Folded T-shirts, and oatmeal sweatshirts and towels. Dusted a rosy film from picture frames. Washed curdled milk from the bottom of a cocktail glass. Vacuumed. Played my limited repertory on the piano. Pulled books from the shelves, read sporadically, finding the flap of the book jacket anchored halfway through *Bleak House,* Ovid's *Metamorphoses,* every single novel and short story by Kafka. There was a huge black leather portfolio of all your renderings, and I rifled through them, amazed that you could draw as well as you did—the esplanade along a riverfront, a museum's arboretum, the grounds of a parochial school—even though you had told me that such drawing was merely "an acquired skill."

We'd agreed that I'd let the machine answer the phone and would pick up only if the call was for me. But after hearing a few of your friend's voices, and thinking they sounded interesting, I couldn't help myself. Explaining that you were out of town on business, I suggested that messages be left with your office, for there was no forwarding number. Most of the callers were miffed to hear my voice, to hear in it the assurance with which I seemed to know you, even though they probably had known you a lot longer than I, and known you well enough to realize that it was uncharacteristic of Sean Paris to have someone answering his phone, or staying in his apartment. I felt subversive—and gleeful.

The first night I stayed at your house I noticed on the bottom bookshelf three slim, leather-bound volumes with marbleized covers made of Florentined paper. I figured they were sketch pads left over from journeys you'd made abroad. I cracked open the third one and found the lined ivory-colored pages of a diary, every page written in black fountain-pen ink. The landscape of the writing on each page had a peculiar up-and-down flourish that hardly seemed like contemporary handwriting but, rather, resembled what I imagined to be the hand of an aristocrat imprisoned for, say, heresy during the Middle Ages. Scanning the paragraphs, I noticed how the word *love* jumped out from the hedgerows of writing, and the initials R.M.

In the first volume, a few pages were filled, the rest left blank. But sandwiched among the empty pages were letters typed double-spaced on thin onionskin bond, folded carefully and placed together like entries in an accordion file. I dared to open one of them and saw that it was written to an R.M. with your signature at the bottom. I glanced at another and found that it addressed the same R.M. person—unmailed letters, I assumed. Were they to a man you once loved? To that man you had yet to tell me about? I was surprised that you trusted me enough not to have hidden the extreme privacy of this correspondence. Or perhaps you'd been in too much of a rush to leave. This made me feel guilty for snooping. I made myself put away the volumes without reading anything.

On my second night in your apartment, a call came in with the noise of a busy street in the background.

"Sean's not here," I said. "Can I take a message?"

"When is he due back?" asked a cultivated yet anxious voice.

"Who's calling, please?"

"A friend. Did you say he was out tonight?"

The man's intent was palpable. "Would you mind giving me your name?" I asked.

There was a pause, during which I thought I heard the phone getting knocked around. "I'll be off it in a minute," the man said irritably to someone else. "What did you say?" he asked me.

"Would you mind giving me your name?"

"My name is José Ayala."

"I'll tell Sean you called."

"Wait a second. Wait a second. Who are *you?*"

I decided to act as though I didn't know who he might be. "I'm a friend of Sean's. I'm staying with him for a while."

"Are you . . . oh, I've actually got to go. Goodbye," the man said and signed off.

And I immediately sensed, no doubt the way you did, that he wasn't as dangerous so much as despairing, and although he might be capable of doing harm, he probably was not evil.

Then again, early the next morning around 7:00 A.M.

"May I speak to Sean now, please?"

"I'm sorry, I'll have to take a message."

"He's gone, isn't he? He's out of town."

"Does that really make a difference? He'll get the message," I said. "I promise."

"I'm sure you must know all about me. I'm sure he told you that I've been calling. He wouldn't just leave and not explain what has been going on here." The man sounded on the verge of tears. "Please just tell me if he's out of town."

"I'll give him your message, okay? Maybe he'll call you back. I'm going back to sleep now." Of course I was fully awake.

"Don't get off the phone. Talk to me for a moment. Just for a moment."

I said nothing. I waited.

"He's a bad person. I just want to tell you that if you don't know that already."

"Okay. Anything else?"

"He's the most charming man in the world, completely charming, but he's got no heart."

"You don't really know him." I merely projected my own concern.

"You're the guy he's been dating, the writer."

I did not respond.

"I know who you are. You're the guy people saw him leaving Splash with the other night, aren't you?"

"Perhaps."

"I'd like come over there and talk to you."

"About my writing?" I couldn't help asking.

"No, about Sean Paris."

"I'm sorry, but that's not possible."

"Sean has things that belong to me that I need as soon as possible."

I deliberated over whether or not to let on that I knew what was between you and José. Finally I said, "You know that's a distortion of the truth. So don't try and trick me."

"So you *do* know what's going on."

I admitted that I'd been told.

"I have this letter from Bobby saying I should get all his stuff back. I have this letter that says—"

"Look, sir, this is not my business."

"Suddenly so formal." He sounded disgusted, but not hostile.

"I want this argument to be between you and Sean."

José suggested I could do everyone a favor by acting as a mediator. "I'm going to call back and read you—"

I said, "If Bobby wanted anything back, he should have asked Sean for it directly." I realized that I'd gone too far with the conversation, indeed, had way overstepped my bounds. I'd ceased to be somebody protecting your apartment and was swiftly becoming an active participant in your affairs, someone you might end up resenting.

"Bobby *did* ask for it—"

"Look, I'm just staying here for a while, okay?" Then I found myself lying. "Sean lent me this apartment as a favor."

"I'll just wait until you leave and then I'll pry my way in."

"That'd be breaking the law."

"Call the police, I don't care," José said. "Because there are too many Sean Parises around. Too many guys getting away with hurting sweet wonderful people like Bobby."

"That's not fair. It's not fair to blame his death on Sean."

"I guarantee that you don't know the whole story."

"Of course you'd say that. You've got an agenda," I said and quietly replaced the receiver.

I stood there in the gathering twilight. All the things I loved in your apartment—the stuffed wood ducks, the collections of smooth sea-tumbled stones, shells and fossils on the mantel— everything vibrated with a cryptic intensity, as if there were clues to your enigmatic past. José had clearly tried to undermine my sense of trust in you. Why should I be permitting him to put doubts in my mind? I tried to be glad I'd hung up when I did.

But there were doubts simply because I'd already sensed something remote in you, something as inaccessible as the yet untold story of your broken heart. In my agitation, I went to the open window and leaned out over Grove Street the way you had done the first night I ever visited. Then I stepped away, stripped myself down to nothing and wandered around the apartment naked. Hot Hudson River wind spiraled through the windows. I felt bereft of something that I couldn't quite name. I went into your closet and picked through the clothing, searching for something of yours to wear.

I found T-shirts silkscreened with places from your past. I admired one from a golf course in Okinawa, but it was the name of a bowling alley in San Diego that I finally brought out and laid on the bed. As I was restacking the pile, I came upon a mound of military fatigues, all block-printed over the rear pocket with the name Monroe. Monroe. A surname? The surname of the R.M. addressed in your letters? Goaded by jealousy, I wondered how exactly you'd come by them, finally imagining that he'd given you one pair every time he made love to you until there were none left. Who was this man? And where was he now?

R.M.'s fatigues had the same impoverished softness of the T-shirts Chad used to wear. After Chad vanished, in order to mourn his vanishing, I had worn his clothes and only his clothes, dressing exclusively in what was his and clearly not mine. In the wrath of my temporary madness, I actually used to believe that dressing like him would bring him back, as though a swath of fabric could actually be patched onto what the fates had already woven. Come back, Sean Paris; come back, R.M.; come back, Chad.

In the closet I also unearthed a small gift box containing two things I assumed had been made by Bobby Garzino: a nubby scarf fashioned of eggplant-and-black silk threads that had a rich texture; a small pillow sewn from a similar fabric with a printed tag on the side that said: *A Dream Pillow, handmade by "The Loom's Desire."* The scarf was extravagantly long. I wrapped it once around my neck and draped it across my chest like a banner. Grabbing the pillow, I walked toward your bed. Noticing a sweet, earthy fragrance, I put the pillow to my nose. It was the smell of mugwort, a gentle soporific herb that I used to take during the time when I had such trouble sleeping. I lay down on your bed, put the pillow behind my head, draped the soft scarf over my groin.

I'd just begun masturbating when the phone rang. I let the machine answer, and after the announcement played, I listened to the message. "Hey," you said. "Are you there?" I stopped playing with myself and picked up. "Hey, yourself," I said.

"What are you doing?"

"Jacking off."

"Uh-oh. Bad timing, I'm sorry. Do you want to speak later?"

"No, I want to speak now. It's always there, so it can wait. Where are you?"

"In the boonies, way up at the top of Montana. Almost in Canada."

"Nice?"

"Dry and cloudless. A perfect way to put all the shit in Manhattan behind me."

"Sounds like you don't want to come back."

"No, I *do* want to get back. Although it *is* rather grand up here in the woods. In fact, it's priming me for Vermont."

"And how's tree tagging?"

"We got some real beauties. How's the old homestead?"

I looked around the room: the rinsed and dried cocktail glasses clustered on a kitchen shelf, the mahogany breakfast table gleaming with its new layer of lemon oil, the neatly arranged stack of bills that I'd put on top of your piano.

"In better condition than when you left."

"You didn't!" You sounded aghast.

"It's different when it's not your own place."

"Sleeping okay in my bed?"

"Seem to be."

"Are you leaving my stuff alone?" You chuckled as you said this, which, I must say, sounded as though you were teasing me, or even making light of what you'd already perceived to be my weakness.

"I've been wearing your clothes, if that's what you mean . . . and there have been lots of calls." I deliberately moved onward. "Everybody's miffed. You certainly do seem to have a lot of friends."

A sigh. "It's been said that I'm a lot better friend than lover."

"Is that a warning?"

"And *you've* sounded tense throughout this whole conversation. Is it only because you were . . . interrupted?"

"No, it's because . . . that guy called, the ex-lover, José Ayala."

There was a lull on your end and I could hear something that sounded like a white-noise machine in the background. "Well, I figured he would."

I relayed the gist of the conversation. However, I found myself omitting the man's attempt to get together to talk things over with me, to discuss you.

"He's jerking your chain, Will. He'll do anything to give me a hard time."

"I realize that. He tried to convince me that you were bad news."

"That would be the thing to do."

"Yet you're sounding pretty unflappable."

"What choice do I have? Anyway, tomorrow I'm coming back. Then we'll log in some time. And you can make up your own mind about me."

But after I said goodbye to you I felt unsettled by our conversation and by the desperation of José who loved Bobby Garzino. I decided to go for a walk and soon was strolling along sultry Seventh Avenue in the direction of Splash. The place was even more crowded than the last time I'd been there. Your T-shirt was tight on me; I'd rolled up the sleeves with the idea of soliciting attention from others. Then maybe I could avoid feeling so vulnerable to you. A steroid-swelled bartender served me a cold Rolling Rock with a leer that instantly perked up my mood.

Soon I found myself in the corner watching the Morning Party playing on the video screen. As the summer was ending and the length of daylight was beginning to dwindle, Splash, in response to popular demand, would keep reprising footage of the Morning Party. Sometimes they would even intersperse footage from the West Coast version that took place in Palm Springs. I was trying to remember what it had been like before I'd grown fixated on you, when I was open to the idea that there still could be others in my life. But that night, when I was staying at your place, when I was still hoping for the best possible things, when I believed that you would be the one whose heat would finally cure me of Chad, I riveted my attention to the video screen until I finally saw what I knew I'd come to see: you dancing with the black man. And as I watched, I tried to assure myself that I was the only one in the world who held a vaunted place in your life, the only one to whom Heartbreaker would finally tell the tale of his own heartbreak.

A hand reached from behind and grabbed my chin. I looked down at the pumped-up, freckled arm of Peter Rocca. "What is this, your new hangout?" he said.

"Looks like it's yours."

"Nah, I'm here with Sebastian. We just blew in for a beer before dinner."

"Sounds like you guys are on again."

"What's it to you? You don't call me anymore."

"It's not like you've been calling me, either."

"It's a matter of pride. The last two times I've seen you, you've blown me off for Sean Paris." Peter looked around. "Is he here with you?"

"No, he's out of town."

"Hey, Sebastian!" Peter yelled. The pompadour boyfriend was standing a few feet away talking to some other guys. "Sean Paris *is* out of town."

I instantly regretted giving out that information and vowed to return to your place immediately, in case somebody hanging out with Sebastian was or perhaps knew Bobby Garzino's ex-lover. I asked Peter why Sebastian wanted this information. "I don't know. Somebody was asking him before."

A moment later Sebastian excused himself from his two buddies and moved toward us in a deliberately slow drift. "Say what?" he said in a sort of growl, edging into Peter with propriety, sparking his dark eyes at me. His face had the usual oblong handsomeness of certain Mediterranean men, his nose prominent yet well formed.

"Sean Paris *is* out of town," Peter said.

"Who needs Sean Paris?" I asked.

"You do." Sebastian flashed a grin of bone-white teeth, one of which was chipped. "Big time."

"Big mouth." I shot Peter Rocca a look of condemnation, then turned back to Sebastian. "He just told me a friend of yours was asking."

"Yeah, so? What are you, Sean Paris's keeper?"

"I'm taking messages for him."

"You move in quickly, don't you?"

"Let's say I have my own inimitable pace."

"I know all about your pace, man. Reminds me of some sharks I seen at the aquarium."

The note of aggression had a familiar ring to it, and I began searching Sebastian's expression for a sign that he might somehow know the person who'd been calling.

"And believe you me," Sebastian continued, glancing at Peter, "I wouldn't be talking to you at all if I knew you still wanted to be a home wrecker."

"Do I count in this conversation at all?" Peter asked irritably.

I turned to him, remembering that cold afternoon many months ago when I'd rounded the corner of Lafayette Street to find him strangling this swarthy, brooding man. "Go ahead," I said. "Take the floor."

But Peter decided to pull his psychiatrist's poker face, and his reticence allowed Sebastian and me to exchange one look of complicity before the lines were drawn again.

"Okay, let's just set everything straight," I resumed in earnest. "I'm sorry if I caused you any grief, Sebastian. I didn't realize how important you were to Peter. So how about if we just say it's behind us? Enough at least so that we can be cordial to each other."

Sebastian calculatedly ran his fingers through his luxuriant onyx-colored hair, almost as though to make a mockery of my ever-thinning pate. He said finally, "I accept your apology, okay?" Then he shoved his finger into my breastbone. "But what you did is not forgotten. Because I'm Maltese," he added by way of explanation.

"I won't even try to fathom that."

"I wouldn't if I were you," Peter said approvingly.

Back at your place, I phoned to check the answering machine at my apartment and retrieved a message from Greg, who, citing an appointment, asked if I could come by the next morning and give Casey his midday antibiotic. In what I thought was an effort to spare his feelings, I'd explained the facts of what was going on before announcing that I was staying at your place. I now left Greg a message that I'd be by in the morning.

Lying in your bed, anxious, it occurred to me that an unslakable curiosity about my lover's past has all too often contaminated my happiness in relationships. Your Florentined diaries held what you'd felt for R.M., whom I did not know, but was curious to discover. Weighing against that was the realization that whatever I might read, besides being out of context, was likely to perturb me even more. And so I lay in your bed, wrestling with my urge to absorb your most private thoughts, and my fear of them, watching the lights of the city stippling the ceiling, looking out into the branches of the courtyard ailanthus. Finally I made my decision.

As I climbed out of bed and crossed through the shadows, I guiltily imagined you sleeping in a motel somewhere in the northern part of Montana, a tall graph of evergreens visible from your window, and beyond that, a dark horizon of mountains with white beards of snow. Like a supplicant, I kneeled down to the musty bottom bookshelf and put my hands on the slim first volume, cracking it to where it held the series of onionskin letters. I selected one and took it to the window to read by moonlight. One random letter, I told myself. No more, no less. This was my final bargain with the Devil of Curiosity. Or so I thought.

Before I began reading, however, I smelled the page: the faint yet distinctive odor of laundry rooms, of a mother's hands scrubbing collars and cuffs, the sweeter smell of a younger man who was better cared for, different from the starchier fragrance of you now, a guy with a nine-to-five job who sent his white and linens out to be commercially laundered.

Okinawa, July 9, 1982
Dear R.M.,
The second time you've stood me up in ten days. Why can't you just call and say you've chickened out? Don't you realize how fucking nerve-racking it is, not to mention humiliating, for me to keep standing there like a dummy in front of the PX and having to see all my stepfather's friends? And the fact that they might be home when you call is no excuse for not calling to say you can't make it. There could be any number of reasons why you'd call me. I'm of age. I'm allowed to have friends . . .

I stopped reading long enough to calculate that in 1982 you would've been twenty-one.

You keep bringing up the possibility of my stepfather finding us out. I know it's a smoke screen. And you know it is, too, you know there are plenty of places we can still meet with anonymity. I hate it when you can't be honest; it makes me feel like a kid. And I'm not a kid anymore, R.M.; I've taken this on completely. I've known you long enough to know that I want to be with you and only you. And you know it, too, and that's why you're afraid that if my parents suspect anything, if my father asks, that I won't lie about it. But of course I'd lie, I'd lie for you.
You've said that I can't really be in love with you, for some reason you don't believe me when I tell you. So then explain to me what is it that keeps me up nights, what is it that steals my appetite, makes my heart race in the middle of doing absolutely nothing? And why is it when you don't call at the appointed hour, I begin to

feel like a prisoner of myself, knowing I have to get through an-
other eternity of an evening until I'm alone again and you can
call? And even then I can never call you.

My parents keep asking me when I'm going back to California;
they can't understand why I'm procrastinating finding a real job
or making up my mind about grad school. They realize I've put my
life on hold, they can sense that I'm waiting for something.

Meanwhile, I'm beginning to lose hope. Because you've stopped
talking about getting transferred back to San Diego. Because you've
stopped talking about our future together. And because the only
time you ever tell me you love me anymore is when you're inside me
and it's hurting me and you just plain forget to hold the words back.

I'm still waiting to hear from you.
Love Always,
S.P.

11

WE TRIED TO MAKE LOVE AGAIN, SHORTLY AFTER YOU ARRIVED BACK in the city, smelling of stratospheric travel, of jet fuel and that sweet reek of plastic audio headsets. You came in wearing your fatigues, your neck branded with a blue-collar worker's sunburn. You threw your arms around me and I was terrified. I kept trying to lick the red line of the sunburn where it bordered pale skin. But all too soon I felt the Marine coming between us, the Marine who once had the power to catapult you into such a state of expectation and desire, the Marine who fucked you until it hurt. Something made me hold back, and then you picked up on it and we ended up lying there, disconcerted.

"God," you said finally, "it's so bizarre because all I could think about on the plane was getting home and jumping on your bones."

"It's my fault," I said. "I'm feeling scared."

You said nothing for a while and finally asked what exactly was scaring me.

I tried to dissemble. "The usual," I said. "Losing my-self . . . getting hurt."

"Well, I'm in the same place. So at least we understand each other in that way."

"I suppose."

"I think it'll be good for us to spend some time together out of the city in another environment."

"I've actually loved staying here," I said, looking down at the haphazard pile of our clothing. "I've managed to get a lot of work done." Then it hit me that you were now willing to leave your apartment unguarded. "What about Bobby Garzino's ex-lover?"

"When José calls, as I'm sure he will, I'll just tell him that I've removed everything Bobby gave me out of the apartment. We'll take it to your place, okay?"

Why hadn't we done that before? "But now he knows who I am, too."

"How does he know that?"

I explained that apparently some of his friends had seen us leaving Splash together. "I don't want him breaking into my apartment, either."

"Okay, understood. I'll just take it all to my office."

From where I lay I could see the rear pocket of the fatigues and the faintest impression of block lettering MONROE. I suddenly felt a stab of guilt over my indiscretion. "While you were gone, I was looking for a T-shirt to wear and I came upon a stack of fatigues with the name MONROE on the back of them."

"Yeah, so?"

"Who *is* this Monroe?"

You waited a moment and then you said, "Monroe was my Chad."

I managed to laugh, although, inside, the breathless, nauseous feeling that swept through me when I first read the letter returned. "Where's he from?"

"Nevis, mainly, though he was born in Michigan."

"Nevis, meaning the Caribbean?"

"He's black," you added by way of an explanation.

Of course! Why hadn't I figured this? Monroe was probably just as magnificent as the guy you were dancing with on the video screen. Maybe you adored black men and everyone—including me—by comparison was inadequate and wan.

"How long has it been since you've seen him?"

"Eight years."

"Do you prefer black men?"

"Not exclusively, no."

I hated knowing how much you once had loved this Monroe. And I hated knowing that your sex with him must have been galvanic and voracious. And now I felt miserable because *our* sex had already gone awry again. But then the phone began to ring, and we listened to it until the answering machine came on and recorded the babel of a street corner and then the lonely sound of dial tone.

"So what else did he say?" you asked glumly. "Did he tell you there are still people in the city who want to ruin my face?"

I smiled. "He says they're waiting to do that till after you break my heart."

"So I guess that means yours will be the very last heart I'll ever break."

"There might even be some distinction in that," I said.

You chuckled and snuggled in closer to me.

"You got all those fatigues from this Monroe guy, huh?" I said.

"Among other things."

That stung me for some reason. I sat up. "Like what? What else did he give you?"

Looking at me, perplexed, you said somewhat defensively, "I don't know. Let me think. A pre-Columbian statue. A tennis racket."

I glanced around the apartment. "So where's the statue?"

"He smashed it toward the end."

I patrolled your expression for a sign of distress. "So he was the violent type, huh?"

"Not very often. And in fact, really only when he was provoked. Although we did fight a lot, verbally. Which, of course, had its dividends."

"You don't need to say that!" And then, "Nothing like sex after a good fight."

"Like coming when your heart breaks," you said with a gloomy smile.

You were facing away from me, and I now could feel your lament, even in the way your dark curls softly crushed against your pillow. So after all these years this Monroe was still vanquishing you. And I now knew that Bobby Garzino was hardly responsible for the tear you shed the first night I learned who he was and how he died, the first night I'd told you about Chad. I now knew that your life had docked with this Marine long before you'd ever met the weaver.

PART TWO

MARINE 🌙

12

WE WOULD SWIM DURING DAYLIGHT HOURS, TOO, BUT HE LIKED THERE to be a swell, preferably a red-flag day with several tiers of combers breaking simultaneously. I preferred late afternoons of calm when the Pacific turned cobalt blue and rays of sunlight bounced in from the west and the foam glowed like phosphorus. We'd follow the string of swimmers' buoys that stretched for two miles down the Santa Barbara coastline, past the Mediterranean bathing pavilion of East Beach, past the marine cemetery looming above the limestone cliffs that plummeted to the nude beach, past the stone balustrades foreshadowing the Biltmore Hotel.

Used to training in pools, we reveled in the greater buoyancy of salt water. It made us believe that we could swim forever. Chad was faster and always pulled ahead of me, and I'd push myself to follow closely the splashing of his feet. But soon he'd gain enough distance so that the darkness of the water would engulf me and I was completely alone again.

Sometimes he'd get far enough ahead that I'd find him waiting for me at one of the buoys, head thrown back into the sun, hair tangled and briny. That grin on his face, and his teeth as white as beached bones—one day, when he was waiting for me like that, he said flatly and without provocation, "You'll probably be the only swimmer." His normally husky voice was particularly rasped.

"Come on." I wondered if he was trying to say that I was some great love of his.

"First and last and in between," he added with a dreamy grin that now reminds me of you. He dove off the buoy and started swimming again.

That day, we'd begun at the beach below the cemetery, had already done a mile down the coast and were on the way back. As I continued following him, I concluded what he'd said had to do with the fact that we both could swim like demons. I was the only swimmer who could even begin to keep up with him. Sometimes it's a lover's strength and not his inadequacy that spooks and spoils the prospect of a future.

But I waited until we finished our swim and were toweling off before asking outright what he'd meant. He grunted and finished rubbing himself with his towel before answering, "You second-guessing me?"

"Just trying to understand."

He bombed me with his wet towel and I found myself clutching at it so that it wouldn't hit the sand. "Just slipped out. Like a little fish that I swallowed," he said sheepishly. "Only meant it as a compliment."

And so I believed. Believed that our love, like our shared obsession for swimming, was a fluke of nature. And that's why his vanishing has kept hurting. He must've had an inkling of what he was going to do a few months down the line, choosing the random life of an itinerant, becoming a man-without-attachments. For all I know, he could now be a seasonal abalone diver, an oil driller working the circuit of remote derricks in the Gulf of Mexico, a chef on a shrimp trawler.

He left in increments before he vanished Big Time. When I was unable to reach him for days, I assumed at first that there was somebody else in his life besides me—a woman, even, because there *had* been women in his past. In 1980, answering machines were practically nonexistent, and falling in love with somebody hard to reach meant calling every hour, calling in the middle of the night and letting the telephone ring twenty, thirty, forty times before falling asleep with the receiver cradled in my arms.

Finally I'd resort to driving an anxiety-fraught fifteen miles from my apartment on Mason Street all the way out to Isla Vista. I tend to see the object of my fascination everywhere I go, even hundreds of miles away from anywhere that might be logical: a car parked in front of a 7-Eleven, a lone figure playing pool in the shadows of a neon-lighted bar. And sometimes when I was driving north on 101 to his place during the daylight, I actually believed that in the swarm of cars heading south toward Los Angeles, I'd see that beat-up Volkswagen with Harvard decals, fenders spray-painted black, careering away from me. I'd pull onto the shoulder and try to figure out whether it was worth continuing the drive to his place. But I always kept going.

Sometimes I'd even head out there at three o'clock in the morning when there were hardly any other cars on the freeway. In his neighborhood I'd drive aimlessly through all those streets of the student quarter, imagine all the undergraduates who were taking my writing seminar sleeping in their prefabricated apartments, innocents. What *would* they think if they knew their instructor was driving obsessively around Isla Vista, spying on his elusive lover? I drove through streets named *Camino* or *Calle:* Camino Pescadero, Camino del Sur, Calle del Barco, Calle Albrogado.

He lived on Del Playa, a street that ran along the ocean, where it was nearly impossible to find a vacancy because every house and apartment was inhabited by an extended clan of surfers. They networked among themselves and managed to squeak their bros into the vacated rooms before any became officially available. Chad didn't surf all that much, he wasn't part of any surfer contingency; nevertheless he had managed to keep his roommates enthralled by his ability to take on the ocean swell in any kind of weather. He'd been granted his own room and his own phone, and if I couldn't reach him, there was no reaching his housemates, and no way of knowing if he had blown out of town, or was out somewhere, or had simply unplugged the jack.

My eyes would turn the corner of that weed-infested driveway before my car did, and I would strain to see if his beat-up Volkswagen was parked there. More often than not it wasn't, and then at 3:00 A.M. I'd be faced with a forlorn fifteen-mile drive back to my solitary apartment and another insomniac night.

If I arrived at a reasonable hour I'd always go in and try to get information from the housemates, who would scratch their sun-frizzed heads of matted hair and murmur in long-toned southern Californese, "Don't have a clue, Will. Hey, Coz, where's our Chad, where's our vanishing Chad gone to this time?"

But Coz never knew and neither did Reese, nor Dino—the one named Tripp was always too stoned to know anything. They were wary of me, these roommates, and often I suspected they withheld information at his request. Had they been poets they might have said that Chad was as unpredictable as some of their favorite combers that gave great rides before switching back and turning them upside down.

But when he was around, we would spend hours, days together without ever being apart. Coexist in the library, in total silence for eight hours or more, I reading Thackeray, he reading Schopenhauer; then we'd hit the pool for 5,000 meters and return. I remember once he came to my house for black bean burritos and

Spanish rice and ended up staying for three days and nights, sub-
sisting on Haas avocados and Mexican papayas and Valencia oranges that I went out and bought for him while he devoured my
Popular Library edition of *The Magic Mountain.* The novel was
all he could talk about for days afterward.

   After he vanished, I badgered his roommates for clues, and
they railed at me for suspecting that they knew more than they
were telling; for they, too, were beside themselves. It touched me
to see how much his leaving affected their lives. For days they sat
together in the living room, shirtless in ragged jams and tar-caked
sandals, getting wasted. They made me tell the story again and
again, how he'd convinced me to swim against my will and how
there were no "last words" as we walked along Cabrillo Boulevard. They dissected my tale like detectives. "So you saw that
boat, yeah? And you told him, right? He definitely heard you?
Okay. Okay. And you didn't even look around to see if he was
there?" It always ended with, "You guys—swimming at night—
what the fuck was with you guys?"

   But they knew we were nightswimmers. They knew Chad. And
in the end they were divided in their opinion of what might have
happened to him. Reese and Tripp were sure that he was dead.
Dino and Coz thought, like me, that he had purposely disappeared.

   For three months the four of them divided his share of the rent,
hoping he'd eventually show up, but finally they were forced to
give up his room to somebody else. In the meantime all his belongings had gone to his parents—except the beloved VW. It lifted
my spirits when they gave it to me, because for a while it allowed
me to imagine myself as him. As I dressed in the few clothes of
his that he'd left in my apartment, as I aped his slightly hunched-
over posture, as I made a ring of my thumb and index finger and
whistled shrilly the way he did when he was out on a board in the
middle of the swell. But all that mimicry didn't bring me any closer
to the mystery of his vanishing.

The times I had actually found him at home, the times signaled by my triumphant sighting of the beat-up, decaled Volkswagen in his driveway, I'd inadvertently run my hands over its rear panel to see if the engine was still warm. Sometimes I'd find him on the back deck of his house, standing among the terra-cotta pots overflowing with herbs and cuttings of aloe, eyeing the ocean and the coastal garlands of kelp. He'd turn to me and grin without surprise and say, "Smells pretty tarry today, what do you think?" Even ten years later the smell of those tarry Pacific beaches depresses me and gives me a headache.

Or: "I was just getting ready to call. Tell you to get your bones up here. Want a beer?"

Beer was usually Corona, clear bottles with the blue painted labels that looked so good in his sturdy veined hands and rang out against the band of his silver-and-turquoise ring. Sometimes it was Dos Equis, sometimes Carta Blanca—but always Mexican. I drank mine quickly to plane down my anxiety. As he took his bottle up for a swig, he'd tell me how he'd gone surfing up at Jalama, that he'd sat in a two-day meditation up near Point Conception, where he alternated between reading Gurdjieff and trying to "key into" the souls of the Chumash Indians before they flew across the water. Yet had he really done this?

Of course I wanted to rail at him for leaving without telling me. But a casual "You should let somebody know you're heading out" was all that I said. "Otherwise it's hard for any of us to know if you've gone in the water and just haven't come out."

"Look, the times we speak are the times I actually get through to you. When I try once and you're not around, I just don't wait." Staring out over the combers, he bent one of his tar-flecked toes on the weathered boards of his deck. "You get very anxious about our communication, Will. You worry about me when there's no need. If I say I'm in love with you, I'm in love with you. I'm not leaving you, I'm just living. If I croaked or something you'd definitely know it."

"How?" I cried. "How would I know?"

He shrugged. "I'd send you a sign." Then he grinned and fixed his black eyes hungrily on me and said, "But even dead I'd fuck with you somehow. Become an incubus and suck your dick in the middle of the night."

"But you'd have to suck it the way I like it. Or else I wouldn't know it was you."

Chad took a huge slug of beer and seemed to reflect for a moment. "I just got this thing about me, Will. I like to go roaming. That's all. I like the idea of being at large, or between two places." He now drained the rest of his beer and brought the bottle down with a hard smack on the wooden railing of the deck and grinned. "I always think about you when I'm gone, anyway."

With that he led me into his bedroom filled with collected driftwood that resembled biblical figures, with ashtrays overflowing with sea glass he'd found up and down the California coast, an entire wall taken up with floor-to-ceiling bookshelves. He drew makeshift curtains made of dyed Indian cotton, lighted several stubby candles that smelled like sandalwood and, facing me, untied the leather thong around his neck that held three blue African glass beads. He put Sting on the record player, gulped his beer and then very gently swept the crumbs of sand from my shoulders. At first our bodies slapped together so hard that the friction of sex raised the room temperature, made the smell of eucalyptus even stronger. As though to cool things down, he grabbed his Corona and poured a line of beer between my pecs down to my crotch, slurped it off me and then put his ocean-cold mouth on my cock.

After that he was much better about calling to let me know when he was leaving town on a whim. In fact he'd make a point of calling me from weird places like Los Alamos, where he supposedly spent an afternoon contemplating the military jets flying in and out of Vandenburg. And I believed him. At Pismo Beach, he swam around the rock formations; at Atascadero, he spent a few days doing volunteer work at the men's prison. The calls were reassuring then. But maybe the reason why he suddenly changed for the better was that he'd already decided what he was going to do. And once he made up his mind, he no longer needed to make his day-to-day whereabouts a painful tease. He was preparing for the cruel mystery of total vanishing.

13

I TOLD YOU THIS IN VERMONT WHILE WE WERE STANDING ON AN incline above the Ottauquechee River, a mile or so before the Taftsville covered bridge. I'd shown you the River Road because I loved its eeriness, the banks overhung with willows, the dark-shingled cabins with spindly steps that scaled down to brackish-looking water that swirled along like televised weather patterns. We'd stopped my car at a rope swing and now I climbed on the hood to gain some more height. Casey sat on his haunches by the rear wheels of my car, his lanky body erect and attentive, waiting to see what I'd do next.

I jumped up and swung down and out over the river like a pendulum, and as I gained the top of the far arc, I let go and plummeted into the water. A moment later there was a splash nearby; Casey had bounded down the bank and leapt in. He swam determinedly toward me, his beautiful hound's head above the water, breasting the slight current with his white chest and the white tips of his paws.

"Good going!" you crowed down to me through your cupped hands. Then you clambered down the bank, grabbed the rope, climbed up again, swung out and dropped into the water next to me.

Farther downstream we could see a rope line of big orange Styrofoam buoys draped like a necklace from one bank to the other, preventing pleasure boats, as well as swimmers like us, from going over the steep falls just beyond the bridge.

"This was my favorite thing to do last summer," I explained as we stood in shallow water and as Casey paddled leisurely back and forth between us. "I used to come here and swing out when I got really depressed."

"Depressed? You mean, over Greg?"

"I even jumped from a few railroad bridges into the White River."

"What were you doing, simulating suicide?"

"Sometimes a little exhilaration is a quick pick-me-up."

You looked doubtful for a moment but then you nodded.

I took you to a place called Lake Echo for a longer swim. There, as we made our way out toward the middle, I could see that you had a fairly even stroke, just needed to keep your elbows higher, to relax and shoulder-roll a bit more, but basically it was all there. I swam a long, easy crawl, watching how the water deepened vaultlike while shafts of sunlight trolled the depths. At one point I dove way down. With my back to the bottom I watched the surface glittering above me like a living mirror, whose silvery skin was broken by Casey swimming in vigilant circles as he waited for me to surface. When finally I could see your body crossing above, I came up for air. "Do you know how to eggbeater?" I asked.

"Eggbeater?"

I explained that eggbeater was treading water with the legs so that one had free use of the hands.

"What's the point of doing that?"

"Besides being the key to playing water polo, it allows you to swim and eat a tuna sandwich at the same time," I said, laughing.

You caught on quickly because your legs were strong, and we hovered there, palms facing, doing eggbeater and kissing water-filled kisses.

As we were climbing back into the car, Casey spotted something dead by the side of the road and began sniffing at it cautiously. You went over to look and then flinched away. A small bird, wings and downy torso complete with a yellow throat, was completely flattened to the road surface like a fossil embedded in stone. One glistening bloody organ had somehow been spared the final crush of car wheels and hung off the remains. It resembled a small brain.

That was the funny thing about the country, I explained, once we were driving to the grocery store. Although it was soothing in all its beauty, in its profusion of plant and animal life, one always saw the remains of violence and heard grisly stories of accidents: drunk drivers felling deer and slamming into hundred-year-old trees, somebody losing control of a chain saw and severing a hand or a foot. I told a story I'd read recently about a guy milling among the tourists at the viewing point three hundred feet above the Ottauquechee gorge. He'd spoken kindly to a couple, who, moments later, turned around to see a pair of black shoes lined up next to each other. The man had jumped off. When they looked far below into the foaming water, they saw the bright red spot of his blood on the stones.

You were quiet. Finally you spoke. "And something about the city makes you think that you can beat dying. Something about a place where if anything goes wrong you can check into one of those mega-hospitals and be kept alive."

I'd been required to remain in New York in order to complete an interview and you'd driven up to Vermont with Casey, spent a few days alone at my place before I arrived. At first you were reluctant to take on the responsibility of a dog, but when Greg got wind of this, he emphatically reminded me how much Casey loved the country. Not wanting to be the cause of a dispute, you had finally offered to take the dog along.

And so you'd been staying in my little red house, probably, I hoped, trying to picture yourself living the life of Will Kaplan, just as I'd tried to imagine myself living the life of Sean Paris on Grove Street. I imagined you working on your landscape drawings in the natural light, then going for walks with Casey in the Revolutionary War cemetery across the street.

We finally arrived back at the cabin. It had been built back in the 1800s as a one-room schoolhouse. The property had changed hands many times since then and had been updated and modernized. The most recent renovations were three-prong plugs and new bleached and pickled oak floors that made quite a contrast to the original aged and unsplit one-hundred-year-old logs that formed the rafters that vaulted up to the sleeping loft, which had to be reached by a ladder.

The moment we walked in the door with our bags of groceries, I noticed that the kitchen clock was wrong. You explained that the night before I arrived there'd been a torrential rainstorm that spewed hailstones the size of cherries. The lightning and thunder had knocked out the power.

"You're actually a pretty good swimmer," I remarked once we were sitting at my round dining table, sipping ice-cold beers that left ring marks on the gingham table cloth. "Especially for not having done it competitively."

You said, somewhat defensively, "I don't like swimming very much. All the river and lake hopping we did today—it's not something I would do normally."

"I didn't realize you were bored."

"I was hardly bored. We were outside. And it *is* beautiful here," you said, taking a swig of your beer. "I just personally feel more comfortable on land. Being a small child in the tropics probably did that to me. A lot of weird things grow and live in hot places. I associate living in Okinawa with constantly checking to make sure there wasn't some kind of creature about to fall on me."

"Like what?"

"Like the worst, ugliest mother-fucking spiders you've ever seen."

"Big?"

Banana spiders, you explained, are the size of a man's hand. Deadly poisonous to small animals. "A bite from one of those suckers is like getting bitten by a rattlesnake."

You warmed to the topic. "They spin these huge cottony webs that have twigs and leaves in them, webs so big that sometimes they stretch across the street between parked cars. There used to be this one web outside my window strung between a shrub and the side of the house. Big enough to catch *birds!* I was always aware of the fact that if I had to escape the house there'd be no way that I could climb out my window. Banana spiders have these long bodies, pointy, and angled legs, very thin. They cocoon whatever they catch and then suck the blood out. When grasshoppers and locusts get caught they usually put up a horrible fight. They tear up the web, trying to escape. And in the middle of all that thrashing, the spider keeps running all over the web, repairing the torn parts, trying to do damage control.

"Then there are the water spiders that were the size of, I'd say, a small doughnut. Those guys can flatten themselves out by exhaling all their air and then crawl anywhere there's water. They've been known to hide under the rim of the toilet and, whenever you sit down, crawl across your ass."

A shudder of disgust zipped through me. "All right, already, enough," I said. "Now I understand why you prefer the winter."

We divided the cooking chores and collaborated on dinner together that first night: roast chicken with lemon and rosemary and

new potatoes, steamed carrots, and broccoli rabe, then fresh rasp-
berries for dessert. Before agreeing upon the meal, however, we
scrolled through many possibilities. You were surprised at the
number of recipes I knew by heart, recipes as diverse as mous-
saka and couscous. I explained that being a child of an early di-
vorce, dividing my time between two parents (both of whom were
superb cooks), I had grown accustomed to two different kitchens
as well as two different sets of culinary likes and dislikes. And
yet you were a much more methodical and nimble preparer than
I was. You measured out ingredients with speedy confidence,
cleaning up carefully as you went along, slicing vegetables with
a dexterity that obviously was part of your ability to draw so beautifully and so precisely.

At one point I tried to open a can of cranberry relish, but the
can opener was unable to grip the lip of the tin. I kept fumbling
until you came over and relieved me of the chore and, without hesitation, effortlessly completed what I'd been unable to do. I could
tell that my lack of mechanical ability was surprising to you. I
imagined that someone like Bobby Garzino, who loomed with his
hands and probably cut things like onions into tiny square pearls,
was the sort to spend hours tinkering with a faltering household
appliance until he got it to work properly.

Later on, after dinner, we sat in the cemetery. Propped between my legs, you were leaning against me and I was leaning
against one of the Revolutionary War tombstones. We kept passing back and forth a bottle of cold Chardonnay. The cabin was
across the street from us now, dark but for one light still burning
in the bathroom. The moon was stalking the horizon, fighting to
break free of an embankment of clouds, but the stars were out in
full regalia and the tombs themselves held a muted luminosity.
The night was a hum of crickets every so often punctured by the
whoop of an owl or the strangled cry of a bird stranded away from

its nest. Casey lay next to me with his head on my lap.

"Up, there goes another one," you broke the silence. "That makes three. Three shooting stars I've seen since we've been here."

"My record is six in one sitting," I said. "But that's when I've spent the night out here watching."

"You've spent the whole night alone in this cemetery?"

"No big deal."

"You didn't find it spooky?"

"Nah, it's beautiful. Especially earlier in the summer when the fireflies are out." The tombs, in their tumbling-down state, resembled pale soldiers collapsing on the last stretch of a battlefield, or perhaps enormous faulty denture work. "If there were any souls of these people hovering around, I'm sure they're long gone. The last person was buried here a hundred years ago. It's not like a modern cemetery with freshly dug mounds."

You laughed. And then you exhaled a trembling sigh.

"What?"

"Nothing. I . . . feel happy here . . . It's so different from the city grind."

"I couldn't be in the city unless I had a place like this to come away to."

"How do you think I feel living there, a person who loves gardens? Sometimes I wonder what keeps me in New York."

"What keeps you there is the axis." I explained that I meant the Manhattan–Fire Island Pines axis. "And in the winter it's triangulated with South Beach."

You digested this for a moment and then you said, "That's an oversimplification, it seems to me."

"So you don't agree?"

I could feel you shrug. "Whether or not I agree isn't important. The fact is that you felt you had to break free of that axis— as you call it. You wanted something different."

"Well, I had to break free of it or else I would never get anything accomplished. Vermont is hardly fashionable with . . . the smooth and the beautiful."

"Come on now, be nice. No sweeping statements about your own kind."

"Okay," I said. "Except that I fundamentally don't feel I have my 'own kind.' "

I sensed a sudden shift in your mood. There were a few moments of significant silence. And whereas I was expecting you to say something that might be discordant or even distancing, I was surprised.

"That may be, but I'll tell you something, Will. I'll tell you straight out. You've got a lot of things that I want in a guy. Intensity, independence, you understand what it's like to be burned by somebody else . . . and yet, well, the idea of having you also scares the shit out of me."

"Don't say that! I don't get the impression that you were scared of that guy in Okinawa."

You sounded annoyed. "How the hell do you know I wasn't scared of him?"

"Just doesn't seem like you were."

"That's your projection. And anyway, I was stupider then. Lots younger. A lot more willing to throw myself into the flame."

"We all were stupider back then," I said. "Nothing had broken us—yet."

"I'll give you a quick difference between you and me." You now swiveled around to peer at me intently with your sad and silly expression. "No matter where we are in the ever-changing flux of this . . . whatever it is—an affair, a relationship—you probably never even wonder why I'm interested in you, right?"

"Why should I wonder about that?"

"Well, I can't understand why you're interested in *me*. And don't even bring up the idea I'm your true physical type or any of that bullshit. Because there're plenty of my type around. And you know how long that fantasy lasts."

"I wouldn't talk about type," I said, defending myself. "But okay, so you don't want to hear your list of virtues?" I said somewhat irritably. "Fine. I won't burden you."

"Top of that list, I think, is that I bring *him* back to you, I think I bring back Chad."

"Who says that's a virtue? If anything, that makes it harder. But obviously the more I get to know you, the more I realize how different the two of you are."

"The other thing is I have the feeling that you've run through the story of your life before with other people, with your other lovers. Whereas I really haven't."

Just then the gleaming eyes of an animal crossed the cemetery, swerving toward us with a feral glance. Casey could smell it and raised his head from my lap. A low growl erupted in his throat. "Look at that," I said. "Look at those amazing eyes."

"What do you think it is?"

"Probably a raccoon. Maybe a possum."

When Casey made a move to pursue the animal, I threw my arms around him and grasped him to me until whatever it was finally scurried away into the darkness.

You leaned back against me. "I'll tell you, though, I've never seen a sky so full of stars. Not even in the South Pacific."

Your past was like some great tidal wave that had been sighted and seemed perpetually to be on its way toward landfall. And as we continued to watch for plummeting stars I said that I was confused about how much time you'd actually spent in Okinawa.

"I was born there," you said. "I lived there till the age of eight. Then I basically grew up around Camp Pendleton in San Diego. But I spent a year in Okinawa right after college with my mother and my stepdad. That last stint was when I met Randall Monroe."

"How long did your real father live with you?"

"I was two years old when he first left us to go to Saigon. And then he came back when I was four. But I think I remember as far back as before the first time he left. The psychologists, the Freudians—whoever they are—say memory isn't formed that early. But I remember lots of things. I remember sunlight in a room and a man with white hair—my father went gray prematurely. He's leaning over me in the crib, dangling these . . . they're like wind chimes. I remember the sound they make, like husked-out seashells gently clattering together. He blows on them. Apparently, there was such a mobile in our house at the time. Made of fish bones and shells and hollowed-out nuts, one of those baby amusements that my mother got rid of early on. Because the noise it made drove her crazy. Anyway, I only ever saw him a few times in my life."

"But when did he die, exactly?"

"Just before I turned eight."

"Was it hard, I mean, how much did you understand what was going on?"

"I understood everything. Plus the fact that my mother was an emotional wreck for so long afterward, for what seemed like forever. But what's more distinct, believe it or not, is my memory of him coming home the last time, the time before he actually went back to Vietnam and got killed. Because there was lots of leadup to his coming home. I kept getting told that my brave, wonderful father was returning, and I was really looking forward to seeing him. The man who'd been sending me these reel-to-reel audiotapes that he made in Vietnam. He would talk to me on them. He would describe his life in his village, what it was like being the commander and the people he worked with. He always finished by reciting a Mother Goose rhyme: 'Jack, Be Nimble,' or 'The Old Woman Who Lived in a Shoe.' And sometimes I could hear the sound of mortar rounds in the distance."

I asked if you still possessed the tapes, but apparently your mother had managed to lose them. How could she have lost something so important? The answer was that even the possibility of hearing the voice of a dead husband had been too much for her.

"But the day he arrived my mother told me at the last minute that she needed to speak to him privately about a few things and sent me next door to Roseanne, her best friend, whose husband was also stationed in Vietnam. I was really upset because I'd wanted to see my father the moment he came and suddenly I was getting shunted next door to Roseanne's and being fed this Betty Crocker chocolate layer cake—I'll never forget that's what she made for me, this pathetic-tasting box cake, whereas my mother always used to make her cakes from scratch. There was supposed to be a phone call that would summon me home. That's how our lives were then, waiting for phone calls—probably why I hate the phone so much. Phone calls from Saigon, calls that sometimes wouldn't come and left my mother so inconsolable that she'd bring me to sleep on my father's side of the bed.

"Anyway, as I waited for them to call me home that afternoon, I was afraid that they might never call me back. Afraid that I would have to spend the rest of my life with Roseanne, eating her cardboard chocolate layer cakes. Afraid that I would be forced to go back to 'the world'—which was what they called the States."

"So you didn't want to go back to the States?"

"No, I loved living in Okinawa, even though I didn't love the spiders or the heat. The States—'the world'—was something you always heard about, something always referred to. But to me it was like the great unknown. . . . Anyway, the phone finally did ring at Roseanne's house. And I was told to walk home.

"I remember hearing their voices as I neared the screen door. And that was strange in itself because whenever I'd come home from next door, the house was usually silent with just my mother there. I went through the back door. But they weren't in the kitchen. So I went over to the end of the hallway that was adjacent to the kitchen. And my mom and my dad were just coming out of their bedroom. I'm standing at one end of the hallway and they are standing at the other end. The light is behind me and they're . . . like these too-dark figures, these dark birds. And yet I can see that my mom is wearing a smile that I've never seen on her before: calm and knowing. That smile really bugs me. And I want to say to her, 'You've been upset for a year, don't act like that! Why don't you tell him about all the times you got so angry! Why don't you tell him about the time you mailed him that nasty letter and how we had to wait all day by the mailbox so you could get it back from the mailman?'

"But then she said, 'Sean, come and see your father.' "

You remembered his cheeks were pink and smooth from shaving, the metal smell of his uniform and his white hair stiff and combed with oil. You got one kiss on the top of the head and then a handshake. But you and your father felt really awkward around each other. Throughout the visit, he was always polite to you, always spoke with soft control. But he was a stranger, different somehow, scarier, less tangible than his own voice that had spoken from all those reel-to-reel tapes.

You swallowed and then you continued. "And then he died. Maybe a month after he went back from that last visit. On his way to get a haircut, he was caught in some cross fire. And his ticket got punched."

Neither of us spoke while the clamor of crickets and tree frogs resounded.

"You sound so matter-of-fact when you say that," I commented finally. Of course that was because you'd lived with it for so long now, you replied. After all, the time your father had been alive was now only a fraction of your life. His death was what you'd grown accustomed to, "like scar tissue," you said.

But I didn't quite believe you. Something in me balked at the way you described a traumatic event as mechanically as a windup doll. And because you then went mute there in the cemetery and, later on, seemed irritable when we walked back to the cabin, climbed the ladder up into the sleeping loft and Casey began whining, begging to be taken up with us.

"You mean to tell me he sleeps with you?" you asked as I made a move to climb down and retrieve the dog.

"Whenever he's with me, he does. He's used to it."

"Don't you think that's a bit overindulgent?"

I shrugged and continued climbing down the ladder. "He's like my child," I said, grabbing Casey under both his front legs and lifting him up, placing his paws over my shoulders. "I'm like his father." Casey watched me with the vulnerable, miffed look in his eyes that always wrenched my heart; he licked me nervously as I prepared to climb the ladder. I held him to me with one arm and used the other to pull us up. He emitted a grunt halfway up and leapt off me as soon as we reached the top.

I sat there for a moment, panting from the climb. Casey went directly to the end of the bed, walked a tight circle and then settled down comfortably.

You watched Casey take his place. "I couldn't let myself be so close . . . to an animal."

"Why?" I asked, suddenly growing aware of the rumor of moths hurling themselves against the screens downstairs and something in me turned cold to what I imagined as your indifference.

"Because I'd get too attached." This surprised me. "And then ten years or so down the line there'd be the loss and the grief and all the people without animals who didn't understand that grieving."

"People like you?" I couldn't help saying.

1 4

LATE THE FOLLOWING AFTERNOON WE WERE LYING IN THE LOFT BED of my cabin, looking up through the skylights. A summer rainstorm was pelting the glass, and we'd just finished making love to the sound of water sluicing through the gutters. Sleepy and torpid and satisfied, I felt emboldened enough to say, "Won't you even tell me a little bit about Randall?"

"What do you want to know?"

"I don't know. How it ended . . . how it began."

You looked up at the rain thrumming against the glass skylight panes. Sighing, you murmured, "The typhoon. It began and ended during the typhoon."

"The same typhoon?"

You scoffed. "No, of course not the same typhoon. Two different ones. A year apart."

"Did it end abruptly?"

"I see you're more interested in the ending than the beginning."

"I'm interested in how he burned you."

You shook your head. "The situation itself burned me. Not him so much. In fact, he left suddenly, just like Chad."

"How come you didn't tell me this before?"

"I'm telling you now. Isn't that good enough?"

"But why did he leave so suddenly?"

You paused and squirmed there next to me. "Because I cheated on him," you said finally. "Simple as that."

That you'd cheated on the man who I assumed was your great love came as a blistering surprise to me. So of course I wanted to know how it had happened.

"Because I suddenly felt him pulling back. He wasn't 'out' to anyone, and we always had to meet in secret. That made it more intense and sexy, but a lot just wasn't discussed. We'd talked about living together in San Diego when he was through with his tour. He was going to work for a company like McDonnell Douglas and I was going to go to graduate school in landscape architecture. But then he started to discuss reenlisting. Continuing to live abroad. He suddenly wasn't even taking me into consideration. So that's why I did it. Because I couldn't deal with the fact that he seemed to be falling out of love with me. I started seeing this cute guy I'd met who taught martial arts."

"But didn't you tell this other guy right away that you were involved?"

"Not the first night. It was one of those situations where you suddenly find yourself in bed with somebody else. But I did the next time we got together. He seemed to accept it. Said all he wanted to do was just to spend time with me whenever we could. I went along with it. I didn't realize it then, but the whole affair was obviously about Randall. I wanted Randall to feel something pulling me away, so that he'd be pulled back. But it backfired. Because the guy got freaked out about my unavailability and couldn't keep himself from contacting Randall. I should've realized that would happen. He told Randall everything. But Randall didn't do anything about it immediately. He waited awhile, a few days. Then one night came and confronted me about it. We had a big fight. And then he left the island without telling me he was leaving."

"But you were in touch with him, afterward? You said you were."

"Sure, I knew where he'd gone—to San Diego. But I had to find out that his tour was over and that he purposely hadn't told me how short he'd gotten—that's what they call it when you get close to the end of duty."

When you finally did get hold of Randall, he claimed he just couldn't admit what he was about to do. Had he announced his intentions, he was afraid that he'd be unable to leave the island. And yet he managed to slip out during a Condition 3 right before they closed the airport.

But I had to understand about typhoons. Almost always, a week before a typhoon begins to hit, the weather is brilliant. Like a taunt. It's so clear and perfect that even if you don't know it's coming, you wonder what's on the other side of such a string of gorgeous days. Like what happens in California before an earthquake and the light sharpens to the point where it seems like it's about to fracture. In Okinawa the perfect weather then gets worse and worse and worse. As if somebody is slowly pulling a shade down on that part of the world. It rains usually about a week before the real body of the typhoon hits full force and the ocean churns into a strange tawny color. The first relentless rains are called Condition 4. That's when the lawn furniture is packed away. When families stock up on sterno, candles, flashlight batteries and books to read during the confinement. When Condition 3 hits—which is when Randall got out—extra food supplies are bought and barrels are filled with drinking water. Condition 2, school closes and windows are boarded with typhoon tape—very heavy tape, like duct tape. Condition 1 means emergency. Caution. Take cover. In the middle of a Condition 1 some of the crazier Marines would actually get drunk and venture down the beach to watch the erratic seas. And often one of them would get swept into the ocean and drowned.

"Imagine finding out you've been left before being forced to stay indoors for a week. It was the worse, most confining week of my life. I knew he was gone and I was going crazy because the phone lines were down and I couldn't call him. And I was completely alone in the house for several days because, on account of the typhoon, my mother and my stepfather had been grounded on the mainland of Japan." You sighed nervously. "I don't think I slept at all that entire week."

"You think he might have met somebody else and just couldn't deal with the conflict?"

You shrugged. "I'll never know, will I? Sometimes it's better to be in the dark than to know the truth. Because you can never know the complete truth about anyone. In fact, you can never know the complete truth about yourself."

And then you told me that he sent back all your letters.

The letters in your apartment! So you *had* mailed them. They'd actually been *his*. Maybe he'd read them over and over again. Read them and then hid them, in a special compartment or a drawer—because he was afraid of somebody finding them. And maybe he had trouble deciding whether or not to mail them back to you. And once he mailed them, perhaps he regretted his impulse, the way you said your mother regretted mailing an angry letter to your father in Saigon and ended up waiting with you all day by the mailbox in order to intercept the postman.

I knew I should confess to having read your private letter, as well as the diaries. But right now, it seemed too risky. Instead, I asked how exactly you'd met Randall.

"He worked for a while in my stepfather's office—my mother remarried one of my dad's fellow officers, a colonel, a few years after my dad died. My stepdad was the one who taught me to love plants and he always encouraged me to build greenhouses when I was growing up in San Diego. Ironically, he got transferred back to Okinawa during my last year of college. Before going to grad school I decided to take a year off, to live in the South Pacific with him and my mother and teach English. A few months after I arrived there I decided to build a lath house so I could grow orchids and protect them from the elements. My stepdad lent me a couple of his staff Marines to help, and Randall was one of them."

"But wait a minute. Didn't your parents know your story?"

A sigh. "I tried to tell them when I was eighteen. Or, I should say, I tried to tell my mother. But she deflected it; all she cared about was that I didn't tell my stepfather. It never came up after that. And I've lived so far away from them that they haven't been confronted with any of my so-called relationships. Randall was so paranoid that he insisted whenever I saw him my parents could never be anywhere near us. Then again, he had a good reason. He did work for my stepfather."

I asked if Randall were really amazing-looking, like the guy at the Morning Party.

You shook your head emphatically and exclaimed that you'd never be interested in somebody so perfect-looking as the guy at the Morning Party, that Randall was rather ordinary, as a matter of fact, but there had been a kind of nobleness in his face. His eyes had been incredibly expressive and bright behind Marine-issue wire-framed glasses.

You didn't much notice him at first when he was helping with the lath house. You were intent on making sure the ventilation was right and the lighting. But then he came back one afternoon when you were tending some fledgling dendrobiums. He'd changed out of his uniform into a pair of tight jeans that showed off everything he had: a wonderful, sinewy body that was tight, compact. He said he'd always loved plants, described his family's sugarcane fields on Nevis—having been born in Miami, he had dual

citizenship. His family sounded pretty interesting: black landown-
ers, a few had been politicians on the island, some white ances-
try although he was pretty dark—one couldn't tell by looking at
him that he was a racial mix. And he had the most beautiful voice,
with a Caribbean accent; he always spoke softly, even when he got
angry, and his voice resonated like a wooden instrument. He could
sing like an angel.

He seemed to know a fair amount about horticulture, so there
was always plenty to talk about. Then there was a typhoon and
some minor structural damage to the lath house and he volunteered to help you repair it. Only then, when he started coming
by every day to help, did you begin to realize he had another interest besides the plants. After a while he hardly seemed so interested in helping as he was in talking. Soon he started fishing
for information: had you ever been in love? Were you involved
with anybody back in the States?

"Wait," I interrupted. "Involved with somebody 'black' in the
States?"

"No"—you laughed—and repeated " 'back' in the States."

Then a month after that typhoon another storm struck the island in the middle of the night. Not a typhoon, maybe, but a pretty
fierce tropical squall. And there were all these tea roses that you'd
just planted outside your parents' house.

"I woke up in the middle of the night and freaked out because
I knew they were just beginning to open and were in a vulnerable
phase. I also knew the damage would've been done and it was already too late to save them. So I just lay there until it got light,
went outside and found that all the roses were pretty much gone.
Petals strewn everywhere like plucked chicken feathers. So many
beautiful ones and they were completely torn apart. I was heart-
broken. But then among all the wreckage of petals and shredded
blooms I saw this one bud. It was absolutely perfect, just beginning to open. I remember it was covered with rain. When I bent

over it, I could smell . . . the nose was faint yet incredible. I don't know what came over me. I just took it in my mouth. Laid it on my tongue, sucked it really gently. The scent went completely through me. And I had this weird kind of . . . I don't know what you'd call it. In a way . . . almost like I came.

"And he saw the whole thing. He'd come over to visit and was standing there at the edge of the property." You grinned. "Then he followed me into the lath house and told me he was in love with me."

I lay there as you said this, speechless in a kind of jealous trance. Jealous of your sensual nature, jealous of such a romantic beginning. For some reason, our storm cleaved and the moon blazed through the skylight for an instant and its light fell on you and gave a pure alabaster wash to your pale skin.

Then you smiled your silly smile and said to me, "Bet you never met anybody who fellated a rose."

Soon thereafter, you fell asleep.

I remained awake, listening to the rain that was booming again against the cabin, to the wind roaring through the trees. I could imagine everything because I'd read your diaries.

Sometimes when your parents go away he comes over. You laze around. You could be reading and you hear floating from the other room this amazing voice like Van Morrison's but sexy, soulful like Marvin Gaye's. His friends call him Belafonte. He's one of the base DJs. You love the satiny darkness of his skin and its soapy smell that faintly hides the smell of his sweat. More musky than the other men you've made love to. You could recognize it anywhere. But it's also a smell of hair oil, of this stuff he uses called Black and White, genuine pluko Hair Dressing. Long Hold Control. Lanolin-rich stuff that's made in Tennessee.

He creams his skin. Rubs cocoa butter into it. He's so worried about dry skin, about graying, about discoloration. Sometimes he lets you do it for him, cream his skin. When your parents are gone he comes over and you rub it into his shoulders, up and down his back and his thighs. You can't help it but you love to keep running your fingers over his body because his skin is so taut and the ridges on his stomach are like carvings. And his pigmentation changes. The skin on his back has this warm, rosy hue to it, as does the skin on his thighs. But the skin on his cheeks and on his forehead has more of a yellowish cast. Sometimes he gets mad at the way you touch and look at him. He says you make him feel like a specimen. And you have to keep telling him he's your first black man, and that the differences between your bodies are intriguing. His foot soles are pale, even paler than the palms of his hands; and when he gets a cut, the healing pink is much more of a contrast on his dark skin than it is on yours. He can't shave every day or else he'll get those gray heat bumps on his face, and his smell changes when he's agitated or when he's about to come.

The two of you leave your parents' compound. Go up to the cliffs beyond the coral beds. The brush tangles into jungle and it's isolated though you can hear the Pacific. He has the most tender mouth, large and pink and powerful. His kisses set off these detonations inside you and he can easily take your cock all the way down to its root and slap it back and forth with the inside of his mouth. He loves it when you lean against a tree and screw his face and sometimes as you're getting there you can feel the mosquitoes biting your shoulders and your stomach and it makes it more intense when you finally come. When he's about to come, his eyes actually film over. And then you both lie there, staring up at the strange-looking trees in the Asian forest. As the daylight bleeds away, you watch how he vanishes next to you, this lovely black man, he just disappears into the darkness.

15

THAT YOU HAD BELONGED SO COMPLETELY AND SO WILLINGLY TO someone else made you more precious to me now. I felt so vulnerable to you. I felt so afraid.

And then early the following morning, a windswept, cloudless morning, the telephone startled us. It hadn't rung since we'd been there. It rang and rang until finally I climbed down the ladder naked to answer it. For a moment there was silence; sometimes because of electrical interference the telephone would shrill of its own accord. I was just about to hang up when somebody finally spoke: "So why don't you ask him." The momentary confusion suddenly burned off like fog.

Telling myself to remain composed, I spoke softly. "What should I ask?" now looking up at the loft to find your gaze locked on mine.

"Ask him to tell you about Bobby Garzino."

"I already know."

"I doubt it."

I took a deep breath. "Why don't you tell me?"

"Because maybe I don't want you to be happy."

"Then what's the point of calling? And how did you get this number, anyway?"

"It's on your other answering machine."

The line went dead. I was aware of the sunlight pouring into the cabin from all directions, splattering everywhere as though we were surrounded by a reflecting pool.

I put down the receiver, turned my palms up and said, "This is getting a little tedious." Up where you still were in the loft, your head tilted sideways, as if you were Casey trying to decipher an unfamiliar command.

You grabbed a pair of khaki shorts and put them on hastily. "Mind if I use the phone?" You climbed quickly down the ladder.

"By all means." I gestured extravagantly toward it.

"I just want to see if my place is okay."

But your neighbor who kept a set of keys wasn't home.

There was a trail that wound up through dense woods to a shack probably two thousand feet above sea level that commanded a panoramic view of the surrounding Green Mountains. From various points along the ascent we could look down into the golden pastures of a high-maintenance horse farm, and the dark burnished forms of grazing Thoroughbreds. The sound of a tractor mowing a field came to us, lazy and distant like the overhead buzz of a propeller plane. Casey kept bounding ahead of us, returning with enormous sticks in his mouth. He'd drop a stick and then streak into the woods, rooting for chipmunks and rabbits. You were hiking ahead of me, and my eyes were level with the backs of your legs.

We climbed until the trail finally reached a level area covered with pine needles, which then led straight to the redwood shack. I could smell the damp mulch of the deep forest.

You stopped and turned around, beads of sweat gathered above your upper lip. "Boy, I'm winded."

"Want to stop?"

You shrugged. "No, we can keep going."

"Okay," I said. "But before we keep going . . ."

"What?"

"I'd like to know what José—I'm assuming it was José who called—was talking about?"

"So would I, Will, believe me."

"You really have no idea?"

"If I did, don't you think I would've said something?"

"I'm . . . assuming. So?"

You rolled your eyes. "Come on, Will, don't tell me you're going to listen to a jerk, now are you?"

I said nothing.

"Okay, wait a minute. You tell me: what awful thing *could* I have done to Bobby?" You held up your thumb. "I didn't give him AIDS." Then your index finger. "I didn't mind-fuck him. I was honest with him, I broke it off in the best way I possibly could. What else could it be?"

I hesitated a moment and then I admitted I'd tried to get José to tell me last week when he called your place. We started walking again, this time side by side on the soft floor of pine needles that led to the mountain shack.

"I wonder if Bobby could have mentioned our sex life," you mused aloud after a moment or so of reflection.

"Well, what about it?" I asked nervously.

"He wanted it to be unsafe with me. He wanted to do all the things everybody used to do back in the seventies but can't do anymore. He said he trusted me . . . and that was so incredibly foolish."

"Well, did you . . . do any of the things?"

"Even if I did, I've explained to you that I've already been tested again."

"Why can't you just tell me?"

"I guess the more you get involved with somebody, the more restrictive those restrictions feel."

"You're not answering my question."

"No, I am, but you're being deliberately thick." A brooding silence came on, and as I was imagining what you might have done with Bobby Garzino, you murmured, "The price of real intimacy has never been so high."

"But why do you think it was that he didn't move you?" And I couldn't help wondering if I, too, had failed or would fail to reach you.

You shook your head. "You know why, Will."

Randall Monroe.

The name itself was forbidding, with its elite sound, the name of some powerful soul, a skilled seducer who could shatter even the most durable heart.

Detecting my inner torment, you frowned. "Now what?"

"Just remembering what you were telling me last night. Remembering what you told me right before you fell asleep."

You looked distressed. "Wait a second. I'm a little fuzzy. Because I really did nod off. What did I say?"

I got a twinge of guilt over all that I'd read in your diary. "You were talking about your sex life with Randall."

"No, I wasn't. I wouldn't."

"Well, you weren't exactly, but I'm sure it must've been amazing."

"Let's put it this way, if it wasn't good wouldn't I be even more the fool to let myself get so fucked up over somebody?"

"There doesn't always have to be fireworks for there to be passion."

"I don't know if I agree with that."

The shack stood before us, facing an amazing panorama of a mountain range, soft layers graduating into the horizon: bluish green peaks, dense with foliage and evergreens without a single bare spot—so unlike the California Los Padres with their sharper summits and sand-colored crotches. The cabin door was kept shut by a weight on a pulley, and we had to duck to pass over the threshold. Inside were a crude wooden table and chairs, a glass oil lamp and a guest book with names and dates and remarks from visitors going back to 1983. With a quick glance we could see that the last hikers had arrived three days before us. We signed our names, went back outside and sat on the wooden porch next to a thorny blackberry patch.

"This great love," I murmured despite myself. "This Randall Monroe."

"I never said he was my 'great love.' "

"The man who keeps you from loving anybody else? The man who robbed you from yourself?"

"Sounds like you're mocking me."

"I'm not. I'm jealous."

"Don't be. It was intense because it was unrealistic with his being closeted. With all the threats of him—or us—being found out, of him being discharged."

You thought of him as a night bird. He worked at the radio station between 12:00 midnight and 6 A.M. twice a week. And you would sneak away to him, ride your bicycle past all the officers' ranch homes, past the elementary school you attended for a year that was once a Japanese prisoner-of-war barracks, past all the traffic signs that advertised "think left" because, several years before, Okinawa had made the transition from driving on the right to driving on the left side of the road. You'd sit beside him in the DJ's booth and listen to him talk to the people who understood English all over the island. He'd speak to them in his Harry Belafonte voice. You'd hold his hand and listen to his voice soothing thou-

sands of insomniacs to sleep. Finally he would cue up a long set of jazz—Mingus, Duke Ellington, Tommy Dorsey—then lead you back to the couch in the green room. You'd always fuck like missionaries because he said he loved to watch your face while he was in you. He liked to talk to you, to tell you how it felt to be there, how tight you were, and how much he liked that tightness. Because that tightness let him imagine that he was the only man, that tightness was why it always hurt and why it finally became a race for the two of you to come before you had to ask him to stop.

"I don't think my life with Randall should matter to you," you said. You picked off a cluster of overripe blackberries, looked at them carefully and tossed them to one side.

"But I've always sensed how powerful the connection was."

"I always seem to get myself in trouble around these matters. Whereas you're such a diehard romantic."

"Romantic? But so are *you*, Sean, don't you see? With your whole notion how someone you love can take a piece of you, make you incomplete. And then searching for what you've lost in someone else. And knowing all along that you'll probably never find it. What do you think that is, if not romantic?"

"I thought you saw some truth in it."

"I do! 'Romantic' doesn't mean 'idiotic,' not to me."

With your dismal expression, you peered off toward the range of distant mountains that graduated into pastel smudges and finally blended into the horizon.

After a while I said, "I just want you to be open to the idea of having great sex with somebody else." With me, I could have added, but didn't have to.

"Will, I never complained about our sex life. Our sex life is fine."

"But how do you expect me to feel when you say sex 'will never be the same' again?"

"I'm not saying it's written in stone. I'm just saying that, so far, since Randall, since ten years. And yet I knew it would be great with him even before he laid a finger on me."

"That's because you'd decided it would be."

This made you suddenly angry. "My body decided, goddammit! It was my body. Natural magnetism. I could *smell* the guy, all right? The smell of him made my fucking toes curl up with desire. I've never smelled a body like that since then, black or white or Asian. And I've had them all. I've tasted a lot of other people."

"But love has to be there to sustain the attraction."

"Yes, but at some point the attraction always dies."

I knew this much better than you knew that I knew. And yet I felt something withering inside myself, some climbing hope dying like a parched vine.

"Come on, Will," you said with displeasure, "wasn't it great with *him?* You said it was amazing with Chad."

"But I've had great since."

"Well, then that's where we're different."

"No, here's how we're different, Sean—"

But you threw up your hands. "I can't take discussing this anymore! Will, if we keep on like this we're going to kill everything good there is between us."

I glared at you, offended.

"All right, go on, then. Just tell me. I know what you're going to say, anyway. You're going to say what other people have said, that I've used my thing with Randall as a barrier, or a smoke screen, something—you'll be sure to give it a metaphor. Because if I can't have great sex, then it follows I can't have great love. Therefore there's no chance that I'll get burned again like I was burned before."

Of course, this had been exactly what I was about to say.

You smiled eerily. "Yet there's this guy I see sometimes. Comes in and out of my life. I don't even know where he lives. He just calls me up sometimes at 3:00 A.M. and asks me what I'm doing.

He comes over, we get it on like a couple of hungry pigs. And I must say, it's pretty damn hot. It comes close. Physically. But as a person he leaves me cold."

I hated hearing about this. I felt queasy. "That's because it's like making love to a phantom," I forced myself to say.

You turned to me with a look of bewildered anger. "Yeah, that's exactly what it is. And it's just the way I like it. I told you once before that I was a better friend than a lover. And *you* thought I was being flip."

"No," I said. "I just hoped it wasn't true."

16

*HE COMES TO SEE YOU ONE LAST TIME BEFORE HE DISAPPEARS. COMES
at night during the typhoon because he knows your parents are
away. Even though the storm is about to be upgraded to Condition
3, your parents decide to travel by helicopter to some important
function on the mainland of Japan. Your mother holds an umbrella
against the diagonal drapery of rain and walks clumsily in her se-
quined ball gown and trips as she tries to hold the umbrella and
maneuver herself up into the cockpit. You're alone in your room,
drawing a plan for a gazebo at the officers' club, when you see him
in silhouette at the window. He's pressed up against the pane like
a mask, dripping water. And somehow you know, even though he's
never done it before, that he's going to barge into the house and
hurt you. It's weird when the one most beloved in the world turns
violent. When the lover's embrace becomes a stranglehold.*

    *He confronts you about cheating on him. Tells you he heard
about it a few days ago and then he socks you in the chest. You can't
breathe. It's as if you're a kid again, falling off a bicycle and get-*

ting the wind knocked out of you. You feel all cottony and numb because it's so outrageous. And yet somehow you've expected it, you've known the moment would come. And you can't fight back. You're crippled because you're in love with him. And it occurs to you that this is the end, the relationship will never be the same, even if he lets you live. That if anything continues there will be no difference between pleasure and pain, and he will crave violence with you like a drug addict craves a fix.

He beats on you until finally you wrench your arms around him to keep him from punching anymore. You scream that you won't fight back. You scream until finally he stops and you both lie there on the rug, both crying. Then he makes the move. You can't believe it, how you just let him do what he wants. And yet, the moment he begins to touch you in the old way, you know that you're losing him. He never utters the words that he's leaving, but you sense he will as he clutches you, finally spits on his hand, lubricates himself and forces in. And you watch his face as you've watched it in the past. Remembering other times. Remembering how his eyes would always lock hungrily with yours, measuring your pain for his own gratification. Remembering how when it was over, and he slipped out, your whole lower half would burn. But knowing this, knowing how it hurt, he would kiss your neck and your chest until you revived and could stand it again. That was how it was.

But now his thrusts are hollow and without love. Now he doesn't even consider that he might be rubbing you raw. And when he finally closes his eyes, it's the loneliest moment of your life.

17

I ARRIVED BACK AT MY BUILDING TO A SLEW OF MAIL, INCLUDING WHAT I thought were several Jiffy bags stuffed with review copies of books that were leaning against the wall of the vestibule. One of the parcels for some reason immediately caught my eye. Instead of having a typed label as most of these packages do, it had my name scribbled right on it. There was no return address. Alerted to something odd and offbeat, I tore open one end and reached inside, feeling something soft and scratchy and jerked my hand out. What could this be?

Tilting the package up to the light, I peered in and saw what I first thought were wood flakes, but then noticed that the pieces were too large and looked more like torn newsprint. A gift, perhaps, that needed a lot of buffering? I again reached in to grope around the roughage, but still came up with nothing. Bewildered now, not even thinking about what I was doing, I punched the bag and a clump of its ripped contents dumped out. Slips of ragged-edged paper caught the air and fluttered delicately down to the floor of the vestibule. Something about that cascading cloud of print now reminds me of a magical moment up in Vermont when I'd once been lucky enough to witness the exfoliation of a larch tree.

Then I realized exactly what I was looking at. Fragments of color and cardboard gave it away. My second novel. It was a copy of my second novel, its cloth cover obviously shorn off and the entire 307 pages shredded.

Gripping the package with both hands, I stood there for a moment, reeling. Who had done it? Not hundreds but thousands of torn pages now seemed to be dusting the floor of the vestibule like snow. I slowly bent down and dutifully swept the floor with my hands until I managed to retrieve every last bit of lacerated print and refilled the Jiffy bag. I clutched the pulverized book to my chest as I walked up the single flight to my second-floor apartment, noticing how the book actually seemed to weigh less now that it was in complete tatters.

Just as I was passing through the apartment door, the phone began ringing. Startled, I dropped the package down on my desk and lifted the receiver.

"You're back."

Brimming with suspicion, I asked, "Who's this?"

"It's Greg, who do think it is?"

I hadn't recognized his voice at all.

"You sound strange," he said. "Are you okay? Is somebody there?"

"No to both questions."

"Well then, what's wrong?"

I explained.

"That's really *sick!*" Greg intoned. "Only a . . . Jesus Christ, only a certified fucking lunatic would think of doing something like that."

I pressed my palm against the Jiffy bag, making a dent in the bulging material.

"You there, Will?"

"Yeah, I'm here," I said barely audibly.

"Are you freaking out?"

"What do you think? I mean . . . I just literally got home and found it!"

"Could it be the guy you mentioned, the one who's angry at Sean Paris?"

"Perhaps that's preferable to thinking it was somebody who hated my book."

We both laughed. But then Greg's saying "At least you haven't lost your sense of humor" annoyed me.

I couldn't help saying, "Your name is in there somewhere, you know. Your dedication. Although by now it's an anagram."

"You didn't say it was *my* book!"

"As if that makes a difference . . . So what's up with you, Greg?" I really wanted to get off the phone.

"I got home and found Casey but no note. I'm just calling to see how your trip was."

"It was pretty good. Anything else?"

"I need to talk to you about a few things. But they can wait. I'll catch you some other time."

"Like what, like what did you need to talk to me about?"

"Obviously this is not the moment."

I was too preoccupied to press Greg the way I normally would have. Casey had spent most of the day cooped up in my car, and I was planning on taking him for a long walk later on in the evening.

"What time will you be coming by?" Greg asked.

"I don't know. Nine or ten. After dinner, certainly. But what difference does it make if you're not even going to be there?" Greg would be at work.

There was a lull. Finally he said, "Yeah, but depending on how late you get there, somebody else might be."

My first reaction was jealousy. And then fear that Greg's new relationship would outlast mine and once that happened I'd feel doubly alone. Why should somebody else—not me—be able to make it work with him?

"Was that what you were waiting to tell me?"

"Kind of."

"Don't be coy, okay? So, is this guy actually living at your apartment or what?"

"No! He just meets me there after work."

Greg had given him a set of keys. That was a big step. I felt oddly betrayed. "Why? *Why* did you do that? Why can't you meet him at *his* place?"

"It's . . . complicated."

I knew what that meant. "You've gotten yourself involved in a triangle?"

"Something like that."

"Look, I don't want some strange man lounging around with my dog."

Greg sounded gratified. "Why? I don't mind that Sean's been taking care of Casey. He even drove up to Vermont with him."

"At your insistence."

"Well, I'm not the one who has a problem with other men."

"Look, what if this guy's lover gets jealous and suspects something and follows him to your place? Then Casey would be vulnerable."

"Spare me the gothics, would you?" There was an irritating silence and then Greg sighed. "Anyway, you'd probably know if his lover, or I should say ex-lover, is capable of something like that."

"I thought so," I said in a huff. "You're being so weird about this—I figured I had to know the people involved. So who are they?"

When Greg hesitated I began churning. "Not one of my exes?" I said.

"There're so many exes that the odds are actually in favor of it."

"Greg!"

"No, he's not one of your exes."

"Then who?"

After a moment, he said, "Sebastian Seporia."

"Very funny, Greg."

"It's no joke."

I was livid. "What? Come on! Get real—Sebastian Seporia. What's with you? You know he's still involved . . . with Peter!"

"Not anymore."

"Oh, Christ, they break up every six minutes. But those two are bonded in blood."

"Well, the bond certainly didn't hold *you* back."

I reminded Greg that when I met him Peter minimized his other relationship. "I never even knew the extent of it until after I'd slept with him a dozen times."

"A dozen times in *two days.*"

"Greg, I can't believe this! After all I've told you about Peter and Sebastian, how could you let yourself get involved with them?"

"Like *you* didn't. Like *you* wouldn't in my position!"

"If I'd known, I wouldn't have. I'd try to steer clear of creating complications."

"Why is it 'creating complications'? You're not seeing Peter anymore."

"What's this about anyway, Greg?" I was furious. "Is it about me? Are you trying to get back at me for some reason?"

"Don't flatter yourself. Sometimes it's nice to get one's rocks off."

"You get plenty of other opportunities to do that. You don't have to choose such an incestuous situation. Don't you understand that Sebastian knows that as soon as Peter finds out he's going to—"

"Who says Peter is going to find out?"

"I got news for you, Greg. You might be quite familiar with the way that Maltese boy uses his cock, but believe me, you don't know jack shit what he's capable of. How did this mess start, anyway?"

"We met at the dog run."

"*He* has a dog?"

"No, he started petting Casey."

Of course. It now made perfect sense. Sebastian could figure out who Greg was because he knew who Casey was—he'd seen me there with the dog. Just then I glanced at my answering machine. "Greg, I've got fifteen messages. What do you want to bet that half of them are from Peter Rocca?"

"I'll take your word for it."

The Jiffy bag full of my shredded novel lay on my desk. This, I reminded myself, was what had happened to me as a direct result of having taken on another life, another lover, someone other than Greg. I wasn't with Greg anymore, so it shouldn't matter so much what he did. So said my voice of reason.

"Greg," I resumed, "does it at all matter to you that Sebastian has it in for me?"

"He's never said anything bad about you to me."

"Yet."

"Look, if I'm having a great time, why should I worry about what's motivating him?"

"Even if it's to make a fool out of me?"

"I honestly don't see how it's doing that. Try not to be so egocentric. Not everything is about *you*, is it? And you're not my boyfriend. Anymore."

With the briefest goodbye, I slammed the phone down.

Needless to say, I hadn't been to Peter's apartment since the night I met you. With barely a hello, he answered his door. He was looking for a key, he explained, and rushed back into the apartment, treading every which way as he continued scouring desk and cabinet drawers and in between chintz-covered sofa cushions. Peter had acquired a lavish stockpile of household goods. His domestic opulence included complete sets of Wedgwood dinner plates, fluted champagne glasses and silverware of a tastefully scrolled Italianate pattern. There were many polished furniture surfaces. If I hadn't known he was a gay man I would have assumed his wedding registry had already been substantially cashed in. Here was the downtown alter ego of an Upper East Side young corporate couple, dressed not in an Armani suit, but in typical skintight fashion, sporting each and every body bulge. Today he had on one of his favorite police department T-shirts, the kind that he routinely collected from precincts all over the United States. This particular one was a gray number from Reno, Nevada. Even though his closets were packed with wool-and-linen trousers and shirts made of the finest jersey, when he wasn't working he'd repeatedly wear cutoffs and the same two or three police T-shirts until they shredded apart in the kitchen's washer-dryer that seemed to be in constant use every time I visited.

I couldn't help saying, "Is Bloomingdale's going bankrupt?"

He turned to me, frowning.

"Where did you get all these . . . things? Get a load of the dinner plates," I said, picking up one that had a gold rim of at least a half inch. "Who gave them to you?"

"I bought them, okay?"

Peter made a couple hundred thousand a year as a phobia psychiatrist and no doubt felt compelled to drop the weight of a few grand here and there on trifles like dishes he'd never use. The guy could barely fry an egg.

I said pleasantly, "All you need is a dining room table."

"Shaddup." Peter laughed. "You can see that I'm in a mood tonight."

"I'm not in such a good mood either. Although it's no wonder you're in a bad mood. I've never seen the place so messy. Must really swell up your anal glands."

"I told you I'm looking for a key. Now don't be a smartass."

It was, to be exact, a spare house key that Sebastian claimed to possess but which Peter suspected was a lie. Peter had given it to him a couple of weeks ago when Sebastian came over to borrow his bicycle. "But then I got it back."

"Even if you *did* get it back, knowing Sebastian, he probably made a copy of it."

This made Peter stop his search and turn to look at me, disconcerted.

"But he still can't get by the doorman," I pointed out.

Peter scoffed. "Like hell . . . he's already done it."

"Well then, you've got to tell them not to let him in unless you authorize it. Put it in writing, for Christ's sake!"

Peter waved me away. "Come on. The doormen have all been on notice for some time now. He simply forges a note from me, or arrives with a piece of equipment like a Cuisinart that he says he has to return."

"Then they're stupider than *he* is." If that's possible, I thought to myself.

"Look, this is not just Sebastian's stupidity," Peter said, making reference to our phone conversation concerning Greg and Sebastian's affair.

I suggested that Peter simply change the locks.

"That's a hundred fifty bucks I'll be out."

"You can afford it." I gestured at the surroundings.

"That's not the point."

"Hock a few dinner plates?"

"If you make one more reference to my fucking dinner plates—"

"What, you'll slug me?"

"No . . . I'll force-feed you my cock."

"You think I'd let you do that, huh?"

Peter's eyes were boring into me. "Will, I can't believe you're fucking with me like this!" he roared.

"Take it easy, okay?"

"Take it easy? I can't believe this whole incestuous situation."

"Pretty tacky, isn't it? Although Greg claims he didn't put two and two together until after they started screwing."

Peter finally sat down on his sofa and crossed his legs. "I must say, you don't sound too upset about this."

"I'm plenty upset." Actually I was glad to let Peter be upset enough for us both. "But, they'll soon get tired of each other."

"Meanwhile you've got somebody to occupy yourself with."

"And you've got a million guys who'd love to date you if company is what you're after."

"I'd like to wring that fucker's neck!"

"Whose neck?" I asked defensively, instinctively protective of Greg.

"Sebastian's."

"Look, the more upset you get, the more you give Sebastian the satisfaction he's obviously after."

Peter had already exasperated me by ignoring the news of my shredded book. But now, at least, he was willing to address the issue of the affair philosophically.

Sebastian had done this kind of thing before, Peter explained. Whenever they had broken up and Peter was dating somebody in the interim, Sebastian always found out about it and then went after the person, in Peter's words, "like a fucking piranha." In this case, knowing I was occupied, Sebastian had set his sights on the next best prey, Greg.

"Well, all I can say is the guy's a schmuck. And you're a schmuck to stay with him. End of story."

"Thanks for being so compassionate."

"Look, I've got my own problems." And then I quickly described again what it had felt like to receive a shredded totem of oneself in the mail. Peter finally seemed to register what had happened. His dumbfounded look let something disturbing dawn on me. "Do you think Sebastian could have done something like that? Would he shred my book and send it to me in the mail?"

Peter scrunched his features and shook his head. "Doubtful . . . seriously, he's too unsophisticated to think of something as, pardon me, interesting as that."

Then it must be the person I first suspected, José Ayala, Bobby Garzino's ex-lover.

Looking anxious, Peter sprang off the sofa, crossed the room and, anchoring his red, freckled hands on the windowframe, stared out at the looming Empire State Building, whose lights were distantly winking in the haze of summer night heat. "Look, Will," he said softly, still facing the great spike of an edifice, "I don't want to stay with Sebastian. I know he's not right for me. He's vindictive. He's possessive. He insults my friends."

"And don't forget that he's a gold digger," I added, glancing at all the exquisite, unused dishes and glassware.

Peter continued as though he hadn't heard me, "I can't bring him anywhere without being embarrassed by his lack of culture, or by his general ignorance of politics, or manners, or anything else. And yet . . . I love him." He suddenly pivoted around, tears making his eyes sparkle. "Frankly, I just can't tear myself away from him. The only way out would be by meeting somebody else."

"You of all people should realize that approach is too messy. The only way out is quit."

"I just can't stand being alone."

"There're worse things."

"Like what?"

"Believe it or not, like having a lover like Sebastian who's a constant pain in the ass. Try a life without him. You'll see." (I was aware of having given myself this same good advice many times.)

Peter went quiet for a while. He came to sit down opposite me on the sofa again, crossing his legs at the ankle, seesawing his knee nervously up and down. "Don't you think I know that?" he murmured. He made a move to get up again, but then, seeming to realize he was acting jumpy, collapsed against the sofa. There was something endearing about the way he reined himself in.

"You know," he finally resumed, "I never regarded your and my relationship as . . . well, extracurricular to my relationship with Sebastian. I mean, in all my fucked-up ambivalence, I was actually hoping it would go somewhere." He now ventured to glance at me sideways.

"Weren't you just hoping that I'd pull you away from him?"

"Maybe. But look, I admire your mind. I can communicate with you. We have great sex. We're intellectually matched. Even so, I'm emotionally chained to Sebastian. And now, because you're with Sean Paris, I've lost the inside track."

I told him I was certain that he would have kept going back to Sebastian. I had never expected anything different.

Peter sighed. "I wish he would leave town. He keeps threatening to move to Florida." Suddenly the phone rang. "Now he'll keep rubbing it in my face, just watch. He knows just how to get to me. That fuck!"

"How do you know it's him?"

Peter sighed again. "Because I know his ring." Then he got up quickly to answer the phone.

18

THE MARKINGS AROUND YOUR DOOR'S KEYHOLE—DEEP SCRATCHES carved into the painted wood—resembled whiskers drawn on a faceless cat, a half-assed attempt at furious art. But it was actually vandalism. A very sad, desperate kind of person did this, I thought, as I studied the scratches. You sat at your dining table, staring at me vacantly, awaiting my reaction. Your green duffel bag was dumped in the middle of the floor, and the clothes you'd brought back from Vermont the day before had yet to be put away and were lying there like entrails dangling from the felled beast of our vacation. With one finger you worried the withered stalks in the vase of flowers that were once freshly cut and thriving around your breakfast table that first morning we'd made love a few weeks ago.

"Why did José bother?" I said. After all, you'd talked to him right before our leaving. You'd told him that you were removing all the "loomed things" from the apartment.

Explaining what had happened to my book in a bit more de-

tail than I had on the phone the day before, I couldn't help but re-
late that act to the gouges on your door.

"Do they have to be related incidents?" You sounded irritated.

"Come on, Sean."

I asked for José's phone number, half expecting you not to
have it.

"Why do you want it?"

I was surprised you'd resist. "To find out if he was the one who
shredded my book."

"Come on, you think he's going to admit it to you?"

"At least I can hear him deny it. I'm pretty good at sniffing
out lies."

"Oh, really? Even in somebody you don't know?"

"In my view, he's the only likely candidate."

Your hands slammed down on the table. "His beef is with me,
Will, not with you. So just leave it *alone*. Okay?"

Frankly, I was puzzled and not just by your anger and by the
fact that you had routinely accepted the damage to your door, but
that you seemed to defend José.

"You feel guilty?" I said. "Or somehow to blame?"

No response. Stretching back in the chair until its front legs
left the floor, you nodded toward the door and said dreamily, "I've
decided not to paint over the scratches. I'm going to leave them
just like that."

"Why?"

"To remind myself what normally sane people can be driven to."

"As if you'd forget."

You raised your arms over your head, until your shirt hiked
up a few inches to reveal the thin dark border of hair between your
navel and your crotch.

When it was time for me to go and walk Casey, we decided to

take a walk through the East Village and then loop west again back to Greg's apartment on Carmine Street. While we'd been up in Vermont, there had been a terrible hurricane down in Louisiana, and the remnants of the storm, which had mostly broken up in the Gulf of Mexico, were just beginning to advance over Manhattan. A humid wind gusted down Grove Street, scattering refuse and imparting to the city air a lingering thrill of its former power. A phalanx of tropical-looking clouds streaked across the sky at such a fast pace that the buildings seemed to be tilting and tumbling toward them.

The moment we ventured outside the squeaky iron gate of the apartment building, you made a point of taking my hand. We began strolling along Grove Street. I'd never held hands with a guy for any length of time in public. Greg and I had done it on a few occasions for a block or two. But this particular attitude lasted longer, and every time I tried gingerly to extricate my fingers from yours, you gripped harder and leered at me. I felt as though I were being tested.

It was difficult to tell whether or not I imagined it, but I thought I saw male/female couples gaping at us explicitly, then glancing away. Were they disapproving or were they trying to adjust to what was quickly becoming a more commonplace occurrence? Two men walking hand in hand was now, in the 1990s, just a minor disturbance in the fiercely urban environment. A gang of teenagers floated along the streets with up-and-down tough-boy strides, swinging a metallic boom box that trumpeted the latest in hip-hop music. "Faggots," one of them sneered. The moment the remark ripped past my ears, you turned to me with a mellow smile that eased the discomfort of being heckled.

"They do it in Europe," you said finally. "Guys walk hand in hand. There it's completely innocent."

"But it's all about camaraderie. Not sexual politics."

And I'll never forget how, suddenly, you stopped and looked at me in sudden bewilderment. "Well, I think it's—" You hesitated.

"What—what are you trying to say?"

"That finally it's beginning to happen, Will," you said barely audibly. "Our relationship."

"I'm already there," I murmured.

But we stumbled into silence after that and strolled along without touching. What had been as yet unspeakable between us when spoken curdled any sense of ease. Did we dread intimacy as much as or even more than death? Had the threat of dying been forged into our shield of self-protection? We walked along Tenth Street until we passed from the genteel respectability of the West Village and Fifth Avenue to the anything-goes funk of the East Village, where pierced body parts, sepulchral makeup, elaborately nihilistic hairstyles were far more cutting-edge than just a couple of guys holding hands.

There had been trouble in Tompkins Square Park, where the homeless were trying to create their own tribal enclave. The police had been forced to intervene and close down what was quickly becoming an unruly colony of the disenfranchised. And almost as though you wanted to test me a final time, you took my hand again as we strolled along the perimeter of the park, where literally hundreds of uniformed cops were standing guard. I felt a few faces panning to follow us, heard what I probably falsely imagined to be disapproving tongue clicks, but then something inside me lifted and I nearly felt free. This was not a test of the cops, or of society. This was a test of *us*, of you and me. And after we crossed the street and continued downtown along Avenue A, after you let go of my hand, you put your arm around my neck for a while.

When we began to head west toward Greg's apartment, I asked if you wanted to go there and then walk with Casey and me. But you shook your head, kissed me on the lips and whispered good-night. Until you vanished I watched you gliding off down Carmine Street.

The moment I walked into Greg's apartment, Casey began jumping up and down and licking me. No doubt he figured I was taking him back up to Vermont. I smelled something different from the normal smell of Greg's macrobiotic cooking of cumin and brown basmati rice. I smelled something sweet and waxy like hair pomade. Sure enough, when I snooped in Greg's medicine cabinet I found a small purple plastic jar of hair dressing cream that I'd never seen before—Sebastian's stash for easy pompadour maintenance, I grimly imagined—as well as a huge pump canister of state-of-the-art lubricant spiked with nonoxynol-9, the ingredient that allegedly would kill the AIDS virus upon contact. The colossal size of the jar to me spelled *Hot Sex with Somebody Else*. "Come on, Casey," I said irritably. "Let's go."

Walking along the West Side piers with Casey loping beside me, I was peering out at the hypnotic twinkle of lights across the river in New Jersey. I was distracted by the glint of a diamond stud. A ruthless pair of eyes, a face welted in scars. Then another face, but this one fat, unnaturally swollen. They charged at me from opposite directions, and as they locked me in with their shoulders, I could hear something crunching on contact. Pains shot up and down my arms. "Let go, asshole," one of them said. "He's your man! He's your man." As Casey viciously tried to lunge at them, I wrongly yet instinctively reined in on his leash. His bark turned into a yelp.

And then I was sitting on the ground, more dazed than hurt, my head throbbing from hitting the pavement, my arms scraped. It took me a moment to realize that Casey wasn't there licking my face as he did whenever I'd fall. The sense of his absence instantly became overwhelming. On one side of me, the molten Hudson River, and on the other side, slow-moving traffic, threads of music piping out tinnily from cars, streams of guys homing between the bars and the water, leaving behind tendrils of obnoxious perfume.

Panic came on me like fever.

"Casey!" I screamed out. "Casey!" People peered at me, alarmed.

"My dog!" Shouting and creating a stir was the only way. "My dog! My dog!" It was possible that Casey, with the sweetest, most trusting face in the world, at that very moment was being dragged along, even tortured by someone, soon to be sold to some illegal lab, held captive, starved, kept in a state of painful neglect for the rest of his short life.

"Casey! Casey! My dog's been stolen!"

In the midst of my shouting, a gruff-looking guy wearing a blue bandanna on his head ran up to me and said he had seen a gang of kids with a dog.

"A black dog?"

Nodding, the man explained that the dog had been trying to get away from them.

This I could not bear. Could not bear the idea of a gang of kids subjecting a dog that only knew the love that Greg and I gave him to the shock of cruelty. I ran in the direction the man indicated, screaming "Casey! Casey! Casey!" before succumbing to the inevitable: calling Greg at work.

He sounded frosty when he first got on the phone, no doubt a holdover from our argument earlier in the afternoon. But when I told him that I'd been mugged and Casey had been taken, Greg's wail of tormented disbelief reminded me that once before he'd been ripped away from a dog. And for an instant I forgave him everything that had happened over Sebastian. "I just don't understand!" he cried. "How could they have gotten him away from you?"

"Greg, aren't you listening? They knocked me down. I must've . . . blacked out. Because they ran away with him."

Once Greg learned where I was, he asked me to call the police while he cabbed it over. It took everything I had to slow down and coherently explain to the police what had happened; then luckily I managed to find you at home.

"Marine mode," is what you called it later. How you ever came up with your plan I'll never quite understand. After taking down the number of the pay phone, you then asked if the other keys on the set I'd given you to the Vermont house were the keys to my apartment, and if the list of the dog owners from the Washington Square dog run was something that could be easily found in my desk. At 11:00 P.M. on a weeknight, surely most of the other dog owners would be home.

Greg arrived shortly before the police, and in the midst of their taking a report the pay phone rang. You'd managed to contact fifteen people on the dog run list before speaking to someone who, as he was walking his own dog, thought he might have recognized a dog like Casey at Fifteenth Street and Third Avenue in the hands of such a group of teenagers. But he hadn't been close enough to make a positive identification and just figured that this particular dog bore an uncanny resemblance to our Casey. The police made a call over to the appropriate precinct, and Greg promptly took off on foot while I was forced to finish giving my report.

"He's pretty good under pressure, isn't he?" Greg said the following afternoon. We were sitting on the futon sofa in his apartment, Casey snoozing between us, his head comfortably lodged on Greg's lap. Greg was referring to your idea to call the other dog run owners, most of whom knew Casey better than they knew Greg or me.

"We were too frantic to think straight," I reassured him.

Greg shrugged and then winced from the black track of

stitches embedded in the left hemisphere of his forehead, the result of a gash he'd sustained when he'd gone ballistic and aggressively dove at the group of kids, screeching at the top of his lungs that they'd stolen Casey. It was a smart move on his part because by attracting so much attention he forced them to release the dog and scatter in all different directions.

"The doctor said there's a good chance I'll scar. But I don't care. It's worth it . . . not to have lost him." His voice cracked as he patted Casey, who let out a pleased grunt and seemed relatively unaffected by what had happened. "I want to call Sean and thank him. Maybe I could take the two of you out to dinner sometime."

"That's not necessary."

"Would it be awkward for *you?*" Greg asked me.

"Not if you felt okay about it."

I found myself once again looking at Greg's T-cell poster, but this time I wasn't so unnerved by it. Noticing me eyeing the poster, Greg said, "You know, I still want you to be the one who makes decisions if anything happens to me—if decisions have to be made."

"Okay," I said somewhat uncomfortably.

Should we put it all in writing? There's somebody at my firm who will do it pro bono. It's probably even more important that we do something like that now that we're no longer each other's significant other."

"I don't want to be resuscitated," I found myself telling him. It struck me how healthy we looked, and felt, two young men on a couch talking, and Greg was only twenty-seven.

"I don't want my parents to come into the city, claim my body and bury me in some dreary place, either." Greg wanted to be cremated.

I began squirming. "Okay, but no more morbid stuff right now."

"What better time is there to get things straight? Especially after what's happened?"

"I don't know."

"And I want my ashes spread near—"

"Come on, Greg, please!"

"Listen to me," he insisted. "I want my ashes spread. . . . in that pine glade where we used to go cross-country skiing. And maybe even some around the red schoolhouse." He paused for a moment and then added, "Although the red schoolhouse has now become *your* new love den."

I told him that shouldn't affect his decision.

Greg sighed, pausing before he said, "It doesn't. Obviously it doesn't, but it's just that it used to be *our* place. Our little romantic place."

"Probably a lot of other people's, too."

"But I never knew any of them." Greg's eyes filled and his chin quivered.

"Come on, don't!"

"You know, Will," he went on, "they only had Casey for a half hour, but during that half hour a million awful things went through my mind. I was really afraid we were going to lose him and just . . . never know what happened."

"I was afraid of that, too."

"I couldn't have handled that."

"I couldn't have either."

19

Throughout September you spent much of your free time in the brownstone garden you'd designed on Charles Street. Most afternoons you'd get home from work, change into a pair of loose faded jeans and a plain white T-shirt, walk the few blocks between your place and the garden, then weed and dig into the twilight. You enriched the soil with emulsifiers and planted bulbs for the spring. Usually two or three times during the week I'd meet you at Charles Street near the time when you expected to finish. More often than not you'd have lost track of the hour and I would either peruse the *Times* or plow through a few chapters of a book I was reviewing until you finally put away all your gardening tools. Then we'd decide between having dinner at a certain healthy Thai restaurant or picking up ingredients for a quick meal back at your apartment, where on a few evenings, it even got chilly enough for us to build a fire in the fireplace.

Toward the end of October I received a phone call from a man who claimed to be José Ayala. When he explained that he needed to speak to me about Sean Paris, I told him there was nothing to discuss and that I hardly thought he had my—or your—best interests in mind. I shouldn't necessarily assume that, he said. At this point I couldn't help but ask where he was from.

"Originally from the Philippines."

I mentioned that the last time we'd spoken up in Vermont I didn't remember his having an accent. There was a reflective pause. And then he said quite definitely, "I never called you in Vermont. I didn't have your number there."

"It was on my answering machine here in New York."

"Ah, but your New York City phone number is unlisted. That's why I haven't called you. Until tonight. Believe me, it's taken this long to find somebody who had it or who could get it."

I let this settle for a few moments. I had still somehow forgotten to ask Directory Assistance to add my name and number to their roster.

Then who had called me in Vermont?

"So how did you end up getting it?" I asked suspiciously.

"Sebastian Seporia," he said without missing a beat.

That son of a bitch Greg! Why would he give Sebastian my number? But instead of venting this, I decided now was the time to ask point-blank about my novel.

José said, "Shred your book and send it to you in the mail?" He laughed.

"Don't sound so patronizing. I'm not forgetting what happened to Sean's door."

"Oh . . . of course. I should've realized." José hesitated for a moment, then said, with seriousness, "I did not shred your book. I now regret what I did to his door. But I did it out of frustration. Because Sean Paris is still in possession of the things that I should have."

"But Bobby gave all that stuff to Sean."

As though he didn't hear me, José continued, "We do reckless things when we're in love." There was a pause. "I always loved Bobby. I guess I can't help despising a person who made him miserable. But it was also his will to get those things back. And that's what I can't get through to Sean. Or to you either, for that matter."

"Wait a minute, you're saying it was in a will?"

Not exactly, José explained, but rather one of Bobby's last requests before he ended his life. He'd written two letters—one to José and one to you. According to José's letter, Bobby's letter to you instructed you to give José all the woven things.

"Sean did mention getting letters from Bobby, but not that particular one. Perhaps he never received it?"

You'd received it, José explained, because it was left for you at Bobby's apartment. At the funeral Bobby's roommate had reported you got it the night you heard the news.

"So he must've read it. He's just not telling you the truth."

Then I remembered the bizarre phone call the first night I ever met you, you asking 'What did *that* say?' and the way you had rushed off into the sweltering late night with the least amount of explanation. Had you been lying to me all this time?

When José spoke again, his voice quavered. "Bobby felt so unloved."

"If Bobby felt so unloved, then why did he purposely give away so many beautiful things?"

"I think you can answer that question better than I can, Will." José paused for a moment and then resumed. "Each gift had a way of saying, I am this beautiful thing. Love me and love the person who gave me to you. Just like some people read books and then fall in love with who wrote them."

José frankly didn't seem a likely candidate for a book shredder. But if not him, who, I puzzled dismally. And why had you never mentioned your last letter from Bobby Garzino?

Almost as though reading my doubts, José said, "If I were you

I'd ask Sean about that letter. And if he denies having it, then you'll know he's lying."

But I was afraid of following the lead of someone at such cross-purposes with you, and more afraid of your lying.

"You should know what a person like Sean Paris is capable of," José went on.

"Why don't you stop being so mysterious and just tell me what you think he's capable of."

"And you don't think it's enough—to drive another man to kill himself?"

"That's a little convenient, blaming Bobby's death on him."

"Convenient?"

"Yeah, I mean . . ." I wanted to be delicate. "In light of the fact that Bobby preferred suicide to dying slowly, dying by degrees."

"I don't think I know what you're talking about."

"I'm talking about the fact that he tested HIV-positive."

A lewd chuckle erupted from José's end of the line. "Oh, *really*," he said exaggeratedly. "Well, that's news to me." And then his voice turned malignant. "Then he must've tested HIV-positive post mortem. Because while he was alive he was HIV-negative."

I went quiet. Just sat there with the phone to my ear and tried to keep breathing. Distracted by a vision, very much like one of those daydreams that appear when I'm driving long distances, a flash of unfamiliar sequences, a burst of conversation that suddenly provides a missing link, a pair of gleaming yet corrupted train tracks laid down in the middle of some northern wilderness.

My mind was reeling. "Wait a minute, you're sure that Bobby was HIV-negative?"

"Yes."

"I thought that a positive-HIV status was why he killed himself?"

There was a steely moment of silence.

"If that's what Sean Paris told you, then you've been had."

No, like me, you assumed it was because of the HIV test results. Because you and Bobby were supposed to get together. Because Bobby was supposed to call you back after the test. And he never did.

"Sean knows exactly why Bobby did it. You just ask him. He's been lying to you."

2 0

I HURTLED ACROSS THE VILLAGE, ACROSS THE VERY STREETS WE HAD walked along that first night when the summer was peaking, when you seemed to know all about *him* and who he was to me before I'd ever told you anything. I was sweating by the time I reached Sixth Avenue and noticed the bell tower of the Jefferson Market Library and, particularly, the clock face half hidden by scaffolding. With the Halloween parade just a few days away, preparations were under way to build a track for the black spider that would ascend and descend the clock face.

But then as I waited for the light to change, I wondered why I was hurrying. We'd have this discussion later, if not now, and I would find out whether or not you'd lied to me. Did I really need to know so fast? And so, when the light finally changed, I continued standing on the corner.

It certainly was a warm night, the last lick of Indian summer, nearly as warm as that day back in August when on a whim you made the ferry crossing back to Long Island. What had made you leave the island? What had you been homing to when you waited at the dock with only a handful of people? After all, the Morning Party had still been in full swing. Why weren't you back there dancing in the froth of summer hedonism? Dancing with that black man? And surely among those thousands there was another compelling man who'd willingly enter your life as swiftly, as completely as I did. But instead you climbed on a boat that crossed the Great South Bay, met Peter Rocca, took a train back with him into Manhattan and strolled into my life.

On your ruined apartment door a note had been written to me in your characteristic imprisoned-aristocrat scrawl. Change of plans. You weren't going to the gym. I should meet you over at the garden on Charles Street.

I headed down Bleecker Street, past our favorite Thai restaurant, which, as a result of the warmer weather, had perspicaciously put out white slatted chairs and flimsy round tables on the sidewalk. The place was mobbed with customers eager to hold on to the idea of summer, particularly buffed-out men in tight T-shirts, with fading tans that would soon need to be augmented by trips to the sun booths.

Outside the brownstone, a pair of iron doors that fitted into the sidewalk were propped open on a pole. I clambered down the metal rungs of stairs that were anchored in cement, then made my way through a dank and narrow basement, with a moldering ceiling just a few inches from my head. Against the cracked cement walls were laid rusted components of old boilers, broken rakes, coiled fluorescent-green hoses. I passed newer materials: gleaming white bags of manure and seeds and, amidst all these relics, a new, shiny metallic shovel. I quietly climbed the stairs attached to the trapdoor on the other side.

And there you stood in profile in the center of a garden steeped in shadow. On a herringbone-brick quadrant bordered in boxwood, whose center, earlier in the summer, had bloomed with begonias. It was nearly dark, and the flanks of plants were irradiated by a blaze of light from the kitchen that overlooked it, a kitchen that was reached by a winding wrought-iron staircase festooned in clematis. You stood there motionless in a pose of bedeviled bewilderment, the most beautiful I think I'd ever seen you.

I watched the dawning of a silly smile. "Hey, you."

"Hey, yourself."

One segment of a flower bed had been hoed up and your knees showed dirt stains from kneeling. I assumed you were planting bulbs. You were soon telling me that, no matter what you did, the garden would never be quite right. One had to tend a garden the way one would take care of a lover. That last remark irked me. Was *I* such a bother?

You said there were just a few more minutes of work to do and then how about brick oven pizza on Houston Street. Although I tacitly agreed, you knew me well enough by now to sense that something was wrong. But you didn't ask right away. You grabbed your trowel and bent down next to what you'd taught me was a caladium, a leafy, banana-like plant with blood-red arterials.

Silent, I watched you making turn-over incisions in the composted soil. There was a great tugging at the center of me, a longing that I was afraid would haunt me for the rest of my life. Finally you stopped digging and looked at me warily. And I told you that I was upset. "José Ayala called me."

"Yeah?" You stood and shuttled the trowel between hands as you wiped each of them carefully on your pants.

"José claims that Bobby Garzino was actually HIV-negative."

You laughed. "The guy will never let up. He'll think of anything to get what he wants."

"I don't think José is lying."

You pivoted away and faced the garden wall that you'd trellised. A bower of grapevines was spilling over the top, just beginning to yellow in the season. "Why are you doing this? Stop getting involved in something that's not your concern."

"The guy called *me*, Sean. I was minding my own business."

You finally turned back to me and I saw the glistening residue of tears on your cheeks. In a moment I gathered that you hadn't lied about Bobby killing himself because of AIDS, that you'd believed it yourself. "And how do we know José's not lying?" you asked in a broken voice. "That it isn't just another ploy to get some kind of retribution, to make me give up the things Bobby loomed for me? I don't care what José does, or what says. I won't give any of it back to him. Because it means something to me."

I mentioned the letter that supposedly revealed Bobby's wishes.

You looked at me without wavering and said, "I never read that letter."

I was dumbfounded. "Are you saying that you *have* it?"

"Yeah, I have it."

"Why didn't you read it?"

"Because I'm afraid of what it says."

But why hadn't you ever told me there was a letter outstanding? In all our discussions about José's phone calls, about his insinuations, you never mentioned the fact that there was this unopened message from Bobby.

Your breath was coming fast and your eyes smoldered in the gloom of the garden. Under your arms there were half-moons of sweat stains from all your hard work. "I kept from telling you about the letter. Simply because I knew that you'd try to coerce me into opening it."

"Of course I would. Because opening it would resolve a lot of things that we don't understand."

"I knew this would happen!" You balled your hands into fists. "I knew that José would do whatever he could to put doubts in your mind. That's *exactly* what he wanted to do, and *exactly* what I hoped we'd avoid."

"The only doubt he put in my mind was whether or not you knew if Bobby Garzino was HIV-negative."

"I haven't lied! And how can you even suspect that after everything I've told you?"

"Told me what?"

"Told you that the last time I communicated with him was before he got the test!" Your eyes were flashing with anger.

"But Sean, now there's information that you've been deliberately ignoring."

"Why does that amaze you so much?"

"Wouldn't you want to know the truth whatever it was? Wouldn't you want to end all this speculating?"

"You're the only one who's speculating."

I couldn't even fathom the idea of getting a letter from somebody, knowing it might contain a last wish and just not opening it.

"Well, that's how you and I differ."

"Okay, but why is it that every time I talk to José he keeps coming back to the same thing: that something in particular happened between you and Bobby Garzino, something that I don't know about?"

"What could've happened?" you roared. "Just *tell me!* What terrible thing could I have done?"

I pondered this for a moment and then I said, "It's probably all in that letter."

"Look, I don't give a fuck what the letter says! Nobody can hold me responsible for the fact that somebody else might have killed himself. Whether or not Bobby was positive, dying was his own choice. He drove himself around that bend. He was sick enough to make it happen."

I had trouble believing you actually meant this. "If that's true,"

I countered, "then what's stopping you from reading his letter? A sick man wrote it, whatever it says."

You said nothing in response to this. Moments passed and with them a flock of Canadian geese wheeled overhead, an expansive natural occurrence in the midst of a city where buildings edged plant life into small, cultivated plots. We watched the birds honking noisily along, and when their cries were finally drowned out by the din of traffic, I looked over at you and felt pity. "You've been hiding something from me, Sean. I've known it all along. I feel it between us even now. So please."

Then surfaced on your face that look of affliction that began long before I knew you, in another country on the other side of the same ocean in which I lost Chad. You extracted a stained rag out of your back pocket, grabbed the trowel, dusted off excess dirt and began polishing the blade until the metal shone. And I waited.

Finally, you said, "I couldn't bring myself to read that letter . . . because I knew that he'd try to make me feel guilty about his choosing to take his life. And I can't handle that. But you're right. There's something else, something that I haven't been able to tell you."

Fear crashed down on me like an icy swell. But I was able to say, "These days when somebody says something like that it usually means one of two things: either 'I've got AIDS' or 'I've got a boyfriend I haven't told you about.' "

"It's neither," you explained glumly. "It's something to do . . . with my father."

The expression on my face must've been comical because you grinned and said, "It's not what you think. It's not sexual."

Two weeks after your father went back to Vietnam that last time, your mother was supposed to get a phone call from him. A phone call that never arrived. She had never seemed so distraught. She kept pacing the house, watching the clock, calling her friend Roseanne for support and bursting into tears. Each day she didn't hear from him she grew more and more agitated. After three days of waiting she was hardly sleeping; she was sure that something had happened to him and couldn't bear not knowing what that was, and wondering if he was dead or alive. She finally reached an emergency communication point in Saigon. Word got back to her that there'd been some sabotage of the village's telephone lines and temporarily all communications had to be made on official radio frequencies. But even after she received that information she kept worrying. She couldn't sleep.

And you couldn't understand it at all. Your father was obviously making her miserable. He'd forgotten to call. He had abandoned you both. Why had he done that? You were angry with him.

Finally the phone call came. And when it did she gushed and blathered in this fake voice. She told him—you couldn't believe this—she told your father that she hadn't been too concerned, that she'd assumed something must've happened to the phone lines and that all along she'd trusted that things would work themselves out.

"I stared at her while she lied to him," you said. "I couldn't believe that she could be so dishonest. And then my father asked to say hello to me. So she put me on. He told me immediately that he missed me and that even though he'd just been back in Vietnam for two weeks it seemed like such a long time and that he was looking forward to seeing me again."

You paused at this point, greatly agitated. Your shoulders pinched inwardly, a sudden hunching over as though you wanted to crumple down.

"But I told him to stay there. I was furious, you see. I told him I hated him. And I told him never to come back to Okinawa."

You stood there silent. Darkness had infiltrated the garden. The damask roses and the Southern magnolias that you'd planted, the copper lanterns began to ebb into the shade. Finally your wounded glance found mine. "The unfortunate thing, Will, is that 'never come back' was actually the very last thing I ever said to him."

Never come back! as the last thing you ever said to your father? *Never come back!*

So you believed that you carried with you the power to kill. And maybe I thought that I could help you let go of that belief.

But I didn't tell you this directly; instead I said I knew that you were capable of great feeling and how it made me sad that you felt it necessary to shut down. I explained that I'd uncovered this tender part of you when I'd read your diaries. I confessed as easily as that.

There was a momentary shudder of hatred in your eyes, a spark of venom, and then your whole face went slack. You began rubbing your thumb over the gleaming blade of the trowel.

"You didn't do that! You're bullshitting me, right?"

"No, I—"

"Why would you do something like that?" you barked, completely incredulous. "Why would you read something that's not yours?"

"But wouldn't you?" I was surprised at your reaction. "Wouldn't you be tempted if somebody left their diaries lying around?"

"They weren't lying around. They were on my bookshelf!" It was as though, to you, the realm of a bookshelf was equivalent to something being kept under lock and key.

"But . . . if you were at all concerned that I'd read something private, wouldn't you have put it all away?"

"Concerned?" you repeated in disbelief. "It didn't cross my mind that you'd even be tempted. Believe me, if I had any idea whatsoever, I would've taken those frigging diaries to my office."

There was now a lull in the argument, a punctuation obviously created by our mutual preoccupations. "Did you read the letters, too?" you asked finally with a desolate note in your voice.

"Just one letter," I admitted.

"Which one?" Your voice was now barely audible.

"The one about . . . the one about how Randall wouldn't call you when he was supposed to. The one about you waiting for him in front of the PX."

You muttered something to yourself and looked momentarily bewildered and finally said, "It doesn't ring a bell."

"I'm really sorry, Sean," I said. "I know it sounds self-serving and stupid, but I actually thought you almost expected me to read them."

You dropped the trowel onto the ground and your gaze was like an X ray prying under my skin. "Are you trying to insult me now?"

"No, I'm not—"

"Why the hell would I want or expect you to read my private writings?"

I quickly explained that I was so paranoid about people reading my writings that I locked my journals in a fire box whenever my landlord needed access to my apartment. And the old man was Czechoslovakian and spoke poor English.

"But you see, you're paranoid and I'm not! I just assumed that when you stayed at my apartment you were there to protect *me*, not to read through my private papers. I was concerned about protecting my place from José. When all along it was *you* I should've been concerned about."

"Sean, remember you joked with me when you called from Montana? Remember you asked if I was leaving your stuff alone? That was when you gave me the idea that you half expected me to snoop around."

Your stare continued, but seemed mistier now, harder to discern. Then it broke and your eyes scanned the garden, at first mildly baffled, then wildly, for something. "This is crazy," you said finally, hurrying over to a bamboo rake clotted with what looked like wet and rotting leaves.

"What's crazy?" I insisted as I watched you beginning to strip the mulch out of the rake.

"I'm forgetting everything I need to do here tonight. . . . What's crazy is your interpreting my phone call from Montana as an invitation to snoop." You suddenly stopped your chore and looked at me with a scowl. Your bare arms were shivering. "Will, we're just different, that's all." You sighed. "Anyway, I've got some more work to do here. I think I'll stay for a while longer. Why don't you just let yourself out."

"Look, Sean, I said I was sorry. It happened early on. And it was absolutely out of line. I admit that, okay? I apologize."

A pause. "If it happens once, it'll happen again."

"No it won't."

You raised your arms as though I were holding you up with a gun. "All right," you said. "It won't happen again. And I accept your apology. But let me get something done."

I was stunned. Being told to leave you seemed like a monstrous request. "Why don't I just sit in one of the chairs and wait for you? Then we'll grab a bite somewhere and chill out."

You faced away from me and, with both hands, shielded your eyes from the shadows in order to survey the back border of the garden. "I'd rather not, Will. I'm afraid I'd rather you just go. I need some time here to myself."

But I still lingered until it became brutally clear that you now intended to ignore me. And then, reluctantly, I retreated across the garden to the coal chute. Before I climbed down the steep ladder, I glanced back, hoping to capture your gaze. You'd already retrieved the trowel from where you'd dropped it and were kneel-

ing again, facing away from me. On one of the green wooden- slatted garden chairs lay a gathering of pumpkin-colored chrysan-
themums that had been carefully picked and sized, their long
stems casually entwined. Who had you picked them for? Had you
picked them for me?

PART THREE

SWIMMER

21

FROM THEN ON I WAS OUT THERE AGAIN, WAITING FOR YOU TO COME
back to me the way I once waited for Chad. My appetite was dead-
ened by remorse and I quickly shed eight pounds. When I did eat,
I consumed foods I otherwise never touched, things like matzo ball
soup and chocolate truffles and blood oranges. Being jilted by a
lover does strange things to the body: mood swings between fits of
elation and distress, cravings that can suddenly turn to disgust.

I tried not to call you so much. And when I did I always began with an apology. I'd invite you to films and other events I knew
you wanted to see. But you either claimed to be busy, or kindly
explained that more time needed to go by before we could see each
other again with any kind of regularity. Ironically, in comparison
to the uncertainty of our relationship's early days, when I had difficulty reaching you, you now promptly responded to all my phone
messages. Perhaps that was because you never intended to make
plans. What else could I conclude but that you were glad for an
excuse to give me up?

Every time we'd speak on the phone, I'd sleep fitfully the same night. I'd dream about losing track of you in the dark corridor of an ocean swim, in the midst of a rip tide. Whenever I'd wake up the loss of you would fall like an anvil on my solar plexus. How can I get *him* to trust me again? asked my weary mind. What should I do to reinstate myself? Yes, you were finally becoming *him*, and your becoming *him* made me wonder if that sense of absence had from the very beginning been encoded within me.

Even though you'd suddenly withdrawn from my life, I felt that I still belonged to you. I started wearing a black length of rawhide around my neck that proclaimed that my heart was still tied. I was spoken for and yet, at the same time, unattached, and something about that communicated itself to strangers. I was suddenly approached by men whom I'd seen around Manhattan for years but who never before had given me a moment of attention. In one-night stands with other men I tried to locate the parts of you that I admired: the wit, the sensuality, the dreaminess, the self-effacing charm.

I picked up a muscle man who took me into a brownstone he was renovating and, as a prelude to sex, asked me to give him a steroid injection. I met a dancer who was unable to find legitimate work and who was forced to give what he called "release massages," the 1990s version of safe-sex prostitution. I met a nervous, angelic-looking guy who, after explaining that "a recent relationship ended abruptly," finally admitted that the relationship had ended because his lover died of AIDS. Those encounters took away the sting of sudden loss while they lasted, but as soon as they ended I felt more despondent than ever.

Sometimes I got so agitated that I had to pace the city to ease the press of affliction. I strolled along the West Side Highway among guys in cut off T-shirts, gold rings flashing from their pierced ears, the air spiced with frowsy colognes. Murmurs of conversation rang unintelligibly to me, and in my mood of alienation

I tried to imagine the gibberish sound of English to a foreigner.
Yet I felt like a foreigner. I felt exiled from your life.

A little more than two weeks after our conversation in the
brownstone garden, I found myself heading out at night along the
promontory of a pier, passing men walking tight nervous circles
in the shadows, a hand riveted to a crotch, or the intertwining
forms of guys necking out of view. Standing at the edge of the dock,
I looked across at the lighted high-rises of New Jersey apartments,
a patch of watery blue sky above them with plumed clouds
smudged in orange by the recent sunset. I could smell the rank
odor of the river. I marveled at how bodies of water constantly
move as the earth itself kept moving, so simple and yet so unfor-
giving.

That night I was wishing that I had told you the truth about
the last time with Chad. Told you how it was at my apartment, told
you I was afraid what happened between Chad and me had something to do with him vanishing. Telling you would only have proved
your theory that Chad had taken a part of me away from myself, a
piece of my own heart that I foolishly believed that I could find
in a stranger. That I might have found in you.

Until those last few weeks with him I never understood what it
was like to want a man inside me. And whenever I felt the beginning of that desire I fought it. He didn't really care that I couldn't
bring myself to be on the receiving end, although sometimes he
joked that we should have a sexual democracy. I told him that I'd
tried getting screwed in the past and that it had been just too
painful. He said that enjoying it was more a matter of trust than
anything else. And he was right. I knew he was right.

I started fantasizing about it, especially when he'd gone on
one of his jaunts and I didn't know where he was. I would lie there
on my bed and let my legs drift apart, imagining. Remembering
some of the women in my life whom I'd made love to, and a certain crucial moment when they let me know that they'd been

aroused to the point that they wanted me inside them. Now, alone, I discovered what that was. Touching myself ignited something in the lowest pit of my being. And then I wondered what it might be like after a bottle of Zinfandel, or after several Coronas. But I was scared because in some way it meant total submission, giving up to him something that had seemed impossible to give.

My apartment on Mason Street. Late afternoon, the sun dipping behind the King palms and jacarandas and the shadows in my bedroom as long-limbed as the trees that cast them. He'd cycled down from Isla Vista, his backpack chock-full of books for studying; he was wearing a pair of rainbow-tie-dyed rugby shorts that rode high on his bronzed legs. "I'm starved," he grunted as he breezed through the door. "What's to eat?"

"Just some Jack cheese and a couple of avocados."

"They ripe, the avocados?"

"I think one is."

His hair was tangled from being blown around by the Santa Ana winds. I asked if he'd practiced water polo and he shook his head and said that there was too much studying to do. Oral exams were coming up. Then he reached into his backpack, pulled out a sourdough round, threw it at me like a football and said, "This should go nicely with the avocados and the cheese."

I forgot to respond because I was already thinking about sex and feeling scared of wanting it as much as I did.

"All right, what's wrong?" he asked.

"Nothing is wrong."

"You're sulking. I know that sulking puss."

"You might know it, but that's not what you're seeing."

"Okay, what am I seeing?"

He hadn't shaved in a day or so and the growth on his face was thickening. His T-shirt, one of his old Stanford ones, was so worn it was coming apart in places, and I could see bits of his torso through some of the holes. I walked over, kissed him once and then tried to pry his mouth open with my tongue. He chuckled and said, "Oh, you're horny, so that's why you're acting so serious."

"Yeah," I whispered, kissing down the cords of his neck.

"What happens if I'm not in the mood?"

I said nothing, just continued kissing him. Finally I brought one of his hands around to one of my ass cheeks. And then he took a capricious sniff. "Have you been drinking?"

"Just a couple beers."

A look of bewilderment on his face, but then he grinned.

The hurt: how can I describe that first moment when he tried to push inside. It cut through me like a blade. I tensed up and he popped out and shrugged and giggled.

"What are you laughing at?" I accused him.

"The look of pure agony on your face."

"Well, what do you expect?"

"I know it hurts. It hurt me the first time with you," he said. "Look, you're the one who wants to do this."

"I know! But can't you go easy?"

He chuckled. "I *am* going easy."

"Then don't get so pissed off."

"I'm not. Don't be so sensitive."

"Just shut up and do it!"

"Jesus Christ, can you at least be sexy about it?"

"It's hard to be when it's killing me."

"I think we're losing the mood here."

And then I grabbed him by the arms. Grabbed him like I would refuse to let him off me until we'd finish what we'd started. "I want to do this," I insisted.

Now I remember that there was a look of dread on his face.

I wish I had a photograph of him precisely at that moment. For in that look I believe lies the answer to everything that I need to know, the riddle of his vanishing.

Why he should have felt dread I don't quite understand. I was the one about to withstand pain for pleasure. He asked me if I had any tequila and I told him there were a few swallows left. He went and grabbed the bottle off the top of the refrigerator, came back into the room, his hard-on bounding between his legs, a line of salt on the crown of his hand. I licked his hand and drank what he poured in a tumbler and what I didn't drink he swallowed. His breath was fiery when he kissed me again, and we didn't try anything for a while, just ground together and kissed and gave each other head. But finally I felt his finger beginning. He leaned over one side of the bed and grabbed the tube of lubricant jelly. I felt his finger again, slicked like an ice-cold probe, and then I shut my eyes and waited.

Hardly as gentle as he promised, he was suddenly all the way in, and the splitting feeling was pure pain, clear as water. I was afraid that I was going to die right there beneath him. I almost wanted to, strangely enough. He grunted something about its being the only way, but by now I was so enraged that I found myself shoving him off. "Wait!" he cried out. "Just wait. Hold on." Now he was the one clawing at me, pinning me, insisting.

"It's too fast. You're in . . . you're doing it too fast!"

But then in the midst of the pawing agony arrived the first hint of numbness which was the curtain before it began to feel good. "Relax," he told me. "You're squirming."

"Of course I'm squirming."

But then a chuckle escaped him.

"It's not funny!" I growled.

He said nothing, so intent was he on his own pleasure.

"I think you should stop," I said.

But he wouldn't stop. I knew he wouldn't, even when I asked him again, when I insisted.

Then suddenly there's a bridge. Getting off no longer has to be so external. He can get me even closer to it, that ache of desire, if only he can reach it. The fullness inside me is suddenly the thing that I've been missing all along when I've come up short, when I've felt I could never get enough of him, of anyone, could never take in the pure pull of his outer limbs. I realize now I can have it all.

And in that moment I became like a madman, bucking and bellowing as I pulled him into me and got off like I never had before and came spiderwebs all over my own face. And perhaps he perceived my new power. He must've realized it because afterward, lying there, we said nothing.

I know I once said how happy I was that last afternoon, but I couldn't admit it to you then. The truth is I wasn't happy, the truth is I'd reached my lowest ebb. Like lying dead and rotted on the bottom of the ocean. No whispers of I love you, no exclamation that it was good. Just silence. The claustrophobic silence when you realize that your lover no longer is a mystery and that the fourth wall of the relationship is finally constructed: complete familiarity. From that silence, I now believe, dawned his desire to swim out beyond the breakwater, a night swim on which he insisted I accompany him.

Now, standing on the dock, I felt my back pocket, and after an initial moment of panic that my wallet had been lifted, I remembered I'd left it at home and that my only encumbrance was a key chain. I hid that in a convenient place between two loose boards. I shucked my clothes and was soon standing in a pair of underwear on the westernmost edge of Manhattan.

And then I was in, a sort of half-dive, half-jump; my foot grazed something hard and slimy on the bottom. I gasped, for the water was chillier than I expected, and it surprised me with a grimy odor. "What the fuck?" I heard somebody say as I did a few head-up strokes—the way Chad used to do when he first began, water polo swimming. I was still bracing against the shock of the cold,

my arms already aching numb. The water temperature had to be
in the mid-fifties.

I began with long easy strokes, dragging my thumb along my
side, elbows high, taking some more head-up breaths to make
sure nothing was bearing down on me. I could feel the yank of a
current, different from the outward pull of the ocean—this was
more like swimming through a constant boiling. After I ventured
twenty-five yards off the pier and looked back at the waterfront,
I could make out several shadowy forms waving. Their shouts
came to me in a strobe-like blare. I stopped and treaded water.
"Hey, man, what are you doing? Where you going? Are you nuts?"

"You trying to kill yourself or what?"

"Idiot!"

I hit things on the way out, soda and beer cans maybe. I never
let myself dwell on what might be floating in the Hudson, just
sliced my way through whatever there was and kept on in the cold
indefinite dark. Certainly didn't have to worry about sharks. The
moment panic hit like a wall, I poured on the speed, just wanting
to get two hundred yards done with in order to come back. But I
just had to touch that point of no return, like a talisman, because
I believed it would bring me around to something that I'd been
looking for.

I finally hit two hundred, stopped and treaded water. The
unguent- black water, my body cold and dumb but my throat and
my head on fire. I'd brought myself out to this unsafe, unlikely
place in the Hudson River at night. Perhaps I wanted to die. And
an old wail left me like a ghost that has, for all these years, been
feeding off a soul. The sound was kin to the howl that left me the
night he disappeared, a crying out that made the Mexican family
who lived below me on Mason Street bang the ceiling with the
broom, just the way they had done earlier the same day when he
and I had made our most raucous love.

But from somewhere up the Hudson I heard the churning noise

of a huge vessel, and I turned to the bouncing glint of deck lights
bearing down on me. The moment before I headed in, it all returned to me: the supreme emptiness of feeling fucked and
unloved, the sense that there was nothing sacred left in me, just
rawness, and all the things I wanted to tell him but never did as
we strolled toward West Beach. In my very last glimpse of him,
there is the look of annoyance on his face, because I was trying
to stop him from swimming along the pathway of the moon. I remember shouting about the sand barge and the foreboding that
pervaded me long before the great wide ocean had separated us.

22

Two cops were waiting on the pier.

As soon as I saw them, I took one backstroke with the idea of turning around and sprinting off down the shoreline, when I heard one of them speaking through a bullhorn. "Hey, buddy, you better get out of that water, now. Right now!"

Flashlights stunned my vision. What could they do to me? I hadn't committed a crime unless swimming in the Hudson River was my crime. But just in case.

I tried to summon up my own voice of authority. "Look, I know what I'm doing! I'm training, okay? For the Around Manhattan Swim."

Although the light beaming in my eyes induced a halo of blindness, I sensed nevertheless that the police activity was attracting a crowd of people to the end of the dock.

"Are you going to get out of the water, or are we going to call a boat and frogmen?"

With a few strokes I was bobbing below them, near the pilings, and any reservation I had about climbing out quickly dissipated when I brushed up against what felt like a floating dead rat.

I was soon standing, like an idiot, smothered with a police blanket, dripping onto the wooden planks of the pier. The cops were squinting at me in a kind of condemning disbelief. I was aware of a crowd of people standing beyond them, but for some reason I didn't care whether or not I came off like a maniac. "You're lucky you're not dead," one said. "Now, I don't want to see you in this water here again. You got that? The next cop will haul you to Bellevue, no questions asked."

With that they took the blanket and left me standing there. The bystanders began to disperse. It occurred to me as I put on my jeans and sweatshirt that the real danger of the whole episode was the possibility that my clothes could have been stolen, leaving me in a Freudian nightmare, naked in a public place. And I hadn't even considered such a possibility before jumping in the water. *Was* I going a little crazy?

Just as I was leaving the pier, I was grabbed by the forearm. It was you. What were *you* doing here? I was elated. Swimming at night could not bring back Chad, but it could bring back *you*.

Dressed in work clothes—a blue blazer and a pair of pleated khaki pants—you'd just left a business dinner and were heading along the piers on the way back to your apartment when you noticed several people scurrying out onto a dock and heard rumors that somebody had drowned. "Normally I'm not the rubbernecking sort, but when they said there was this guy in the river, of course I had to look."

"Did it cross your mind that it might be me?"

You raised your eyebrows and I now noticed that your cheeks had reddened. "Yeah, it did, unfortunately. And I was hoping it wasn't."

You were quite obviously perturbed, whereas I was just delighted to see you. And so I asked you what was wrong.

"What's wrong?" you mocked me. "Come on, what do you think is wrong? I'm concerned, can't you see that? I want to know what you were doing."

Your reaction was, at first, bewildering to me. I was swimming—what did you think I was doing?

"Come on, Will, you're talking to *me*. Why are you giving me a line?"

"I'm not giving you a line." After all, it hadn't been the first time that I'd done something similar to this.

"In the Hudson River, in November no less." You abruptly turned away from me and exhorted, "Come on, we better start moving. You're soaked!"

I had been unable to towel off and my clothes were showing huge damp blots, although by now my hair was almost dry. The wind drawing in from the river was surprisingly arid and buffeted our backs.

"So how have you been?" I asked after we had walked away from the pier and were heading along Christopher Street.

"Been the same. What about you?"

I tried to sound hopeful. "Getting better."

A pause. "Well, that's good."

"Dating anybody?" I couldn't help asking.

You turned to me with a scowl. "You know I'm not dating anybody, Will."

"How would *I* know?"

"What would be the point of getting involved immediately with somebody else?"

"It happens. I mean, you're the one who withdrew."

We walked a few paces before you responded. "You know why I had to withdraw. I saw that I was driving you crazy. And that was driving *me* crazy."

Your attempt at such an oversimplification was maddening,

but I didn't want to begin a heated discussion so soon. We strolled another half block in silence before you finally spoke again. "Look, I just don't want you to suddenly start acting weird because we're not seeing each other."

By weird, did you mean swimming treacherously?

"You know what I'm talking about."

And then it dawned on me, that you were assuming that my despondency over you had driven me out onto the pier and into the water. Maybe you thought I was in the process of killing myself—like Bobby Garzino. And I was about to explain how you'd completely misconstrued my actions—that, if anything, my swimming out there had a lot more to do with Chad—when I realized that you would never understand. What drove me to swim couldn't enter your comprehension because you never really grasped how much that relationship or his vanishing has affected my life.

Your face was full of caring and concern when you suddenly turned to me and said, "You must be cold."

"I am a little bit."

"Do you want my jacket?"

"No, Sean, I'm fine."

"You sure? I don't want you to get sick or anything. The Hudson is no swimming pool."

"I'll take a hot shower as soon as I go home."

We walked a few more paces. "You know, it'll probably take a while for you to get across town to your apartment. Wouldn't you rather come by my place . . . *just* to take a shower?"

Just to take a shower.

You wanted to help but also wanted me to know that any such gesture was purely platonic.

"That's not necessary."

"There's no reason to stand on ceremony."

"Believe me, I can wait until I get home."

You shrugged, somewhat miffed by my refusal.

"Clearly a *friendly* offer," I couldn't help saying.

"You don't have to be so cynical."

I stopped walking and faced you. "You know, Sean, it's true I've been pretty depressed these past few weeks. But, believe it or not, the prospect of a friendship is not going to kill me."

"Never said it was going to kill you."

Well, you certainly act like it, I almost said, but didn't.

"In fact," you went on, "I was perfectly happy the way everything was. I only pushed for a change when I saw you couldn't handle a relationship."

"No, because you were angry about my snooping around, because you were angry about my intrusion."

"I got over that pretty quickly."

"Well, I'm glad to hear it." I forced a lighthearted tone.

"Will, the point I'm trying to make is that I'm not relieved to be out of this, the way I think you imagine I am."

I didn't believe you. It seemed that there was still a part of you that expected, perhaps even wanted me to remain fixated, which made it difficult for you to believe my explanation that I had merely been swimming the Hudson River in the middle of November.

You said, "I just wish you'd stop trying to figure out everything about me. It scares me off. It's not going to make you feel any better. And it's certainly not going to get rid of any ghosts."

I digested this for a moment and then said, "Giving up, letting go happens naturally, Sean. It's human to give up the spirit of one love only when we finally commit to another."

"No, I don't agree. We have to give up the ghost first. Be free. Only then be with somebody new. Otherwise one ghost-love gets replaced with another ghost-love. There's no real content. Just another form, another outline that we fill in with the same exact longing we had before."

We continued in silence along Christopher Street and down Bedford until it was necessary for you to veer off toward Grove. You explained that you had an early day tomorrow, said goodbye and kissed me gently on the lips. And that kiss was a lot more than I'd expected, having expected nothing.

23

"YOU'RE NOT GOING TO DUMP ALL OVER ME," GREG SAID. "JUST because . . . of what happened with Sean. I'm not your fucking scapegoat! And for the millionth time, I didn't give Sebastian your telephone number. He could've found it out in any number of ways. He could've looked me up once and saw the two listings and put two and two together. Either that, or he pressed star 6–9 once when he was over at my apartment right after you called."

"Star 6–9?"

A new phone feature traced the last person who had called and called them back directly. Hadn't I heard about it?

I'd heard about it but was unaware that it was now saturating the consumer market. But apparently star 6–9 had been available for the last six months. Greg had signed on for it because his phone already came equipped with a digital readout. And Sebastian, who'd been there several times when I'd called, conceivably could've scanned the monitor and jotted down my phone number.

We were having this contretemps at Greg's apartment as he

was getting ready for his night job. Wearing only his boxer shorts, he was ironing a dress shirt. He was clearly getting nervous about being late for work. "And in fact," he went on, "for your own self-protection, if somebody gives you their home number off a phone sex line and you call them directly, it means that they could conceivably get your number and call you back after that at all hours of the day or night."

A horrifying thought. "Only *you* would think of such a per-verse-case-scenario," I said.

"Why do you think it's called star 6–9?" Greg threw me one of his typical 'I know you inside and out' looks as he steam-pressed a shirt arm. "Just troubleshooting yet another possible paranoid fantasy."

When I accused him of being flip and unsympathetic, Greg's face reddened. He uprighted the iron and slammed it down on its tin tray. "Now, just wait a second here. Who stayed up with you until three in the morning Halloween night? Who missed two parties and the parade because you were feeling so dismal?"

"Well, you'd have been depressed, too."

"No shit. Look, I wanted to take care of you. But I easily could've fed you a couple of Xanax, put you to bed and gone out."

"Maybe you were being helpful because you were secretly glad."

This made Greg seethe. "You know one of the things I hated about being involved with you, Will? That you always saw a black hole in the middle of everything. I couldn't even tell you you fucked me good without your thinking there was some qualification to the compliment."

I managed to smile.

Greg continued, "Look, you know my opinion of the situation. From what you've said, Sean has never been able to handle a re-lationship. The claustrophobic type that bails out when things get a little uncomfortable. You saw it coming a mile away. And now that it's happened, you're going to realize: better now than later."

"Here's the pot calling the kettle black."

"Look, I never claimed I was perfect." Greg peeled the shirt off the ironing board and held it up to the light. He scrutinized it for creases, then his eyes found mine. "I've apologized for hurting you a million times. I don't know what you want."

"Well," I complained, "for starters I'd like it if you'd stop dorking Sebastian."

Greg fixed me with a stubborn gaze. "What's he got to do with anything?"

"He's hateful."

"Did I ever tell you to stop dorking Sean?"

"Sean wasn't involved with anybody else."

"What's the big deal, Will? I mean, Seb is just a fuck buddy."

"Oh, he's Seb now. Your fuck buddy Seb who happens to despise me."

"That's not"—Greg paused—"necessarily true." He grabbed a bottle of starch that was standing next to his ankle and sprayed a wand over his shirt. "Anyway, he knows my loyalty is to you."

I said nothing for a while and watched Greg finishing up his shirt, listening to the gurgling of hot water in the iron, hot water sizzling into steam. "I think I blame myself for making you into such a hard-ass," I finally said. "You weren't nearly so tough when we first met."

Greg shrugged and headed over to his closet. "Yeah, well, I lived with you for long enough. What do you expect?"

"Just what I want to hear."

Greg had turned away from me and was trying to select a pair of dress pants. "I'll admit that I was threatened by your thing with Sean. You made it sound like it was some grand passion or something."

It *is*, I wanted to reply. But I said nothing because Greg had already told me that in his opinion throughout those few months with you I'd been on edge, expectant, hardly my old self.

"I must admit it really got to me when you went up to Vermont with him . . . to our old place. And then that night we almost lost Casey, even though I was nearly out of my mind, I noticed his smile. A smile that could crack a safe." Greg turned to face me again. "So factor all that into my hunch that nobody can get too close to a guy like him. Principally because a guy like him has no real devotion to anyone. And that with Sean Paris you were basically spinning your wheels."

At this point, Casey got up from where he'd been lying next to Greg's refrigerator and sauntered over to a plastic pumpkin chew toy that squeaked. He picked it up, squealed it a few times, then brought it over and dropped it in my lap. Petting him, I tossed the pumpkin a few feet away and Casey pounced on it and began a wrestling solitaire.

"Don't get him riled up right before I have to leave," Greg warned as he finally selected a pair of dark trousers and stepped into them. He put on the dress shirt and buttoned it up swiftly.

"I think I'll take him with me tonight, to my place," I said. "If you don't mind."

Greg now showed me the most compassionate face I'd seen thus far in our conversation. "Mind? I wish you'd take him to your place more often."

"Maybe I'll start doing that."

Once Greg was dressed and ready to go, and after I'd put on Casey's leash and collected a few of his chase balls, I said, "So exactly how often *have* you been seeing Sebastian?"

Greg broke into a grin. "God, you're really fixated on this thing with Sebastian! Once a week . . . at the most. But I'll be honest with you, he *does* talk about Peter a bit too much."

"Don't you get it? They can't live without each other."

"Well, fucking around with me is surely a strange way of being unable to live without Peter!"

That was when I pointed out it was the only way to dilute the terror of real intimacy.

Casey and I escorted Greg to the subway and then we dropped in at the dog run and threw some balls around until Casey got tired. We took a little stroll after that and eventually wound up back at my apartment. Like a vigilant heart, the red answering machine light pulsed with a message. Your recorded voice said, "Hey, Will, it's Sean here. Just checking in to see how you're doing. Give me a call, whenever you feel like it."

We were still speaking maybe once or twice a week. Nevertheless, the lags between those calls felt endless, like great flat stretches of a monotonous landscape. I kept thinking that during one of those perfunctory phone calls you'd come to your senses, that missing me would eventually get the better of you, but it never happened. And to think that only recently you'd said that it was finally beginning to "work" between us. Though I knew why we'd split up, there was still an injured part of me that kept appealing, "What happened, Sean, what happened?"

While listening to your message, I watched Casey trundle into the kitchen and sniff around for his food bowl in just the place it used to be when he'd lived here with Greg and me, a bowl that had since been retired to the cupboard. When he didn't locate it, he fixed me with a baleful look. And I got sad. Because I realized that during those four years with Greg and Casey I'd probably come the closest to living in any sort of normal, domestic bliss.

24

I FOUND MYSELF AT SPLASH ONE NIGHT, WATCHING VIDEO FOOTAGE OF the Halloween parade, the variations on drag and vampires and androgynes on stilts that I'd deliberately missed. This year there seemed to be a surprising number of eunuchs weaving in and out of the costumed regalia, innocent-looking boys with golden tresses; it made me wonder if there is a movement afoot toward sexlessness. After the parade shots was threaded some footage of a rather drab-by-comparison Veterans Day picnic. Thanksgiving was now only a week away, and for the first time in many years I'd deliberately made no plans. I hardly had much time to feel sorry for myself, however, when I noticed a hot blond giving me the eye. It's scary how deep depression can suddenly burn off like fog when a number is overtly making his interest known. And there's always that moment before you get into conversation and hear how he speaks, when you allow yourself to imagine this guy will be the one who will willingly spend the weekends reading with you and seeing films, who'll prefer spending time in Vermont instead of

on Fire Island. But usually the moment he opens his mouth you
know at best it will be a one-night stand.

Nevertheless.

Eyes finally locked, we were grinning at each other, and as I
strolled toward him, suddenly somebody tugged my shirtsleeve.

Another man, an exotic with golden skin and eyes glossy like
Mediterranean olives, dark, wavy hair, diminutive. If I hadn't already set my sights on the blond I might have been more friendly
to this guy.

"Are you Will?"

I checked to see if the blond was still enthralled; he looked
bewildered by the fact that I'd allowed his gravitational pull to be
thwarted.

"Yeah, I'm Will." I sounded brusque because I wanted to keep
moving forward.

"I'm José Ayala."

I now turned to gape at him. And the hunky blond shriveled
into a passing thought. "God! I've wanted to get ahold of you!" I
exclaimed.

"I guess I should've given you my phone number that time we
talked."

José glanced at the scowling blond, now retreating back to his
original perch. "I don't want to get in the way of anything."

"Don't worry about it. That was just my loneliness rearing its
ugly head."

"Well then, you've come to the right place."

I grinned and asked what *he* was doing at Splash.

"Same as you. Deluding myself that I might get laid tonight."
We both laughed.

"I never expected you to be handsome," I said boldly.

"You thought I'd be a troll?"

I considered this for a moment. "Honestly, I don't know what
I expected."

"The one whose love is unrequited has to be ugly, right?" José grinned.

I agreed that it's a dismal assumption. And I reflected back on your ideas concerning what exactly constitutes a *fatal attraction*.

José was dressed better than most of the people in the bar. He wore a pair of black jeans and a white cashmere crew-neck sweater that showed the bones of his clavicle and the beginning of a taut, slightly built chest. Unconsciously rattling the ice in his cocktail glass, he asked if he could buy me another beer. I explained that I'd soon be leaving.

"Anyway," he said, "should I assume because you're here that you're . . . alone again?"

I nodded. "You must've heard."

"I did, actually."

"Sebastian clue you in on that one?"

José frowned. "I haven't spoken to him since . . . Is he still seeing your ex?"

"No, thank God. Greg finally blew him off. Sebastian finally starting bad-mouthing me."

"That was loyal."

"Well, that's one dividend of gay life. Your former lovers often become your best friends." As soon as I said this, however, I realized what an insensitive comment it was in light of what had happened to Bobby Garzino.

"It's kind of like a wartime mentality," José conceded as he gulped back what remained of his drink. "Our side has got to stick together . . . especially these days."

I asked him how he'd been able to recognize me. He surprised me by saying that he checked one of my books out of the library (the one, ironically, that I'd thought he'd shredded) and had looked carefully at the author's photo.

"I still haven't figured out who shredded my novel."

José appeared concerned. "Honestly, it could have been any-body."

"Promise it wasn't you?" I was smiling.

"I swear to you on my mother that it wasn't."

I looked over where the blond had been standing and found him speaking to a short, barrel-chested boy who had more hair on his head than I, and bigger proportions, and was younger.

"I'm going to get that drink now," José said. "Sure you don't want anything?"

"You go ahead. I'll just wait here."

José coolly approached the bar and confidently snagged the attention of the shirtless bartender, who served him promptly. There was something of the patrician in this little guy, I decided, a charming sort of assurance, which seemed quite a contrast to the person whom I'd imagined desperately gouging up a wooden door and placing importunate calls from pay phones. Why did he get so stuck on Bobby Garzino? Then again, such obsessive be-havior could easily overwhelm most people who found themselves in a similar predicament. When he returned, José asked if you and I had broken up before you quit your job.

The question threw me into confusion.

"You didn't know?" he said.

"I haven't heard from Sean in a couple of weeks now."

"Well, he left work 'suddenly.' So says the receptionist."

"Bugging him at work again, huh?" I managed to say, despite a burgeoning anxiety. "Even I never did that. Not even in my most dismal hour."

"You never had an ax to grind."

"How do you know?"

"I guess I don't know, really."

There was a brisk silence and I was about to leave when José said, "Look, I want to apologize for telling you things that maybe you didn't want to know."

"They certainly had their desired effect."

"My object wasn't to break the two of you up."

"You're going to have a hard time convincing me of that."

"Well, if you really believe that, then why are you talking to me now?"

I pondered this. "I don't know why, exactly. I guess because I'm intrigued. Intrigued that we're both connected to the same man in different ways."

"Me in a more hostile way," José amended. "Though of course that's over now."

I doubted that but suppressed saying so. When I reminded José I had to be going, he asked if he could take me to dinner sometime.

I looked at him shrewdly. "What for?"

"As a gesture of thanks."

"Come again?"

"I feel I owe you. I finally got all the loomed things back. Sean brought them over one night and left them in a box at my door, and they were lying there when I came home. I figured you had something to do with their being returned."

I grabbed a cab hurtling along Seventeenth. Gave the address on Grove Street, leaned forward in my seat, gripping the door handle, cringing whenever we snagged any traffic. The rest happened like clockwork. A young couple who lived upstairs happened to be leaving the building the moment I arrived and, recognizing me from all the nights and mornings I spent there, let me in.

The ruined door had been spackled and repainted, the marks of José's anguish completely eradicated. I tried it and, to my surprise, it swung open.

The beloved apartment was like a struck stage, hastily abandoned, and not quite denuded of props. The furniture was gone;

so was the piano; the walls were bare, with gaping holes from where pictures had hung; and all the stuffed birds and butterflies had taken spectral flight. Left were a digital clock-radio and a box of moldy paperbacks. The floor was strewn with paper clips and pieces of broken tile that I recognized from the garden on Charles Street. In the closet hung a torn houndstooth jacket. An ugly brown sweater was wadded up in a ball and stuffed into a corner.

How could you do this to me, Sean, knowing my history? Were you punishing me for not accepting you as you were, for trying to squeeze meaning out of your blighted past?

Your drafting table had remained behind, the Tensor lamp lying on its white surface, next to a box of nearly dried watercolors and a caked paintbrush. There was also a pocket-sized photograph of a small child with blond ringlets, the pudgy face unmistakable, the eyes even then glacial and piercing. Across the front of his T-shirt was stenciled a picture of a bayonet as well as the slogan "My Daddy is a Marine."

My back to the wall, I slowly let myself down until I was sitting on the bare floor. Then I broke down and my sobs echoed burlesquely. Through bleary eyes I finally noticed the telephone placed on top of the answering machine that was blinking like the last living organ in a chilling corpse. I went over and pressed the play button and this is what I heard.

Beep. "This is a message for Sean Paris. Please call Delia at Citibank Visa 800-678-4567. It's November fifth at five thirty-five."

Beep. "Sean, this is Dan Telebon from work. It's uh, 10 A.M. on the seventh. I need to talk to you about the Santa Fe house. Can you call me as soon as you get this."

Beep. "Sean, this is Howie Rosen from Barneys. Remember me? How ya doing? Give me a call at work. Oh, and by the way, those pants have come in in your size."

Beep. "Sean, this is Robert Sirjane. November tenth. We need you to get in contact with us on several matters that are pending. Please call as soon as you get this message."

Beep. "Sean, this is Howie from Barneys. I understand you haven't picked up your pants. Give me a call at home or at work. I can always bring them to you after work if necessary."

Beep. "This is a message for Sean Paris. Please call Sabrina at Citibank Visa. We need to speak to you by midnight on the twentieth of November."

Beep. "Sean, this is Robert Sirjane again. It's the fifteenth of November. You have not contacted us as you promised you would. I'm sorry, but I've had to authorize accounting to withhold your final paycheck until you can help us clear up some of the loose ends here. I need you to contact the office as soon as possible."

Beep. "Sean, Howie from Barneys. Please call. I'd appreciate it."

Beep. "Sean, it's Mom. We haven't heard from you. We're leaving San Diego for a month and I'd like to talk to you before we go."

A spooky recognition came to me: I hardly knew this man.

Beep. The sounds of the street. Like when José used to call. "Hey, Sean . . ." says a jaunty-sounding man with obvious confidence. "This is Tom Whalen, the . . . gentleman you met on Bleecker Street. I've been thinking about your beautiful face. Thinking about us getting together again. Being close. I've walked by your apartment a few times, saw your light on, but just didn't . . . well, just didn't want to bug you. I'll call you again. 'Bye, beautiful."

That message singed me like hot acid, but I quickly went numb when I heard the following:

Beep. Pause and a sigh, but this time a sigh that I recognized. "Hey, Will, it's Sean. I don't know why I think you're going to hear this but I somehow think you are." Your voice rose on the last word. "I wonder why. Obviously I've left. I . . . had to leave. Where am I, you might ask. Well, right now I'm at a pay phone at a truck stop outside Minneapolis. In fact, from where I am I can see Lake Superior. I'm driving out to Seattle to visit an old friend of mine. Anyway, here's what I'm asking you to do. There's a pile of mail that I left behind. On top of the mantel. I mean, it should be there, I've paid rent until the end of the month, so the apartment should still be how I left it. There's a letter that's been opened. It's *the* letter. I finally read it. If you could just read it yourself, okay? It explains everything better than I can, why I've been acting weird, why I had to leave." A sigh. "Why I couldn't admit something, something that I should've told you from the very beginning, but couldn't. I'm gutless, I guess. Right now I'm not in the best of circumstances to go into any explanation. If it makes you feel any better, nobody else knows that I've left. Nobody knows where I've gone. But I . . . I love you. And I'm sorry. Beep.

July 31, 1990
Dear Sean:

The doctor says I'm in perfect health. My blood count is fine, HIV negative, normal T cells, normal everything, but I still want to die. I feel guilty because I know there are guys right now in the hospital who would trade places with me, guys who would willingly exchange their sickness for this . . . how else do I call it—unrequited love? But everything is relative and since I haven't lived through a life-threatening illness I can't make use of that contrast to get myself back on track. It doesn't help me to think about them, even to force myself to visit the ones who won't make it beyond a few more weeks, because my own misery still won't go away.

And my misery is living without you and the rest of my life now seems like too long a stretch to go. Yeah, maybe it won't always be this way, but the fact of the matter is I'm completely exhausted. There's nothing left in me. I can't last.

What makes it so bad is that I know you've never felt the same about me. I still can't believe it. I still can't get over the fact that it didn't work out with us. Because once when we were together, I felt that we belonged, that you were the one I was always meant to be with. How could I feel this so strongly if it weren't true? How can I ever trust myself again? José is the only man who has ever completely loved me, he deserves this devotion, but I find that I cannot give him what he wants. So, in the end, I can blame no one but myself. And that's another reason why I want to do this.

Sean, you feel nothing for me. And I still can't accept that, try as I might. I still can't quite believe your reaction last night when I finally told you that I wanted to die if we couldn't be together. How can you be so cold to somebody who cares so much for you?

Maybe by doing this I will make it possible for you to feel again, maybe I will make it possible for you to treat someone else the way you should have treated me. Maybe I will force you to reckon with the power of yourself on someone else. And if I can accomplish that, I do accomplish something in this life.

And I would like you please to return to José all the loomed things that I made for you. Selfish perhaps, I just want him to have them since he can't have me.

Bobby

2 5

I TOLD NO ONE ABOUT BOBBY'S LETTER. I LIVED WITH IT LIKE A SACRED relic. Kept it in a compartment in my desk. Took it out sometimes and reread it. Bobby's final implication mellowed the pain of my losing you; I could understand how imperative it was for you to withhold the truth. For had I known the truth any earlier I certainly would've doubted you; it would've been too scary to relax in your open arms, even to rest my head on your shoulder. I now knew that you would never change.

A long time after you left town, I had these recurring dreams. The dreams began with Chad, who has become one of Loie Fuller's Chinese dancers in the Yeats poem "Lapis Lazuli." Dressed in Asian silks, he wears a long black braid down his back. He whirls around my apartment, then sits down at a piano. "Spirited fingers begin to play." And after sounding the few notes of a nocturne, he turns to me. His dark Latino eyes now become your fatal arctic-blue eyes. And those eyes tell me to drive to the coast, to undress on a dark beach, to take on the Atlantic's dark freezing rollers until my body goes numb.

In late January I got reinvolved with Peter Rocca, basically because there was no one else even remotely interesting and I was lonely and because Sebastian had gone off to Malta for a few months. Peter was familiar ground, and that was much less threatening than sounding a whole new relationship. On Valentine's Day, he and I went for a Dutch-treat dinner at Provence, then back to his place for sex, our usual wild Sexual Stations of the Cross. In the midst of it all there was no mention of valentines.

Afterward, when we were lying in his bed, shrouded in oxford cotton sheets, I was actually looking forward to spending the whole night with someone I admired who was warm and familiar. And I found myself relating Bobby's letter, which by now I'd read so many times I could recite it verbatim. Peter couldn't understand why I'd kept the letter to myself for the past few months. I insisted that I'd wanted to keep it to myself. Besides, Peter hardly told me everything that went on with him.

"Well, pardon me for being thick. But I'm not quite sure what Bobby was going on about. Sean told him he never loved him. What was Sean supposed to do: get back together with Bobby because Bobby was threatening to do himself in?"

"It's not that," I said. "Sean just kept a lot of things from me. He wanted to make it seem that Bobby killed himself because he was sick. I asked Sean several times if he was telling me everything. He said he was. And yet, he never told me about that last desperate phone call."

"Sean probably just convinced himself that Bobby was using him as an excuse."

I glanced out the window at the Empire State Building, whose upper stories were lighted crimson in honor of the defrocked saint. "But sometimes I wonder if Sean suspected or even knew that Bobby was actually HIV-negative."

"I wouldn't be surprised," Peter said.

"It's not so simple. Sean's not that much of a liar, Peter," I said.

"Never said he was a liar. He just believes what it's convenient to believe."

I remembered what had been revealed to me in the garden on Charles Street, the "never come back" story. But I refrained from telling Peter because I was afraid he'd cast doubt on that, too.

"Believe it or not, I haven't once stopped thinking about that night you went off with Sean," Peter resumed. "Seeing you guys walking away, seeing you brushing up against each other. I wonder why I can't get it out of my mind. That night . . . you and Sean made me feel like I was going crazy."

I leaned over and kissed him. I said, "That night I was cavalier. I'm sorry. I promise I'll never do anything like that to you again."

Seemingly satisfied, Peter lay back, arms cocked behind his head, his stomach glistening with the sweat from our sex. Although he was loath to admit it, he'd finally buckled under the pressure of fashion and now shaved the little bit of hair there was on his chest. Fucking hypocrite, I'd said to him the first time he seduced me again and I noticed the stubbly difference. He explained to me that while Sebastian had been away he'd had a brief fling with a model who got him high one night and shaved him, and now he was forced into keeping those superhero tits trimmed. Growing it back was unbearable—all the itching.

"You miss Sean, don't you?" Peter asked gently.

"I hate to say it, but I do," I admitted just as the downstairs buzzer rang.

Peter sprang out of bed to answer it. I was staring at his naked butt when I heard him exclaim, "Oh, my God. No! Tell him no! Tell him that I'll get it from him tomorrow. Tell him I'm sleeping." There was a pause. "Well, then tell him I fell asleep with the light on."

"Sebastian," he said when he turned around again, as if I couldn't figure that one out. I'd been operating under the impression that Sebastian was gone until March. "Shit! I should've realized he'd come home early just to spy on me."

"Well, after all it *is* Valentine's Day," I couldn't help pointing out, noticing how orange Peter's pubic hairs looked in the direct light.

He sat on the edge of his bed, clearly perturbed. Finally he murmured, "He knows you're here. That's the problem."

"What makes you think that?"

"Because that's what the vacuum cleaner is all about."

"The vacuum cleaner?"

"Oh, I forgot to mention that. He's downstairs with my vacuum cleaner."

Apparently Sebastian had borrowed one of Peter's vacuum cleaners before he left and had never bothered to return it. Once before when he brought back something he'd borrowed, the doorman let him through without buzzing Peter. "He figures with any household item he can get upstairs without my knowing he's in the building."

"But wait a minute, why does he think you're here with somebody? Or is he just that suspicious?"

"Didn't you take a piss after we had sex?"

"So."

Even though we were so high up, there was a place uptown from Peter's building where, with a pair of binoculars, Sebastian could actually peer into the bathroom. "From there he'd be able to see that whoever took the piss wasn't me."

I stared at Peter dumbstruck. "You're joking."

"I wish I were."

"I can't believe you put up with this nonsense!"

"Well, 'this nonsense' is about to come to an end," Peter said, just as the buzzer blared again. I shook my head because I knew such nonsense would never end. All I could do was watch this beautiful naked man, afflicted by unholy love, hurrying across his pristine apartment toward the intercom. Did he and I and Greg and everybody we knew choose unwisely because we were by nature more comfortable with unhappiness? "Yeah," Peter said into the intercom phone. "Tell him absolutely not!"

"They say he wants me to come to the window," Peter declared.

"So talk to him."

"I don't want to!"

"You've got to deal with this sooner or later."

In a reluctant fury, naked Peter threw open his window and leaned out into the cold February night. "What do you want from me?" he yelled down to the street.

"You fuck!" Sebastian shouted back. "I come all the way back to be with you and you're *with somebody*. And I know who you're with! You're with that fucking asshole Kaplan!"

Some pair of binoculars he's got.

"Well, why didn't you tell me when you were coming back?"

"I wanted to surprise you, okay?" Sebastian screamed and then broke down into frustrated sobs right there on the sidewalk.

When Peter glanced back at me he looked aggrieved. He leaned out again into the cold, his body by now crimsoned from exposure. "Come on, don't do that, Seb," he now hollered with surprising tenderness. "Just go home. I'll call you in a half hour."

I ventured to look out the bedroom window and saw the most pitiful sight in the world: Sebastian bent over and blubbering, gripping an upright vacuum cleaner as though it were a life preserver. He finally began trudging along the sidewalk, the vacuum cleaner trailing behind, bumping over ice patches and the irregularities in the concrete. Watching the finale of his jealous rage, I suddenly knew with great certainty that, of course, he *had* to be the one who'd shredded my novel.

"Why don't you just go be with him," I said once Peter had

closed the window and was standing before me, shivering, with his arms crossed over his chest.

"You see what an infant he is?"

"But he loves you," I pointed out. "As a matter of fact he adores you. And infants do grow up eventually."

Peter shook his head. "It's so hard with him. Even the simplest things with him turn complicated."

"That's what it's all about, Peter. Relationships. You must see something in him; after all, you've been with him for a few years now."

Peter suddenly noticed I was beginning to get dressed. "Hey, where you going?"

"Home—where else do I have I go?" I said, resolving to myself that this would be the last time I ever slept with Peter Rocca.

2 6

WE WERE CROSSING TO FIRE ISLAND ON THE FERRY WHEN GREG declared that he had applied to law school. He listed all the universities, some of which were located outside of New York City. We were sitting down next to each other and Casey was wedged in between us.

"Does that mean you're going to take my dog away from me to another city?"

"Suddenly he's just *your* dog."

"You know exactly what I mean."

"Well, not if I get into Columbia or NYU. They're my first choices. I don't want to leave New York. Unless I happen to snag Harvard or Yale."

I asked Greg if he stood a prayer of getting into those schools and he tried not to look too proud as he announced that he was 99th percentile on his LSATs.

"You make me *sick*," I said, elated for him. "Ninety-ninth percentile? One day you decide to go to law school and the next day you're in the ninety-ninth percentile! You're going to be a lawyer, Jesus Christ, you're going to be a lawyer just like the rest of New York City!"

"Just think, I can represent you. Do all your contracts. Make sure the big multimedia companies don't fuck you over."

"You must be dreaming. That'd be like holding up the Chinese army with one gun." I appraised his Fire Island outfit: a dress shirt cut off at the sleeves and skimpy denim shorts. "You'll have to clean up your act. Can't go to torts class looking like that."

"Easy A," Greg said, spreading his legs and leaning back against the bench railing.

Born-and-bred New Yorker that I was, I'd never before been to Fire Island Pines, and it suddenly dawned on me that there wasn't even one woman on the boat. "We could be going to Mount Athos," I pointed out, just as the drone of the engines dropped a notch and the ferry began listing to the right, shifting its course to head into the harbor of the Pines. From where we sat we could see a string of weathered-looking houses on the bay side of the island. Although we were situated below an overhang, a harsh splash of sunlight was sprawling across the bottom half of our legs.

Once we disembarked, we went immediately to the house of a man whose golden retriever played with Casey at the dog run. As soon as the dogs were settled in an enclosed yard, we joined the throng of bare-chested men, dressed in either shorts or bathing suits, milling down the boardwalk toward the prefabricated pavilions that served the Morning Party. The Gay Men's Health Crisis was sponsoring the event, and all proceeds would go toward reinforcing the various fronts of battling the epidemic. Our tickets came in the form of pink plastic wristbands that had to be worn in order to enter the dance floor. They reminded me of hospital bracelets; how macabre, I thought, to wear hospital bracelets to a party.

Laid over the sand, the dance floor quickly filled with thou-

sands of men who were already heavily drugged before they began gulping down the rum punch being served by the cheerful
hosts. I found few sober-looking people in the crowd. The majority of the men in attendance were beautiful, but to me the beauty
was either improvised or exaggerated: too much emphasis placed
on a perfect hairstyle, sets of heavily pumped-up tits and big arms
that didn't match stick-thin legs. I saw great wide backs in tandem with sunken chests or huge chests coupled with undeveloped
backs. I saw beefy arms that didn't correspond to the size of the
chest and vice versa—all of it, it seemed to me, the half-baked
results of working out to be beautiful instead of working out to be
fit. There were some knockouts, certainly, but they flaunted it
with every last ounce of purpose. What will they do when they hit
forty, fifty, I couldn't help wondering. What will any of us do?

Greg and I danced for a while, and that was comfortable because we could touch each other, as we moved in tandem, and he
could put his back to me and spoon as we danced. But then he ran
into a guy he'd been dating on and off, and I was honor-bound to
give them a wide berth. After making plans to meet me at the five
o'clock ferry, Greg with his friend took a stroll to some more se-
cluded area of the beach. And as I watched them walking off, I
had to forcibly dispel the creepy feeling that Greg's Morning Party
date looked a lot like me.

However, once I was alone again, I grew even more aware of
the passion of the mob, the narcotic faces thrown back into the
sun, faces bowing over to inhale the latest in designer drugs that
conveniently came in tiny amber bottles. Then a great laurel of
tanned and muscular arms linked together in so many frolicking
tribes—all of them inspired by the sexual throb of carefully selected music. Never before had I been so aware of the pressure to
pursue physical perfection, to be unblemished and youthful at
the dance. I could even understand why people were tempted into
and consumed by the triangle—the New York–Fire Island–South

Beach triangle. But then some cloud heads crossed the sun and the stain of a shadow drifted over the crowd, and I grew aware of the thinnest of membranes separating us from the rest of the rest of the world: the false belief that pumping up would be our protective armor against the plague. And I remembered that the death sentence of Narcissus was wasting away.

When I found myself dancing with another loner, a guy with a nice ostentatious build, I mentioned that I was thinking about going for a long swim in the ocean, and he told me that he was also a swimmer and asked if he could tag along. I think he could tell that I was serious about the swimming.

We left the party and stripped off our shorts down to Speedos and in a flash we were out beyond the breakwater, hitting the smooth back of the swell and beginning our flight along the shoreline, matching stroke for stroke. Through my goggles I could see his perfect underwater S motion, the final backward thrust of the hands before the high elbow recovery. I hadn't risked a tandem ocean swim since Chad, and I was reminded that with it came the responsibility to keep an eye out for the other swimmer, to make sure we didn't jam together in a cresting wave or brush up against each other when we least expected to. At one point during the swim, I glanced back at the Morning Party, and the image of the dancing that flashed back over the surf was a great, writhing tangle of snakes, the sort that would crown the head of Medusa.

The swimmer invited me back to his house for a drink, but I wasn't in the mood to be with a stranger, and besides, there was very little time before I had to meet Greg back at the dock. In fact, by the time I arrived he was already waiting with Casey, looking concerned. He'd just pulled five blood-engorged ticks off our dog.

"I hope they're not the Lyme variety," I said.

"You can't see that kind."

"So then what are you so worried about?"

"When you pull the ticks off, sometimes the heads stays in

and can float in the bloodstream and do things like stop the heart."

"And a meteor can strike Fire Island." I smiled and Greg seemed to calm down. I asked him where his "new friend" had gone to. Apparently the guy felt like dancing some more, but they had a date later on in the city.

"Must be nice to look forward to that."

He detected my edge of jealousy. "Look, you could have any number of dates. I saw guys cruising you today."

We both stood with our backs to the breeze that was whipping in from the mainland. "You know, at some point, you've just got to give somebody else a chance," Greg finally said.

"Yeah, well, at the moment the idea is too depressing." I cited some of my Morning Party observations. Greg listened carefully and shook his head. "I know what you're saying, Will, but we're all like this to a certain extent—yourself included. And the fact of the matter is it's been nearly a year since Sean split and you haven't really dated anybody."

"Except for Peter," I pointed out.

"Peter doesn't count."

"I guess I'm getting there, slowly."

"Getting there maybe, but definitely torturing yourself along the way."

"Torturing myself in the most beautiful of places," I amended and gestured toward the ocean front.

We boarded the ferry along with only a scattering of others; the majority of men were still reveling. Greg met some people he knew, people I didn't even recognize. How strange, it seemed, that in two years away from me he'd reassembled a whole new world for himself, a world in which I was not automatically known by everyone. The moment the boat steamed away from the slip I wandered off along the upper deck to find solitude. I leaned over the railing of the boat and admired the water in the Great South Bay, its deep indigo.

I found myself remembering the time when Chad and I got up early one morning to go deep-sea fishing. Nearly eleven years ago, but Jesus, I could remember everything about that day: not a single flaw in the California sky, and the Monterey pines spiking the grounds of his apartment building, and the maple syrup smell of these thistles that used to grow along his driveway. And the way he shaved hastily in the dark and his tanned cheeks showing pinpoints of blood from the razor burn. How he went down on me as I was driving us to the dock, even though I told him I was so tired it probably would take me ten years to come. I remember saying that, *ten years to come.*

And I remembered the part of Bobby's letter, the part about "the rest of my life now seems too long a stretch to go." Bobby was dead, though I still couldn't quite believe it; and yet, before he died, he was able to feel something so acute as to make him choose not to feel anything more at all. Yes, he was gone now, but how could he really be gone, and how could his intense love for another man completely vanish with his leaving? Why couldn't I let go of Chad? Why couldn't I let go of you?

I closed my eyes and asked whatever higher power there might be to just tell me whether Chad was alive or not, to show me some sign that either he'd died eleven years ago, or he'd just left me. Please, I murmured to the water pulsing alongside the boat, leaning closer to it, smelling the mucky brine of the bay. Let me know one way or another and then I promise to move on.

The part I still cannot understand is what possessed me to let go of the railing. Balancing my stomach on the bar, I was leaning forward, craning to kiss the face I suddenly saw before me, a waxen face with a startling dark gaze flecked with the silvery dorsals of the fishes swimming inside his head. And then the boat lurched unexpectedly and its forward thrust left me out of balance. I was like a juggler's ball thrown high up into an arc and slowing to that stationary point where its upward force and gravity meet. But then

a hand brought me back into the forward motion of the boat—
Greg's hand jerked me back to myself.

I was startled by the spooky look on his face.

"What the fuck were you doing like that?" he fumed.

"Nothing, I was just—"

"Do you realize what you just nearly did?"

I shook my head. I peered at him but he seemed so many fath-
oms away.

"I'll fucking kill you if you do something so stupid."

"I was just . . . I was just smelling the water," I finally
protested.

"*Smelling* the water," he mocked me. "It looked like you were
getting ready to jump."

The shoreline of Long Island loomed only a quarter of a mile
away. "Greg, if I was going to jump, don't you think I would've
done it out in the middle?"

"Who knows what you would've done?" he exclaimed. "I'll be
honest with you, Will, sometimes I think you're turning into a real
nut job." And yet he sounded relieved.

"I didn't know I was acting weird."

But then I felt him stiffening next to me, suddenly attentive.
"Jesus Christ," he muttered. "I don't believe who's on this boat!"

Before I could ask who Greg meant, I instinctively glanced
toward the bow of the ferry, where I noticed that you'd been standing, watching us.

E P I L O G U E

AND I TELL YOU EXACTLY WHAT I TOLD GREG. I WASN'T ABOUT TO JUMP.
Then I'm staring out over the water, dead inside, mute to you when
you tell me I scared the shit out of you, that you were just about
to run over when you saw Greg grabbing hold of me. My eyes rivet
to the cutting wake. I wish you'd just go back to where you were
standing. We'll be docking soon.

"Come on, Will, don't be like this. Just talk to me a little . . . Why do you think I came out to Fire Island today?"

I shrug. How long had you been back? Had you ever really
gone away?

"Won't you even look at me?"

Unyielding silence.

"So what's with the bandanna on your head? . . . You don't
have to cover up the fact that you're balding. You're beautiful,
Will. Your balding head is one of my favorite things about you."

Spare me the compliments.

"I would've called you but I was afraid that you would refuse to speak to me. I guess I was right. Then I thought you might be out here today. That you might be curious about the Morning Party."

I look around for Greg and Casey, but they've slipped away to another part of the ferry. The engines are beginning to wind down, we're approaching land, and I suddenly feel the urgency of wanting to know what will happen next.

So I finally dare a full look at you. Your hair is longer, gelled a bit to relax the curl; your skin is tanned, and your eyes are still a piercing blue. I hate you for looking good. And what's worse is I can see a certain soulful glimmering in those eyes.

The dock is encroaching on our one-way conversation, so you breach the silence again. "I had to come back to New York. Because I couldn't let you be left twice."

I'm now compelled to speak. "I don't understand."

"I didn't want to be like *him,*" you explain.

This sort of perception is what in the beginning so quickly broke down my defenses. But by now it has taken a toll. I still can't believe you could leave without telling me, after all we talked about, when you knew it was the worst possible thing to do to me. I wait another moment and then say, "But you *are* like him. You vanish when you can't handle somebody's devotion."

There was more to it than that. I'd heard the phone message at your apartment, hadn't I? Your neighbors said they saw me going into the building. When they forwarded all your mail, the letter you'd left me was missing. Had I read the letter?

I admit to you, I read it. "But you still could've stayed, Sean. It might've been hard, but you could've faced it."

"You're absolutely right, okay? And it's embarrassing to have to admit that. Because at least you had the guts to leave yourself open to me. At least you were willing to risk falling."

"What a fucking line," I say as the boat makes its final approach, as I can feel the other passengers charging up to return to the eternal pleasure-seeking that goes hand in hand with living in New York City.

You move in closer until our shoulders are jammed together, and as I edge away you say, "I just want you to tell me honestly what you were doing leaning out over the water like that. Were you about to take another one of your unexpected swims?" The ferry sounds its horn and the passengers begin gathering their belongings.

I remember Chad. I remember the voyage out to the Channel Islands, where, just off Santa Rosa, the boat intersected a school of blue porpoises. I remember how they rushed the side of the boat like a Marine battalion, their opaque, gentle eyes catching light, how they seemed so content in their powerful locomotive freedom. Sunlight coming from the east glinting on the surface of the water like silver lures, and Chad, shirtless, was leaning over the railing as I am now.

He was watching the porpoises undulating, watching the power of their waving tails, and the blue ridges of Santa Rosa were soaring out of the mist behind his haloed head. "Christ, what a life," he'd said. "I wouldn't mind a life like that."

"Your life is okay," I told him. "You can live on land. You can go swimming whenever you want."

He turned to me, his black eyes squinting. "I love you," he said. "And I'd love to do it with you right now."

"You always love it when you can't have it."

"I guess I love what's impossible," he agreed, saluting the porpoises, who were finally abandoning their escort. It is one of my fondest memories of him.

You repeat your question. What had I been doing leaning over the railing? Had I been about to jump off the boat? You must still be afraid that what happened to your father and Bobby Garzino might soon happen to me.

But I'm also afraid because I don't want you to leave again.

I'm afraid because I don't know what I mean by this confession and that I've told you everything in the blink of an eye.

I realize it isn't a bid to bring *you* or *him* back, but rather an exorcism.

Still, you want an answer.

The boat kisses up to the dock and Greg is now walking toward us, Casey straining against his leash to reach me. Waving to them, I grab my bag and hoist it over my shoulder. And then I tell you that I was praying.

CPSIA information can be obtained at www.ICGtesting.com
Printed in the USA
236260LV00001B/67/P